BEST OF
BEST
GAY
EROTICA
2

BEST OF BEST GAY EROTICA 2

Edited by

Richard Labonté

CLEIS
PRESS

Printed in the United States
Cover design: Scott Idleman
Cover photograph: Phyllis Christopher
Cover models: Michael Soldier and Dick Wolf
Text design: Frank Wiedemann
Cleis logo art: Juana Alicia
First Edition
10 9 8 7 6 5 4 3 2 1

"Just Another Night at the World's Greatest Diner" © 2000 by Dimitri Apessos, reprinted with permission from *Best Gay Erotica 2001*. "I'm a Top" © 2001 by Otto Coca, reprinted with permission from *Best Gay Erotica 2002*. "Five a Day" © 2000 by Jaime Cortez, reprinted with permission from *Best Gay Erotica 2001*. "Snow" © 2002-2004 by Jameson Currier, reprinted from *Best Gay Erotica 2003*, first appeared online at VelvetMafia.com, and was published in *Best American Erotica 2004*, ed. by Susie Bright (Simon & Schuster); reprinted with permission from *Desire, Lust, Passion, Sex* (Green Candy Press, 2004). "Neighbors" © 2002 by Trebor Healey, reprinted with permission from *Best Gay Erotica 2003*. "Natoma Street" by JT LeRoy, reprinted with permission from *Best Gay Erotica 2002*, originally appeared in *The Heart Is Deceitful Above All Things*, © 2001 by Bloomsbury USA. "A History of Barbed Wire" © 2003 by Jeff Mann, reprinted with permission from *Best Gay Erotica 2004*. "The Bachelors" © 2002 by Douglas A. Martin, reprinted with permission from *Best Gay Erotica 2003*. "Baying at the Moon" © 2002 by David May, reprinted with permission from *Best Gay Erotica 2003*. "Frantic Romantic" © 2001 by Alistair McCartney, reprinted with permission from *Best Gay Erotica 2002*. "For Hire: A Date with John" © 1999 by Sean Meriwether, reprinted with permission from *Best Gay Erotica 2001*. "Everything's Gone Green" © 2002 by Marshall Moore, reprinted with permission from *Best Gay Erotica 2003*. "A Bedtime Story" © 2000 by Jay Neal, reprinted with permission from *Best Gay Erotica 2002*, originally appeared in *American Bear*, Dec. 2000/Jan. 2001. "Wake the King Up Right" © 2004 by Mike Newman, reprinted with permission from *Best Gay Erotica 2005*. "Losing It" © 2001 by John Orcutt, reprinted with permission from *Best Gay Erotica 2002*. "Positive" © 2001 by Andy Quan, reprinted with permission from *Best Gay Erotica 2002*, also appeared in *Positive Nation Magazine* (April 2003) and was reprinted in *Best Gay Asian Erotica*, ed. by Joël B. Tan (Cleis Press, 2004). "Pink Triangle-Shaped Pubes" © 2004 by Alexander Rowlson, reprinted with permission from *Best Gay Erotica 2005*, first appeared in *fab magazine* (January 2004). "Prolonged Exposure May Cause Dizziness" © 1999 by Sandip Roy, reprinted with permission from *Best Gay Erotica 2001*, also appeared in *Best Gay Asian Erotica*, ed. by Joël B. Tan. "Corncobs" © 2003 by Dominic Santi, reprinted with permission from *Best Gay Erotica 2004*, also appeared as "Maiskolben," in the collection *Kerle im Lustrach* (Bruno Gmunder, 2004). "Going Down, Going Down Down" © 2003 by Simon Sheppard, reprinted from *Best Gay Erotica 2004*; reprinted with permission from *Boyfriends from Hell*, ed. by Kevin Bentley (Green Candy Press, 2003). "Cocky" © 2001 by Mel Smith, reprinted with permission from *Best Gay Erotica 2002*. "Warm-up" © 2000 by Mattilda a.k.a. Matt Bernstein Sycamore, reprinted from *Best Gay Erotica 2001*; reprinted with permission from *Pulling Taffy* (Suspect Thoughts Press, 2003). "Knowing Johnny" © 2000 by Bob Vickery, reprinted with permission from *Best Gay Erotica 2001*, first appeared in *Men* magazine and subsequently in *Cocksure* (Alyson, 2002). "Straight Boy" © 2002 by James Williams, reprinted with permission from *Best Gay Erotica 2004*, first appeared in *...But I Know What You Want* (Greenery Press, 2003). "Huh?" © 2003 by Ron Winterstein, reprinted with permission from *Best Gay Erotica 2004*.

For Asa, my own Best Gay

TABLE OF CONTENTS

Go to page 132

Introduction
Richard Labonté

Choosing "bests" for a "best of the best" is, at best, a sub-jective exercise. The 108 stories selected for the *Best Gay Erotica* books between 2001 and 2005 were, after all, as good as they get.

Here's how I picked the stories for this second volume of *Best of Best Gay Erotica*: First, I asked the judges for each year—Randy Boyd, 2001; Neal Drinnan, 2002; Michael Rowe, 2003; Kirk Read, 2004; and William J. Mann, 2005—what their favorites were. Then I opened each book, and jotted down the titles of the stories I wanted to reread—a worthy filter, since I live a life of "too many books, too little time," and never make time to reread books.

My loss.

In "What We've Always Done," his introduction to *Best Gay Erotica 2004*, Kirk reminded me why fiction—good erotic fiction—can be a constant companion: "These stories will find homes in the minds of questioning youths from tiny towns, who will dog-ear pages and perhaps secure the book away in their own hiding places." He also pointed out: "Each story will contain passages certain readers will return to, knowing that those magical four paragraphs will get them off every time."

After reading the twenty-three stories suggested by the judges, and the several dozen that jumped out at me that weren't already on the judges' lists, I had narrowed *Best of Best Gay Erotica 2* down to, um, sixty-six stories. Some authors were represented two or three or even four times; that trimmed the possibilities to, er, fifty-four stories—coincidentally, half the total in the five volumes from which they were being selected.

Whew. It was quite a weekend. Wore me out. Lots of magic paragraphs.

Much of the magic comes from the pens of lusty and celebrated erotic writers like Simon Sheppard, Bob Vickery, James Williams, Mel Smith, Dominic Santi, Jay Neal, and David May—regular contributors over the years to dozens and dozens of porn anthologies of whatever persuasion (and they have about a dozen one-author collections to their credit, as well: check out their author bios for further reading). Their literary skills make a hot story blaze hotter.

It comes, too, from a posse of crossover authors like Sean Meriwether, Jeff Mann, Marshall Moore, Mike Newman, Andy Quan, Douglas A. Martin, Jaime Cortez, Sandip Roy, Alistair McCartney, Trebor Healey, Jameson Currier, Matt Bernstein Sycamore, and JT LeRoy—writers and editors whose body of work embraces erotica with gusto, but also includes collections of essays, volumes of poetry, sheaves of magazine and newspaper criticism, books of nonfiction, many megabytes of online journals, and about a dozen novels among them.

And it comes from writers like Dimitri Apessos, whose first-ever published story—in *Best Gay Erotica 2000*—was reprinted in *Best of Best Gay Erotica*; his second, from *Best*

Gay Erotica 2001, is reprinted here; Ron Winterstein, whose story—in *Best Gay Erotica 2004*—marked his first appearance in an anthology; and Alexander Rowlson—whose story in *Best Gay Erotica 2005* was another first. This series consistently publishes the early work of queer writers, and I'm pleased that their tales are included in this best of the best.

I'm also pleased that John Orcutt and Otto Coca—both from *Best Gay Erotica 2002,* both recommended by Neal Drinnan, that year's judge—are here. I worked with John and Otto at A Different Light Bookstores in San Francisco and New York in the last century, solicited their stories for consideration early this century, and was glad that Neal judged them good enough to be included—both then and now.

As I wrote in the introduction to the first volume of *Best of Best Gay Erotica* (which featured stories from the 1996 to the 2000 editions, and remains in print): many thanks to the five judges with whom I worked. Despite their own different styles, ages, interests, and even nationalities (one Canadian, one Australian, three American), they each brought to the books they worked on the same sharp eye for both literary quality and erotic lustiness. Thanks also to the writers whose stories are reprinted here; to all the contributors whose erotic fantasies and fevered talents and literate imaginations have made the *Best Gay Erotica* series possible; and to the thousands of readers who have made these books best-selling successes for ten years…and counting.

And, as always, thanks to Frédérique Delacoste and Felice Newman, pioneering purveyors of the ultimate in quality erotic reading.

Richard Labonté
Perth, Ontario
January 2005

Just Another Night at the World's Greatest Gay Diner
Dimitri Apessos

"I want a chocolate shake with that."

"You do, huh?"

"Yes, please."

"Here you go!"

And with that, Durrell does his ridiculous little Chocolate Shake dance. He always does this when people order chocolate shakes; he positions his arms outward, bent at the elbows as if he's doing the Twist, and shakes his ass around in a belly-dance motion. It's a joke, of course. Durrell's black. Chocolate shake, get it? But, as always, the hapless tourist does *not* get it and sits at the counter, staring, confused.

Durrell sighs.

"I'll get your shake, sir," he concedes, disappointed and defeated.

With that, the hungry tourist turns back to his *USA Today* and Durrell walks over to the ice cream machine, which happens to be positioned right by where you're sitting. In response to his failed joke, you smile widely and shake your head at him in disbelief.

He smiles back, while pouring chocolate ice cream into the shake glass, and leans over to whisper: "I am so over this shit!"

You smile, understanding. Durrell is one of your best friends in New Orleans, and you can always rely on him for a free meal, but in return you have to listen to him bitch about all the ridiculous things drunken tourists say and do all day. You know he's not really bitter about it; after all, drunk heterosexuals and testy homosexuals are the occupational hazards of working in any restaurant on Bourbon Street, let alone the Happy Leprechaun, the only gay diner you have encountered in your many travels throughout gay America. For every sleaze from Jackson, Mississippi, who comes in and tells him how good he would be to him as his "white daddy," and for every straight frat boy who walks in accidentally looking for a burger who gets hostile once he puts two and Cher together to ascertain he is the only heterosexual in the entire restaurant, Durrell has the consolation of making and spending more money than any nineteen-year-old should know what to do with. French Quarter tourists may be obnoxious, but they tip well.

As if reading your thoughts, Durrell puts down the shake glass, uninterested in serving this poor tourist who didn't get his joke, and sits on the counter to talk.

"You should have been here earlier," he relates. "You know that hot blond stripper from Procession? Claude, or whatever he's calling himself today?"

"The hustler one?" you ask.

"Honey, they're *all* hustlers," he answers. "Anyway, he was here earlier with this big daddy from Florida or some shit, and we was packed, so service was slow, you know? Well, this daddy starts yelling at me that he wants his food, and he can't believe the service is so bad. And the stripper knows me and comes here all the time, so he's, like, whispering to him 'sit down' but this daddy won't listen so he comes up to the counter and starts yelling in my face that he knows the owner and is gonna get me fired and all that."

"Shit, what did you do?"

"I didn't do nuttn', I don't deal with trash like that. But Mike, the cook, gets in the way and yells at him, 'Look, just because you're paying your hustler by the hour, it don't mean you'll get your food any faster! Now sit down and shut up, or get the fuck out!' and this daddy just stands there wit' nuttn' to say but then the stripper gets up and starts yelling at Mike..."

"What was he yelling?"

"Oh, you know: 'Watch what you say. You don't know me!' That kind of shit. As if there's anyone in the Quarter who don't know that he's a hustler."

"Right," you agree.

"Right! So Mike says somethin' like 'I don't need to know you' and the hustler makes to come around the counter and Mike starts hitting him on the head with a frying pan!"

"No shit!"

"No shit! So there I am, twenty minutes after walking in, and I have Mike beating this hustler on the head with a frying pan while the hustler is trying to choke him to death and the daddy is trying to pull them apart, yelling at the hustler, 'Remember, I can't have the cops show up! My wife knows the sheriff!' It was some funny shit!"

You smile.

"I can't believe Mike lost it like that," you say.

"Well, he'd been on for fourteen hours at that point," Durrell explains. "Adam called in sick and Brad couldn't get anyone to fill in, so Mike just stayed on for a double."

Just another night at the Happy Leprechaun, you think to yourself before asking: "So what happened with the hustler and the daddy?"

"Oh, so the daddy pulls out this big wad o' cash and yells at the hustler, 'Stop choking him! I can't have the police come here and see me! Just take this money and stop choking him!' So the daddy gives the hustler this big wad o' cash and runs out of the restaurant and the hustler stops choking Mike, gets his food to go, and leaves."

"You gave him his food after all of that?"

"Why wouldn't I? He got it in Styrofoam; it's not like he was staying here to choke anyone else. And he tipped me, like, twenty bucks!"

Yup, just another night at the Happy Leprechaun.

"So, is Mike fired?" you ask.

"Why would he be fired?"

"Ummm...because he beat a customer on the head with a frying pan, maybe?"

Durrell gives a sneering giggle before saying, "Oh, please. Mike could drop his pants and piss on the grill and they wouldn't fire him. Why, I can think of five or six guys who come in here every day to eat, just so they can hit on him..."

"Wait," you interrupt. "I thought Mike was straight!"

"Exactly!" Durrell responds with a smile. "Well, he calls himself bi, but I don't think he's ever even been with a guy..."

"I am so over everyone in this damn town calling themselves bi," you squeal. "I swear to God they should get with the program!"

"Well," Durrell continues, refusing to acknowledge your interruption, "you know how the queens down here go nuts for straight boys..."

"That's sick," you say, and you mean it. Of all the sleazy things that have bothered you about New Orleans in the three months since you moved from Indiana—and there are many—this is probably the worst. The weekly visitors from Mississippi and Alabama, coming in to stock up over the weekend for a week's worth of sex before going home to their closeted lives; the huge turnover of staff in every bar and restaurant, which allows every manager to treat their employees like dirt; waiting in line for hours to use the bathroom at the clubs because there's always more than one person to a stall: all these things bother you, but you laugh at them anyway. But the obsession that every gay man in New Orleans has with hooking up with "straight boys" reveals so much self-hatred—so much denial—that just thinking about it brings you down.

The phone rings and Durrell answers. It's his on-again/off-again boyfriend, as you can tell immediately by the way his face prepares itself for a long conversation. Balancing the phone between his shoulder and cheek, Durrell reaches into his tip jar and hands you a dollar, motioning with his eyes a plea for you to play something on the jukebox. You find the motion kind of rude and play three songs from the Lulu CD just to punish him. When you come back to your seat at the counter, he is hanging up the phone.

"Bitch," he calls you, as Lulu's version of Bowie's "The Man Who Sold the World" starts to play. "By the way, your roommate was here earlier and he got in a fight, too."

"What about?" you ask, not sure you really want to know.

"There was some guy from Miami here who started yelling at him about his T-shirt. Started calling him a Communist and stuff, and your roommate freaked out and went off on him."

"What T-shirt was he wearing?" you ask, although you know the answer, to see if Durrell knows, too.

"I dunno," he answers. "The red one he always wears with the guy from *Evita*."

You have no time to educate him on the history of Latin American Communism, because the door opens and in stumble—drunk and probably sleepless for more than forty-eight hours—four "ladies" you know well: Bianca, Autumn, Michèle, and Sabrina. Ranging from "drag-for-pay" to "heavy hormone treatment," the four of them have become something of a menace around town, going in and out of bars and restaurants all night—every night—scaring the straight tourists with their bitchy catcalls and loud, androgynous laughter. With them, tonight, they have a boy no older than twenty, who seems to enjoy being taken along for a confusing ride.

"Have you heard from Nicole?" Durrell asks you, realizing that within a few seconds all opportunity for serious conversation will be gone.

"We've been playing phone tag," you barely have time to answer before the four "ladies" reach your spot on the counter and, without a break in their loud laughter, kiss you and Durrell hello.

"Hello, girls," Durrell greets them, switching instantaneously from butch to queeny. "Where's Miss Derrick?"

"Oh, girl," Bianca starts, "you wouldn't even believe what Miss Derrick got into! We were at La Ho-Down, when…"

You start to listen to the story when the stumbling boy who is escorting the "ladies" around town sits—or rather lands—on the counter seat next to you and extends a hand in your direction.

"Wassup, dude," he sputters with a huge chemical grin on his face. "I'm Andrew."

You look at him, unsure of what to make of his greeting. From up close you see that he is probably only eighteen or nineteen years old, visibly rolling his ass off on ecstasy and God-knows-what-else, and incredibly good looking. Underneath his curved baseball cap you see two steely, smiling gray eyes, the focus of a gorgeous, chiseled young face. He is wearing a tank top and baggy jeans and has a perfectly formed upper body—through nature, rather than exercise. Everything about him, from his outfit to his way of speaking, screams "straight boy."

"Hello," you answer, shaking his hand. "I'm Lawrence."

"Wassup," he asks rhetorically as he takes your hand and transforms your handshake into some kind of strange, brotherhood clasp. "You work here?"

"No," you answer. "I bartend across the street. Just getting a snack before I have to be at work in twenty minutes."

"Cool, cool," he nods a little too expressively, revealing just how hard he is rolling at this moment. "Man, this is a crazy town…"

"Yes," you agree. "Where are you from?"

"Michigan," he answers. "I just got in this morning, and I've been drunk since I stepped off the train. My girlfriend's coming down to meet me tomorrow, so I'm getting in as much partying as I can, ya' know?"

"Yeah," you answer, trying to avoid his beautiful, inebriated stare. A less-experienced man would have asked how he—a straight boy from Michigan—ended up escorting a group of trannies and drag queens on his first night in town, but your time here has taught you not to ask such questions. Anyway, you're pretty sure he'll tell you, regardless.

"So, right when I got off the train I asked this kid that was hanging out at the station where I could get some rolls—ya know?—" he starts recounting, meeting your expectations. "He told me I had to hit the gay bars on Bourbon if I wanted to find good shit. I mean, I don't care; I was in the rave scene back home so I got lotsa' gay friends. Are you gay?"

"Ummm," you falter. "No, I just like to get my cock sucked by young boys."

"Right on," he nods, completely missing your joke. "So I'm waiting outside this club, Narnia—you know it? And these dudes here come by, and they were, like, 'Oh, you're so cute!' so they gave me two rolls for free and I've been hanging out with them since."

There's a lot that you find funny about this story, but nothing amuses you quite as much as the fact that he just referred to Bianca, Autumn, Michèle, and Sabrina as dudes. You look over to see if they noticed, but sadly they did not. (They are too busy, still relating to Durrell what happened to Miss Derrick and pretending to ignore the obvious fact that every pair of eyes in the entire restaurant is staring at them.) Dudes, he calls them, despite the fact that they are all in dresses and three of them are wearing fake breasts.

Just another night at the Happy Leprechaun.

"So," you say, to keep this boy talking and to keep the laughs coming. (You don't have to be at work for another fifteen minutes, anyway.) "Are you rolling right now?"

Instead of answering verbally, he leans over, putting his face within two or three inches of yours, so that you can observe his dilated pupils. The proximity makes you nervous and excited. This boy is beautiful. Fucking straight boy! Fucking trannies, bringing him here!

"I see," you respond to his pupils, looking away awkwardly.

Impervious to your discomfort, or perhaps because of it, he puts one toned, tanned arm around your shoulders and whispers in your ear: "So, dude, is this place as fucking gay as it seems?"

"Gayer," you answer.

"Since I've been in town, all I've seen is gay bars and dudes in dresses," he confides in you. "I mean, when I was thinking of New Orleans, I was thinking of chicks showing their tits for beads, ya' know?"

This boy is so far gone that all sarcasm is wasted on him, but it makes you feel better anyway, so you agree: "Yeah, I'm pretty upset about the lack of tits, myself."

"I mean, nothing wrong with gay people!" he interrupts.

"No, of course not," you say to support him, with mocking jovial tolerance.

Suddenly he leans over even closer and squints, trying to

concentrate on your face, from within a haze of ecstasy, as he asks, in all seriousness, as if he just processed your comment from several minutes ago: "So, you get your dick sucked by dudes, huh? What's that like?"

"It's okay," you answer, nodding, and trying to stop yourself from bursting out laughing. You can't wait to tell your roommate about this. "It's not bad, you know?"

"But," he prompts you further, "is it better than a chick?"

"Depends, you know?" you lie, as if you've ever had an interest in receiving oral sex from a girl. Then, in your best Donnie Brasco voice: "Depends on the dude and the chick, ya' know?"

The gravity of this response is too much for straight rolling-boy Andrew. He withdraws his arm from around you, in confusion, takes his baseball cap off, rubs his short brown hair, then puts his hands on the counter and looks at nothing in the distance, emphasizing with: "Wow, dude..."

This joke has gone far enough. You have to be at work in ten minutes, so you excuse yourself and go through the kitchen and the courtyard of the Happy Leprechaun to use the bathroom. (The bar you work at has the nastiest bathrooms in all of the French Quarter, so you always do your business at the Happy Leprechaun before you report for duty.) Your surprise is considerable, when, after taking a long piss, you open the door of the bathroom and find young Andrew standing in the courtyard, a confused look on his face.

You suppose that he, too, has to piss, so you say "Wassup?" and try to squeeze past him. Instead he leans over, right as you pass next to him, and, half-falling over you, tries to kiss you on the mouth. It's a sloppy attempt, even for a straight boy, and you push him away. To put it simply, you can't believe this shit.

Then, right there in the empty courtyard of the Happy Leprechaun, in front of the open bathroom door, Andrew kneels in front of your feet and looks up at you with a gorgeous, mischievous grin. With a svelte, too-experienced-for-a-straight-boy move, he turns his baseball cap around so that the visor faces backward, and starts licking the bulge in your pants. You look around. No one is watching, other than the security camera, but no one ever checks that anyway, so what the heck.

You're already hard, so you push his face away from your crotch for just a second, and undo the button of your pants. With the same grin on his face, Andrew leans back toward you, undoes your zipper, and pulls out your cock. (It is a universal truth that no one ever wears underwear in New Orleans.)

Once again, with style that belies his claims of inexperience, he bends his neck to approach your dick from underneath and gives the shaft two long, playful licks. He pulls back for a second, looks up with an expectant smile, and puckers his parted lips in precisely the width of your cock. Then with one swift motion, he lunges forward and takes your entire shaft in his mouth, moaning with hunger. He pulls back and forth twice, never fully releasing your tip from his mouth, and then slips his mouth off you and slaps your mushroom head against his cheek. As if he's been starving for this exact taste, he takes your cock and manically wipes it over his lips, his nose, and his eyes.

You take his baseball-capped head in your hands and force it back onto your cock. With a girlish squeal, he accedes to your demand and allows you to set the pace. He puts his hands on the back of your thighs and squeezes them with delight as you fuck his face with steadily increasing speed and furor. You bring his head down on your crotch again and again, forcing him to take in every inch of you, as he moans and slobbers with each deep swallow.

You remove yourself from his hungry lips for a second, then you turn your body and his head slightly so that his back and his head touch the tall walls of the courtyard. With him cornered like that, you push your pelvis back and forth on his face, fucking his mouth rhythmically, while he moans in accord with the pace you're setting. You look down at his chiseled cheeks, his beautiful, half-opened eyes, his backward cap, his bronzed body accentuated by the bright-white tank top, and once again you say to yourself: I can't believe this shit is happening. He reaches up and is now hanging on to your exposed buttcheeks, as you rape his supposedly virgin lips, closer to coming with each forceful thrust.

Recognizing the twitches of the muscles on the underside of your cock, he pulls you out of his mouth, looks up at you with begging lust, and whispers: "I want you to come on my face, dude!"

With his left hand he jerks off your shaft while he kisses and sucks on your tip with furious hunger, and you see that he has opened his own fly with his right, and is banging away at his own large, handsome dick with equal earnestness.

Your tip feels as if it's on fire, your shaft muscles contract with an explosion of joy, and you squirt a heavy load of thick, white jism all over his pretty, straight-boy lips. He moans with delight, and as you look down you see his own cock pop with white foam like a champagne bottle. But your own cum keeps flowing, too, for several seconds, wetting with milky spunk his forehead, those cheeks, his long, boyish eyelashes.

As he kisses and sucks the remaining jizz off your cock with yelps of incredulous lust, you see your slowly drying cum drip from his face and down his long, smooth neck to wet the top of his previously clean tank top, outlining his finely shaped pecs. His moans and kisses are dying down as exhaustion begins to hit him, and you push him away and zip yourself up. You are late for work.

As you straighten your pants and shirt, standing at the exact same spot where you fucked his face, he collapses to the ground with mock-ecstatic fatigue and lets out another girlish giggle. He looks up at you from the dirty courtyard floor with his big eyes full of expectation, all pretense of heterosexuality gone from his recently abused face.

"That was great!" he yawns, childishly stretching his body out on the ground. "Wow, dude!"

Afraid that he is going to ask to see you again, or meet you after work, or, even worse, admit that there is no girlfriend arriving the next day, you walk away without a word. You step into the kitchen, and from there into the dining room of the restaurant, as "To Sir with Love" dies down on the jukebox and Bianca finally concludes her story to Durrell.

"So Miss Derrick, she turns to him and she says: 'No, you *don't* know me, you understand? Cause I'm here incognegro!' Incog*negro!!!* Can you believe that bitch?"

Durrell and the "ladies" burst out in deafening laughter as you pick up your backpack from the counter and wave goodbye to all present. They all wave back, and you hear behind you a customer nervously complain: "Ummm, I'm still waiting for my chocolate milkshake..."

As you close the door and step out onto Bourbon Street, you faintly make out one of the "ladies"—or perhaps Durrell—yelling in response something that sounds a lot like "Eat my ass on a shitty day!" to the poor, thirsty tourist. You look at your watch. You are officially five minutes late for work.

As you cross the street and think of an unnecessary apology, you tell yourself: Yup, just another night at the Happy Leprechaun.

Baying at the Moon
David May

...And shall you, gliding in your silken shirt,
Deny the hidden bruises of your flesh,
Not boast the livid honour of your hurt?
Come; if they fade, I'll brand you deep afresh.

—VITA SACKVILLE-WEST

New England is dotted with small towns like this one, villages with empty factories and warehouses that had once been the centers of their economies, empty brick buildings set along rivers and shorelines, buildings converted to shopping centers, offices, and loft apartments with startling views of New England sweeping past village scenes of churches, storefronts, centuries-old houses, markets, and schools—silver-blue winters, burnt-orange autumns, the oppressive green of summer, the brilliant yellow light of spring: views from homes like ours.

I watch him in our kitchen while I'm supposed to be working, watch him move with cool efficiency as he chops, slices, grates, tastes, stirs, and smells. He is manly as he does these things, as I never knew a man could be in a kitchen. I admire him as he goes about his business, calm and collected, confident. I watch him and smile, content with my life. After so many near misses, after too many tears, we are together.

He looks at me, smiles.

"You're not done, are you, Sir?"

"No, not yet," I answer.

He shakes his head, not daring to chastise me, nor wanting to.

"They'll be here before you know it."

"They" are our dinner guests, people he's collected in the few years of our life here: the women who own the antique store down the road, the Unitarian minister and her husband, the gay biker couple in the next village, Jake and his new Dutch boyfriend, the mayor and her historian husband. Their combined presence will mean activity, noise, and conversation. I know he's right and that I should get back to it.

"And you want that grant."

"This is my grant proposal, not yours, boy."

He beams.

"Yes, Sir."

As usual, those two words give me an instant hard-on. I'm tempted to order him to suck my cock right then and there, knowing that he'd obey me in an instant, eager, smiling, and without question. But I also know that this interruption might interfere with his preparations, leading him to apologize for a meal that falls short of his expectations. He would apologize repeatedly, blaming only himself, even when it was my interruption that caused the shortcomings of the meal, shortcomings apparent only to him.

So I only smile instead. Going back to my work I realize once again that I am, as I am every day, happier than I was even a moment before.

Barry was dancing the first time I saw him. He was also

probably high, he tells me now. Jake and I were at the Pleasure Dome after the Folsom Street Fair, and Barry was in the center of the dance floor, moving his whole body in time to the music, arms above his head, eyes closed, oblivious to me and the world. He wore calf-high boots and worn Levi's undone at the waist. He was shirtless, a thick chain locked around his neck that I didn't understand the meaning of despite all the boys in collars and on leashes I'd seen that day, not even when Sam (red-bearded and as hairy as me) pulled on that chain and locked Barry in a kiss that lasted uncounted minutes, a kiss I watched with awe and envy.

"He's a beauty, all right," Jake yelled in my ear over the din of the music.

"What's with the necklace?" I asked my friend.

"He's the other man's slave."

Hearing those words, I was more in wonder than before, more in lust with the lithe, sweaty body, its muscles accentuated by just enough hair (almost as blond as the rest of him) to make him man enough for me. His fair beard, like Sam's, was full but carefully groomed, his hair buzzed short. I ached (yes, that is the word) to kiss him, to hold him. I wanted my seed in him. I wanted to mark him as mine.

"Then he's definitely taken?" I asked Jake, trying to make light of my pain and disappointment.

Jake laughed, not sensing the storm of lust and frustration raging inside me.

"Yeah, Joey, I think so. But as usual, we've both spotted the perfect *shegetz*."

"I'm a *shegetz*," I reminded my friend.

"You're Italian, Joe. That doesn't count."

This was (and is) an old joke between us, and we laughed as always.

Jake and I have been best friends since third grade. He told me he liked guys (and was in love with a Waspy beauty he played tennis with) while we were still in high school. Ten years later I told him that I also loved men. Fortunately for us—or maybe unfortunately—we always like the same guys (blond icebergs, Jake calls them), so there was never any question of our being lovers, only of competing for the same guys.

"You're sure about this, Joe?" Jake asked me when I told him that my marriage had been a mistake, that I'd fallen in love with another intern, my handsome Nordic Todd. "You're not just doing this to be fashionable?"

"Yeah, Jake. I'm just doing it so I can be closer to you, faggot."

"Who're you calling 'faggot'?"

"I'm calling me a faggot. And I figure if I'm going to be a faggot, I can at least be a man about it."

Which is when Jake hugged me, like I had hugged him ten years before. And we kissed each other on the cheek as we had done then and ever since.

"You're such warm people," my Danish wife once commented when she saw our usual embrace. Her voice had the same tone of disappointment and disapproval it had when she discovered that I was Italian rather than Jewish and why the Jew she was flirting with that night at the student coffee shop would not respond to her. Had I not loved her as much as I did, I suppose I'd have been too hurt to be her second choice, but she was so beautiful that I was flattered to be just that—until I met Todd and he turned my life upside down with a single kiss.

Jake and I danced together the rest of that night, or until it was time to hit Blow Buddies. As we danced, I watched Barry dancing without stop, his face beatific. I watched while the sweat made tiny rivers down his torso to form a damp spot at his crotch, and down his back to form another one in the ass crack of his Levi's. I wanted to bury my face in his ass, to lick up the sweat and inhale his scent.

He was like some great cat, a lion basking in the pleasure of the music, in the shifting lights surrounding him, in my admiration, in his Master's love. Yes, he was the cat, content and lying in the sun: I was a dog, alone in the darkness, howling at the moon and afraid I'd never attain the thing I wanted most to love.

I shot my load so many times that night at Blow Buddies, each time thinking of the still-nameless beauty dancing half-naked with his Master and never noticing me. Every mouth I kissed I pretended was his. But imagination can take a man only so far.

I flew back to Boston the next afternoon and life went on as before. Except when I jerked off and fantasized about him, about his kiss and the feel of my dick in his mouth or butthole. Other than those moments alone, I forgot about him. Instead I searched for love among the men I met at home, always accepting lust when love wasn't offered.

"You're husband material," Jake—ever the amateur therapist —said a few months after I told him I was gay. "That's why you got married so young. Some men are lovers and some men are husbands. Most men are one before becoming the other. But you're a husband by temperament. Like me. We'll take sex, but we want love."

After I got back from San Francisco, I asked him during one of our frequent phone conversations what he thought about Masters and slaves, about Dads and boys.

"It's an intense kind of intimacy, Joe. Why? You think you might be into it? After what we saw, I'm not surprised. Leather looks damn hot."

"I keep wondering what its appeal is. And, yeah, it turns me on."

"Then explore it," he said. I could almost hear his mischievous smile. "I am."

It's great having a best buddy who gives you permission to be yourself.

The next summer in Provincetown, I saw Barry again. And again he was dancing, bare-chested and chained, with his Master. Again I watched them kiss, watched in desperate wonder at their shared passion. Again he didn't notice me.

After the bars closed I went down to the docks and slapped around a boy who almost reminded me of my nameless beauty, slapped him around and pulled on the chain locked around his neck as I fucked his face. He accepted my cum gratefully, then asked me to fuck his ass. I was happy to comply, but I knew it wasn't the same as having a boy of my own.

When we were done, I asked him where he was from.

"San Francisco."

"I should've known. All the hot bottoms are from there."

He laughed. "Thanks."

"What's your name?"

"Matt. I'm here with my Owner."

I was startled by the carelessness with which he said this.

"Does he know you're here?"

"He's over there," Matt said, nodding toward a particularly dark and busy corner, a cluster of moving shadows filled with grunts and groans, with murmured promises that would fade at the first hint of light.

"You're so casual about these things out west."

Matt shrugged.

"I guess."

Then he kissed me and reached for my cock, already hardening again.

"Up for another round?" he asked with a crooked smile, handing me another condom.

How I wanted someone to smile at me like that all the time, to look at me as Barry looked at Sam. As always, I took what I could get. When I shot my third load I looked up at the moon, full and heavy, half hidden in the clouds of a coming storm, and howled.

I did my best to forget about him. And for a while I did. Then, a few years later, Jake and I headed to London for what had become our annual vacation together, as usual sharing a hotel room but not a bed. Every night Jake and I took a black cab to the leather bars.

And, yes, there he was again. This time he was being led around the Hoist on a leash by his Master, licking the boots of strangers. I put myself in their way so that my beautiful man, my nameless beauty, would lick my boots. They approached and I met Sam's eye. We nodded, and there he was: Barry, groveling at my booted feet. I put one boot behind his neck while he licked the other. Eventually he made his way past my boots to my leather pants, and then to the codpiece. I looked at Sam and he nodded, signaling me to unleash my fat cock from the leather codpiece and let it find its home in the deep, warm, wet throat waiting for it.

I looked back down at Barry, at his eager mouth grasping the codpiece between his teeth, his eyes looking up at me for permission. I nodded and he pulled it loose. My cock burst out of its confines, fast and furious, slapping him across the face. He let out a small cry of surprise to see the size of it, but opened wide without a second's hesitation. It was even better than I'd imagined, more wonderful than I'd dared hope. His mouth engulfed me. I was swallowed whole and I cried out to know such pleasure, such beauty. I put one hand behind his head and fucked.

Sam drew closer, caressed my pierced nipples through the thick hair that covers my entire chest and torso, and kissed me. Our beards met before our tongues, igniting the space between us. Even as we kissed, I screamed to the ceiling—and came. Cum shot out of me in thick streams. I could feel it explode from the very base of my balls. Ribbon after ribbon spurted, all greedily swallowed by my nameless beauty, the perfect vehicle for my seed.

Sam finished kissing me, and I pulled Barry to his feet. Finally, for the first time, I kissed him. After aching for that kiss for so long, it was an even bigger release than cumming down his throat had been. To hold him at last, to feel the softness of his lips and the bristle of his stubble-length beard, was the purest joy I'd known until that moment.

When our lips parted, Sam was standing there smiling.

"Hey, thanks, buddy."

"Yes. Thank you, Sir."

"Sure, pal." I nodded to his slave. "Boy."

"You're American like us?"

"Afraid so."

"Then let me buy you one."

Yes, the camaraderie of Americans meeting abroad. We introduced ourselves. I found out that they were from Chicago, that Sam's work allowed them to travel a lot, and that my beloved boy's name was Barry. Barry said little, letting his Master speak most of the time. But he smiled a lot, and whenever his eyes met mine I saw pleasure in them, pleasure in his subtle smile, like a cat lying in a patch of sunlight and lifting its face to better enjoy the sensation of the sun's warmth. I didn't tell them that I'd seen them in San Francisco and Provincetown, that I'd wanted Barry for years, that I envied what they had. I only exchanged email addresses, knowing I'd never contact them for fear I'd make a fool of myself should I ever see them again, should I ever see Barry again.

I went back to the hotel before Jake did and jerked off I

don't know how many times thinking of Barry. His mouth was so incredible; I could only wonder how good his fuckhole must feel. I wanted it but didn't dare hope for it. Once again, I was alone in the night, baying at the distant, unattainable moon. But it was a moon I'd now been to, a moon warm and beautiful and fantastically familiar, a moon that might perhaps be within my reach.

After that I fucked and flogged men whenever I could: men who said they were boys, boys who thought they were men, hot bottoms who wanted to please me and wear my collar for the weekend but also to live their own lives from Monday to Friday, men who wanted only the one night and no more, men without any sense of self who wanted to immolate themselves in mine, and hungry slaves hoping to hook me as their Master/husband and so land the plum role of doctor's wife. This last group disgusted me. I wanted my man to be my boy, yes, and to own him; but I also wanted him to be his own man, capable of self-sufficiency; otherwise, of what value would be the gift of his person to me? I had no real sense yet of what I wanted that man to be, other than my ideal of Barry, but I knew that he would not be a wife. I'd had a wife already, and I didn't want another one—of either sex.

I also learned that whatever pleasure and pain might be shared with these men, when there was no heart connection, no sense of mutual regard, affection, or respect, there was no satisfaction either. It didn't matter how sweet his ass was, how deep he could inhale my cock down his throat, how much pain he could take from a single-tail whip, or how I made him scream: if we didn't care about each other, at least a little, I didn't care about the sex. How much more wonderful would it be, I imagined, when I found the man/boy of my own, the one I could love forever?

Fast-forward a few more years: I was in Chicago with (of

course) Jake. He had just broken up with another boyfriend, so we headed to the Steamworks. Nothing like plentiful, anonymous sex to ease the pain of lost love, we figured.

I hadn't been there but a few minutes, it seemed, when I found myself surrounded by a bevy of big blond midwesterners, kissing them, feeling my ass being eaten, my pits licked, my nipples chewed, my cock sucked. I gave myself over to the flood of sensation, eyes closed and happier than I'd been in a while. Then I heard a grunt, a groan, and a sigh that told me—what? I don't know, but I opened my eyes and looked out the door of the room we were in and across the hall into a room with a sling. A man was stepping away from the sling, shaking his spent dick of excess juice, stepping aside to reveal who was in the sling—my angel: Barry. Our eyes met.

I shook off my cluster of farm boys (as I'd dubbed them) for the one whose fuckhole I'd longed for for so many years, longed for almost as much as I had for his kiss. I shut the door behind me, smiled, and stepped up to the sling, to the sweet hole puckered and ready for me to fuck.

I reached for a condom.

"Fuck me raw."

"No, I can't. I won't."

"Yes, you can. The others did. It's all right."

"No, it's not, Barry."

At the sound of his name, he looked up at me and, recognizing me for the first time, started to tremble. I saw tears in the corners of his eyes. To quiet him, I leaned over to kiss him, to comfort him. Then I noticed that there was no collar around his neck. Something was very wrong. I pulled him out of the sling, held him close.

"Come on," I whispered.

I laid him down on the mattress and held him close, kissing away the manly tears, caressing the hard, hairy body I wanted to know every inch of, to study for years to come.

"He's dead, you know."

"Sam?"

"Yeah. Master died in that plane crash last summer. I was supposed to join him in Paris a few days later. And…"

"It's okay, boy. I understand."

"Do you? Do you know how I feel? Do you know how it feels not to care if you live or die?"

"We've all lost loved ones, boy," I said, perhaps too severely. "As much as you hurt, you don't have a monopoly on pain."

He was quiet a moment, looked into my eyes, and reached up with his mouth for a kiss that I was glad to give him. Then his hand reached for my cock.

"I want you to fuck me."

I reached for a condom. He didn't resist this time. I lifted his legs onto my own strong shoulders, and entered paradise.

"Oh, baby…."

"Sir?"

"Oh, baby, baby…."

"You like it, Sir?"

Not since Matt under the pier in Provincetown had I met a man who could grab my dick with his fuckhole like Barry was doing now. He squeezed on my cock, then relaxed his hold on me, varying the tautness of his hole with the intensity of my strokes. This was not a passive bottom who lay still, expecting to be pleased. This was a man who sought to pleasure his partner with all the skill he could muster, with at least as much skill as most of the men who fucked him must have offered him that night.

"Baby, baby, it feels so good. It's so fucking amazing, boy, it's so fucking incredible."

And then he did that thing he does, that thing I have no words for and can't describe, that sent me over the edge, screaming into the abyss of orgasm. I shouted so loud that there was a sudden pause in the constant chatter of the bathhouse beyond our little room, a stunned silence followed by nervous laughter and knowing guffaws. I collapsed on top of him, our bodies colliding, slick with sweat.

"Baby."

"Sir."

I almost said, "I love you" but didn't dare. Even if it was true.

We kept fucking, each of us cumming time after time. He was focused on me, and I on him. We were our own little world, an eternal moment that could never be repeated or lost, now that we were together. Or so I told myself, so I hoped he felt as well.

I bent him over my knee to spank him between fucks, twisted his nipples, then held him down as I raped his hole, spat in his face, but never stopped kissing him.

At some point I heard Jake calling my name, and realized that we would have to end it sometime.

"I never want to let you go."

"I don't want you to, either, Sir."

"Are you ready for that?"

"Master has been dead more than a year, Sir. It's time I decided."

I kissed him again, losing myself once more in the softness of his lips, in the bristle of his beard.

Jake called my name again.

"Come on, boy. Let me introduce you to my best buddy in the world."

Four in the morning found the three of us at a diner on Halsted eating lousy burgers and trading tales.

"You don't remember the first time I saw you, Barry."

"Yes, I do."

"You think it was in London, but you're wrong. It was at

the Pleasure Dome in San Francisco, right after the Folsom Street Fair. You were dancing with Sam and I thought you were the handsomest man I'd ever seen. We both did. Ask Jake. He was there."

Barry shook his head.

"I don't remember seeing you there, but I was probably high. It was years before that, though. You don't remember? It was in high school."

"Not in Wakefield? Wakefield, Massachusetts?"

"Ayah. You were a year ahead of me. And I had such a crush on you. But I also thought you two were lovers and I used to follow you around hoping to see the two of you kiss, just so I'd know I wasn't the only queer in town."

Jake laughed.

"You weren't. Trust me."

"One time you were shooting hoops at the park and you caught me watching you through the fence and one of you asked if I wanted to join the game. I was scared shitless and ran. But later I always wished I'd gone in and played ball with you guys."

"That was you?"

Barry nodded.

"Yes, Sir. And when we saw you in London, I recognized you immediately—even with the beard you had then. I was so glad to finally get to touch you. Master said I could suck one dick that wasn't his that night. And I'd wanted yours for so long."

"Synchronicity," I murmured half-aloud, in wonder that our mutual longings should have lasted all these years.

"*Beshert!*" Jake said with sudden finality. "It was meant to be!"

Our courtship progressed slowly, if steadily. We both knew where we were going, knew that we were heading for the same destination, and we took our time getting there. We traveled back and forth, Barry more than me, and spent every available holiday and vacation together.

Sam's death had left Barry financially fixed, if rudderless. His mourning had turned into depression that devolved into a self-destructive spiral. Occasional drug use became a constant, and unprotected sex with strangers the norm. By some miracle, he avoided infection or worse. Sometimes he credits me for bringing him out of the miasma of his pain, but that's a gross exaggeration. All I did was appear at the moment when he was ready to bring his life back into focus.

"Synchronicity," I tell him.

"*Beshert!*" he responds.

Now that he didn't need to work, he could do what he really wanted, which was to go to graduate school, to study and teach. He applied to schools all over New England, thinking he'd attend the school closest to me and Boston. Then, on one of his weeklong visits (a week he spent collared, often naked, periodically flogged or whipped, and occasionally chained), I told him that I'd been offered a job at a teaching hospital in New Hampshire. He looked at me strangely.

"Where in New Hampshire, Sir?"

I told him.

"They just accepted me into grad school, Sir."

"Is it where you want to go, boy?"

"Yes, Sir. It was my first choice," he said. "Synchronicity."

"No," I corrected him. "*Beshert!*"

I woke up this morning to find him next to me, awake, sitting on the edge of the bed and looking out the window at the slowly moving river this former factory town was once dependent on for power and transportation. I reached over, touched him, and he turned to me with his usual smile.

"Sir," is all he said, all he ever needs to say.

I pulled him to me, kissed him hard, held him tight, spread his legs, and fucked him through the convenient hole in the back of the union suit he wears to bed during our New England winters, fucked him without so much as spit between us. He opened to accept me, opened then squeezed tight. Now that he's mine, now that he wears my collar, he is where I plant my seed. That's how I mark him as mine. I do what no one else is allowed to do. The collar is only the symbol.

I think of how my wife had demanded my help on occasions like this. She was, quite naturally, insisting on equality in our marriage, something Barry neither wants nor needs. His self-confidence and my belief in him are all that matters—that, and the chain around his neck and my seed in his body. We are two orbs circling each other, reflecting our love back and forth, two planets dancing in perfect sync.

Just before our guests arrive he showers and puts on a fresh shirt. Then, because there is time, and because I need it, he sucks my cock, successfully drawing the cum from my balls just moments before the doorbell rings. As always, his timing is impeccable.

At dinner, the local historian again remarks that one of the town's founding families shared Barry's surname. Barry's response to this information is polite interest. He knows already that he is their descendent but refuses to take credit or blame for this accident of birth.

"You're such a great cook," the minister's husband remarks. "It's almost enough to make me want to be gay. Honey, why don't you cook like this?"

His wife shakes her head and rolls her eyes, this being a tender point between them.

The women with the antique store laugh, delighted to watch the foibles of their heterosexual neighbors. The biker couple shares a smirk with each other, and us.

"That's not fair," Barry says with his usual modesty. "Cooking is just a hobby for me. And I don't have a congregation to respond to at all hours. Besides, we eat very simply most of the time. Often it's just soup and bread."

"True," I agree, not saying that the soup is one he makes himself, the bread fresh because he's learning the art of baking it, that canned and frozen food are a rarity in our kitchen unless prepared by him. No one knows the trouble he goes to when he cooks, or how well we live. Like all New Englanders, he likes it that way, the exact details of his personal life kept a mystery.

I smile at him, prouder than ever, my cock hardening again.

I watch Barry the next afternoon working at his desk, absentmindedly petting the cat that sits next to the keyboard, purring. I fucked and flogged him the night before as a reward for our successful dinner party. Then fucked him again this morning, making sure he shot his own load before I gave him mine. He hums as he strokes his cat, content with the warmth of the healing welts on his back, with the feeling of my seed deep in his guts, with the touch of his cat's winter coat. Then he notices me watching him and starts to stand up.

"Sir?"

"It's okay, babe. Just admiring my boy."

"Your boy who's turning gray, Sir."

"As if that could make me love you less."

He laughs, crossing the room to my chair where I've been working on my grant proposal, and sits at my feet. I stroke his short hair and beard, happier than ever to have captured my mysterious Other in the crook of my heart. He leans his head against my leg to better appreciate my touch and sighs deeply, tendering a kiss to my free hand.

Together we watch Barry's cat stretch, jump off the desk,

stretch again, and step noiselessly across the carpet to our dog lying in a patch of winter sunlight, absorbing what warmth he can from it. The dog lifts his head to the cat's soft salutation, to the gentle touch of the cat's paw on his muzzle. They touch noses in greeting before a brief but well-mannered exchange of affectionate grooming, and the cat curls himself up with the dog, purring loudly.

The dog wags his tail, content.

A History of Barbed Wire
Jeff Mann

It itches as I write this, my new tattoo, first tattoo. Black barbed wire wrapped tight around my right biceps and triceps, a desire that took decades to distill. Four times a day I dutifully rub lotion on it, study the design in the mirror, watch it peel and heal, try to discern its history.

First, a boy in southern West Virginia, a drizzly March day. I'm helping my father run barbed wire along a new pasture fence, from locust post to locust post, then about a corner oak. We tug the thorny wire carefully off its roll, pull it tight, and staple it to the wood. Always there's the knowledge, the dread, the slightest chance that a tautly stretched length of wire might snap. I remember stories: the farmer in an adjoining hamlet, the sudden accident; the way the wire, too tense, turned on him just as a rattler abruptly betrays the snake handler's confident piety. In my imagination, this man I never met is naked, lying in the meadow grass, his beard the thick copper of August light. The barbed wire's wrapped about his torso, the dark hair on his chest is rilling with rain and scarlet, a

March drizzle such as this is lapping away the blood. "Pull it tighter," orders my father. I start nervously, and one of the barbs pierces my thumb. Wincing, I lift the wound to my mouth, lick off the red stain, the taste of rust, waiting for the sound of a whip in the rain.

High school loner, I'm reading my first gay novel, Patricia Nell Warren's *The Front Runner*, trying to imagine the track star and his coach making love. Finally I must face what I am. The local mountain men have always frightened me, but now I realize that I also desire them, though I know my lust, if expressed, would be met only with contempt and violence. Brought up on stories of courage—Confederate soldiers, Greek and Roman heroes—I'm trying to decide what manhood means in light of this problematic and uninvited homosexuality. I want to become the sort of man I desire, I want somehow to absorb the apparently effortless masculinity of country boys. Boots, beards, chest hair. Denim jackets, pickup trucks. Tattoos.

In my early twenties now, I'm escaping into university anonymity, buying my first leather jacket, swaggering self-consciously into my first leather bar, cultivating roughness, learning how to drink bourbon straight. That red-mustached bartender, veins cresting the pale ridges of his biceps—his eyes meet mine. Back in his apartment, Steve lights a votive candle, slowly strips for me, pulls lengths of rope from beneath the bed. I tie his hands to the headboard, knot a bandana between his teeth, and take a doubled-over belt to his perfect ass. He groans when I enter him. In the candlelight, his eyes are moist, his eyes are bright.

A decade later, I take my turn in Richmond. The cock gag's buckled in tight, the rope cuts into my arms, wrists, and ankles. I'm a martyr drunk on too much mescal, seduced by a leather couple who've been looking for a sacrifice. Drew, black-bearded, his shoulders dense with muscles and tattoos, holds me down. Tom, ponytailed, ruthless, expressionless, drips hot wax over my nipples. I sweat, buck, shake my head, bite down on rubber, a muffled beggary, wrestling against them. They force me back against the mattress, their tongues and mustaches ranging over my body, and then they arch together above me, their kiss a keystone. Drained saint, exhausted, replete, I fall trembling against Drew's big tattooed shoulder. Gently he smoothes my thinning hair, runs a finger through the sticky opal puddling on my chest.

In St. Mel's Church in Longford, Ireland, I sit in the pew, watching locals pray, wondering what tragedies they are wrestling with. Somewhere near are the graves of my ancestors, blood two hundred years removed. My youth's almost over, my temples are slowly silvering. Before me, Christ opens his robe to reveal his heart, which is tightly wrapped in thorns. Suddenly I remember the corner oak, at the angle where two fences meet, back home on the farm. Barbed wire again, its intermittent fangs my father and I wrapped around the tree's expanding girth (the wood widening within like concentric circles a skipped stone sings across pond water). Over the years, into rough bark that tight barbed wire will slowly sink, then be swallowed up, a sharp suffering disappearing beneath the skin.

Ireland still, Sligo now. Above the door of the Cathedral of the Immaculate Conception, Christ is stretched in gleaming marble upon his cross. Drunk on pub Guinness, I want to ascend somehow—ladder or levitation—run my fingers across the painful arch of that carved chest, stroke the long hair and beard. My last lover still arches beneath me so, at least in memory, summer afternoons stolen together, his husband safely ensconced at work. A rainstorm rips the white oak leaves, rival gods wrestle within our bones. To the bed, to this

crucifix of sheets, I tie him tight—the way we both like it—
then hurt him gently, hairy savior, gym-pumped imp. I run my
mouth over soft black moss, hard curves of chest, shoulders,
biceps, cock, till our skins are splashed with magma. I bury my
face in the sweaty fur between his pecs, wishing time would
cease on this spot. I know what nothing surpasses, the world's
beauty held entirely in my arms.

All my lonely youth I dreamed of marriage, and now the
domesticity I dreamed of seizes me fast. Television evenings,
cookbooks, monogamy. Conversations about lawn, house,
and car. Hum of the dishwasher, the air conditioner. Days
spent behind a desk. I want some reckless, irrevocable gesture,
some proof that a little youth, a little edge is left.

Context can eroticize almost anything. In gay porno I
buy, magazines like *Drummer, Bear, Bound and Gagged*,
tattooed men are tied and tying, sucking, fucking, flexing,
posing. In the campus gym, I study athletic college boys
as they sweat and strain. Tattoos dark against pale skin
and muscle-bulge. Designs delicately drilled into shoulders,
biceps, calves. Sophisticated body art, long ago superseding
the trashy, primitive tattoos I remember on hillbilly boys of
my hometown. Even middle-aged, it's instinctual: incorporate
what you find desirable, make it your own.

My mother, my sister, now my lover—how they've tried to
keep out my wilderness, my warrior, my extremes. The first
tattoo I wore was temporary, a rose wrapped around a dagger.
Then the henna flirtations: a thin black armband in Rehoboth
Beach, a few tribal swirls across one shoulder. No drunken
adolescent spontaneity here. Now I take years to contemplate
consequence, to make decisions that are permanent. For
months, sadly dick-whipped, I'm wheedling my dubious
spouse for his approval. Meanwhile, I carry around designs in
my backpack, pull them out in the evenings, stand before the

mirror, roll up my right sleeve and hold them up to my arm. I wonder how badly it will hurt.

It's a snowy spring equinox. Into Ancient Art I step for my long-postponed appointment. Pulling off my coat, sweater, and shirt, I stretch out bare-chested in the padded chair. Patrick is one of the best tattoo artists in the region. He's young and handsome, with blue eyes and a scruffy blond goatee, colorful Celtic designs swirling along his thick forearms. I wish he'd tie me down and stuff a rag into my mouth before he begins. Instead, he pulls on rubber gloves, sets out tiny pots of ink, and then the needles begin to bite and hum.

A small proud pain, almost a pleasure: nails, honeybees, wild rose thorns. A minor test of strength, sweat rolling down my sides like spring thaw. When Patrick bandages me up, a little over an hour later, I'm sorry that it's over. Now barbed wire's tied about my arm. Appetite's inscribed, flesh is emblematic. I shake his hand, pull on my clothes and my respectability, and stride out into the snowstorm, flakes coming down thickly now in slate-gray dusk.

What we want's indelible, unlike so much we know, those transitory passions that wash over us and trickle away into meaninglessness. Something like a scar, but chosen, free of accident or random circumstance. Here art's eternity and body's ephemera reach some compromise. As if ink might redeem the page, might lend meaning. It's scrimshaw, rope burn, rough touch that does not evaporate. Thorns wrapped around the heart of the Sacrificed God. A naked man bound tight, strength in restraint, learning to submit, letting go, learning the pedagogy of suffering. A message which will not erode away, like epitaphs in rain, which will perish only when its medium smolders reluctantly at the edges, like wet paper, then takes to flame.

Everything's Gone Green
Marshall Moore

It's too early to call Dave. I think it's eleven. Besides, I feel like a freshly hatched pod person from *Invasion of the Body Snatchers,* still slimy and smelly and stumbling over my own feet. Dave told me to give him a call but I'll take a shower first.

Last night I went out to dinner and to hit a couple of clubs with friends after my roommate flaked out on our plans, and look where it got me. I had a fantastic time, sure, but I'm paying for it in blood this morning. The sun burns down on my face and, outside, a streetcar clatters by. Every limb feels as if it had been sawn off someone else and glued to my overheating torso. Very *Jeepers Creepers.* I even look the part, a twenty-something actor in one of those slasher flicks about virgins impaled on gardening tools, the only penetration they'll ever know. No, how about this scenario: I'm a *Firestarter* extra, about to spontaneously combust here in bed, sweat sizzling off me for a few seconds before streamers of flame burst out of my chest. There are hangovers and then there are hangovers. This has to be some kind of record.

"Fuck," I croak. My mouth tastes like I blew some guy with a gym sock over his dick instead of a rubber. It's never a good sign when you wake up in the morning and the first word you utter is *Fuck*.

I went to Tulane. I know a bit about drinking and how to recover. These days my impression of a grown-up is pretty convincing: I don't have many hangovers to subdue. The skill stays with you. Some aspirin or Alka-Seltzer, that's the thing, and Gatorade. Any of those sports drinks will do, but Gatorade is the original, the one, the true, the green syrup that helped me win trophies on the track and swim teams. Slurp enough of that shit and you'll feel like a god. Especially if you were out all night with your rowdy friends pouring beer down your throat. If that doesn't work, try something stronger: I recommend Red Bull, but all those energy drinks in the narrow cans are interchangeable. As long as it contains enough caffeine, vitamins, and herbal supplements to send a retiree's heart into arrhythmia, it'll do.

Dave. A group of us met for dinner at a new Thai place in the Mission. He came as a friend of a friend's friend, or something like that. Somebody's plans changed. I never did figure out his connection to the group. He was there. That was enough. The restaurant was too loud for me to follow the details of the story when Andy, a guy I'd gone out with a few times, introduced us. *Josh, this is…what's your name again?* Airport runways are quieter than most of the restaurants on Valencia, and as much as possible I ignored the guy on my right, Simon, who was sleeping with my friend Lance. Simon reeked of cigarette smoke and wore glasses with blue-tinted lenses. He spoke through his nose in this grating, weary *I'm above all this* drone. Let him talk to his dinner plate. I was more interested in the darkly good-looking guy on my left. Besides, he was one of two people at the table I could actually hear. Lucky me.

Dave Buenaventura, long black hair in a ponytail, handsome almond eyes, olive skin, just thinking about the way he looked at me last night in his car. He'd driven me home. I invited him up but he said, *Let's wait,* then leaned over and helped himself to a slow, lingering kiss. When, after some making out, I undid the top three buttons of his shirt to kiss the top of his chest, he gasped, *You found my spot.*

Yes, that's enough to keep me here in bed a little longer, those words…and the way he writhed when I licked his Adam's apple a second later.

He denied wearing cologne when I asked about the scent.

"It's just soap," he said, running a hand through my hair.

"It smells too good to be soap."

He shrugged and I resumed the kissing. A nipple. The other one. I flicked them with my tongue and made him gasp again. Under his shirt, this iridescent silvery thing he had on beneath a battered leather jacket, I went exploring: the smooth expanse of his abs, the suppleness of his skin. White men don't have skin like that. It's as if there are no pores. The skin is burnished metal that has warmed up and learned to breathe.

Yes, all this happened in his old Mustang convertible, which I have to say is kind of a ridiculous car for these narrow, vertical San Francisco streets. We fogged up the windows like a pair of teenagers. I stopped short of letting my hand roam south of Dave's navel. If he wanted to wait, then I'd be a gentleman and show some restraint.

I wanted to keep kissing him until my mouth went dry and his razor stubble chafed the skin off my lips, but a yawn interrupted me. All that alcohol. The late hour. We'd been dancing. It caught up with me.

Dave chuckled, all the more intimate with his face two inches from mine and his lips shiny with my spit. He ruffled my hair.

"You're not why I yawned," I stammered.

"Go upstairs and get some sleep, handsome."

I nodded, suppressing another yawn by biting my lower lip and locking my jaw.

"Guess I should." I looked at him. His face—half in shadow, half suffused with a surreal orange glow from the streetlight down the block—radiated affection. I leaned over and gave him another quick kiss. My lips tingled from the sandpapering he'd given them with his stubble. "Although I don't really want to."

"I don't want you to, either, but…" Dave left the rest unsaid. Which was fine.

I opened the door, had to shove. Old Detroit iron. A precipitous Noe Valley grade. Wrenching myself out of the Mustang took speed and dexterity worthy of a Cirque du Soleil acrobat. That door slamming shut would have guillotined a limb. Gravity sucks. Dave rolled down his window, and I leaned in for a goodnight kiss.

"Nice meeting you," I said. "I was supposed to see the new *Scream* movie with my roommate but he flaked out. Lucky me."

"No, lucky me." Dave nodded. "Call me tomorrow, okay?"

"I will." I slowly pulled away, turned, took a step toward the front door of my building. The usual battle raged between the big head and the little one: Turn around and invite him up! No, don't, you're not a horny college kid anymore! To compensate, I walked more slowly than usual, in case he had a change of heart and called out for me to wait a minute. Just think about the moment when you've got him in bed and his shirt and jeans finally come off! No, Josh, don't think about that. I fished in my pocket for the front door key, had just opened it when I heard what I'd been hoping for:

"Hey, Josh!"

I froze. The front door probably woke a few people when

it swung shut. Do I show him the shit-eating grin or let it fade before turning around? I took a couple of steps back in Dave's direction.

"What's up?"

"You never got my number."

So much for my buzz.

"I can't believe we forgot that part."

"We were having too much fun," Dave said. "Hold out your hand."

He wrote his number on my palm with a marker, then blew on it to dry the ink.

"Goodnight, handsome man," he said.

None of that insomniac tossing and turning last night, no mummification among my own linens. Nope. I passed out the second I got horizontal, a bit rueful that Dave wasn't here with me, also glad he'd gone home. The fun could wait. My eyes wouldn't stay open. My consciousness dropped like a stone down a well.

Getting out of bed this morning seems less and less likely, not now, not yet. I'm dying for about a gallon of Gatorade and maybe some Excedrin, but an electric sort of inertia takes over. I keep coming back to what I imagined last night: Dave the pagan sex nymph, here in my bed. Discovery, laziness, the opening credits of a putative romance.

My hangover has receded to a dull anesthetized roar, my hands roam across fabric, under, exploring. He's wiry. Not the kind of guy you'd find at the gym, but there's no fat on him anywhere. He runs, I think he told me. Narrow hips, cock lengthening in its lazy way after I slide his jeans off. His eyes are closed. For the first time, I notice his long lashes. I want to kiss them too, but those full lips compete for my attention.

Okay, even with a vicious hangover I've still got a boner. This comes as faint surprise. I pull the blinds shut, and once I'm out of the sun's glare I feel better. It's enough of a boost for me to decide that wriggling out of my boxers is worth the effort. I could always pull my dick through the flap in the front but somehow that isn't where I see this fantasy going.

Is he circumcised or not? You can never tell. At first I pretend he's not, and then I substitute a cut version to see which I like better. I can't decide. It's him. It's his. Once it's in my mouth, will it matter?

Some guys require lube to jack off but I'm not one of them. I prefer a dry hand. It's a different kind of friction. Something about lube has a numbing effect, makes the sensation more removed, less immediate.

Salt floods my mouth, seawater. I didn't tell him not to come in my mouth and he didn't warn me first. I'm okay with that. It's him. It's his.

I come faster than I was expecting to, and the volume isn't my usual gush. The semen sort of falls out of my dick. Dehydration. The pleasure courses through me, then subsides quickly, leaving me drowsy, more depleted than I was at the start.

Dave.

I grope for a towel. They're under the bed. When I wipe the congealing remnants of my fantasy away from my chest, off my wrist and hand, I see what slipped my mind: Dave's number. My bones turn to rubber when I look at my palm and see blurs. The numbers look like camouflage. Something in my semen has broken the ink down into its component colors. Some blue. Mostly green. The 415 area code is unmistakable, but the rest? At the end, a 7. The digit before that, either a 6 or a 5. Maybe a couple of zeroes.

Cum dissolves ink. Who knew?

I stare at my hand. It's a horrifying moment, as if I'm partially possessed. Think of *The Evil Dead*. Whose hand is this, anyway? Who let the demons in? Whose friend was Dave, and who introduced us? Did he tell me where he lived, what neighborhood?

After a few minutes of hypnosis from the greenish blur in my palm, I tumble out of bed, put on a robe, and make my way to the kitchen for the Gatorade and the phone. If I have to call Information as well as everybody I know and a lot of people I don't, I'm going to track Dave down. I am. But first, I've got to do something about this hangover.

Corncobs
Dominic Santi

Iowa farm boys understand about corncobs. When your asshole's itchy, there's nothing in the world like lubing up a rack of fresh bumpy kernels, grabbing a handful of peeled-back husk to hold on to, and nosing a pointy tip up against your pucker. The cum stain on the wall behind me was still there from the first time I pressed a corncob all the way up my ass. By the time I was nineteen, I'd become an expert at nurturing, and then using, the especially large cobs of hybrid corn growing in the experimental plot that started just beyond the far edge of the barn.

I'd never considered cornholing myself to be a gay or straight thing. I knew I wasn't interested in chicks, at least not as anything more than friends. But I wasn't interested in any of the guys I knew, either. The only men I'd ever felt anything for were old enough to be my grandfather. That was way too weird for me to consider being "attracted," or even "interested." I mean, we're talking *old* guys here, you know? Like my friend Tom's Uncle Deke.

Deke reminded me of the rough farmers in pictures of

the Depression, which wasn't all that long before he'd been born. He called himself an "old coot," and he rode his tractor wearing a ribbed tank top and an old straw hat and bib overalls that he only hooked on one side. When his shirt was wet with sweat, I could see his nipple showing through, surrounded by thick, gray chest hair. His eyes twinkled when he laughed and ruffled Tom's and my hair like we were puppies. We were both eighteen then and seniors in high school, but I used to have wet dreams about Tom's uncle taking me over his knee and spanking my bare ass while my dick rubbed against the rough, heavy denim covering his thighs. I dreamed he spanked me until I came. I woke up on my belly with my covers bunched up between my legs and covered with cum. I knew I'd been humping the bed in my sleep.

I never told anybody about those dreams, or about the crush I had on Mr. Perkins, the FHA club advisor. He'd almost made the Olympic swimming team when he was in high school, way back before he went to Korea. He was the first teacher I ever heard talk about "same-sex attraction," though he was talking about cows that fell in love with each other and saying thank god for artificial insemination. I laughed along with everybody else, but I wondered—if cows could do it, could bulls maybe do it, too? I watched him from the corner of my eye when I knew he couldn't see me. Mr. Perkins always wore suits, and the bulge in the front of his pants would have done a bull proud, even though he was soft. I told myself I absolutely did not want to know what his dick looked like hard, or if it got real drippy when the foreskin peeled back over his cockhead, or if his cum smelled salty and musky, but still tasted creamy when he licked it from his hand—like mine did.

The only time I'd said anything to anybody about thinking about older men was during graduation week. I'd confided in my best friend, Tammy, that I'd love to have a muscled, hairy chest like my senior English teacher. Tammy had wrinkled her nose and reminded me that Mr. Bartell's chest had gray hair and he was going to retire the next year. I got all huffy and told her I was just speaking hypothetically, but she gave me one of those looks like she did sometimes and laughed. She told me later, after I'd figured things out, that she'd known I was gay when she met me, but since I was so busy being a macho asshole with my football buddies, she hadn't bothered to mention it.

For the longest time, I figured maybe I was just one of those weird people who didn't really want to hook up with anybody else. So, like I said, when I started playing around with corncobs, I didn't think of it as being a gay or a straight thing. It was just something that made my asshole feel mighty damn good and made me come real hard.

By the second summer after I graduated, my folks didn't particularly hold me accountable anymore for what I did in my free time. They said that since I pulled a man's weight to ensure the success of the farm I was eventually going to inherit, I deserved a man's privacy, so long as they weren't getting calls to post bail or crap like that—which they weren't. On the hot August night I picked the biggest hybrid ear, though, my face still heated when I thought about my plans for the evening. We sat down to dinner with Tuck, our hired hand, and I muttered something about wanting to do some leather working later in the loft while I still had some light.

Nobody paid much attention, though Tuck nodded and said gruffly, "I admire your work, boy. You've got a good hand."

I muttered a quick "Thank you," blushing even more as I stuffed mashed potatoes in my mouth. Tuck's voice was thick and growly, and he laughed a lot, but I was usually too tongue-tied to talk around him. He was at least as old as Mr. Perkins, with short, thick gray hair and clear blue eyes. But Tuck worked harder than any of the younger hands we'd had.

In fact, he knew more about growing corn and farming than anyone I'd ever met, even though he only had an eighth-grade education. His face was rough and weather-beaten, and the thick gray fur covering his chest and back glistened when his muscles rippled in the afternoon sun. I couldn't help the hard-ons I got when he walked by me, smelling like hay and sweat and, one time, grease from working on the tractor. And I couldn't stop wondering if the huge bulge in his crotch was all thick, manly dick.

I took a bite of roast beef, concentrating hard on my dinner and trying not to think about either Tuck or Tuck's dick or the new hybrid that everybody was talking about. While they were discussing overall yields and market quality, all I was interested in was what I was going to do with the huge ear of corn I'd picked that afternoon. It was a good twelve inches long and three inches in diameter. My ass was itching for the feel of each and every one of those bumpy little nobs sliding through my sphincter. I just knew that cob was going to give me the best fuck of my life.

The low rays of the sun were still streaming over the western fields when I climbed the ladder and pushed open the door to the part of the loft I'd claimed for myself. Nobody ever bothered me there. Dust motes danced over the comfortable nest I'd made in the hay. Since I liked getting fucked on my back, I'd custom designed the "mattress" so one blanket-covered area was shaped like a regular bed, complete with a white cotton case on the pillow. That end faced away from the window, so I wouldn't be blinded by the setting sun. The far end, the one toward the entrance to the loft, had hay bunched up under the sheets, so when I spread my knees and tipped them back to my shoulders, my lower back was supported like it was on a huge pile of pillows. That let me keep both hands free to either beat off, or like tonight, indulge in some serious ass play.

Earlier that day, I'd laid out my supplies. A huge bottle of lube and a pile of fresh cum rags rested on a towel in the middle of the bed, along with four corncobs—a little starter one, a medium-sized warm-up one, one the size I usually used to fuck myself, and finally, the *pièce de résistance,* my huge, beautiful hybrid. It glowed bright yellow in the evening sun, its strong husks green and sturdy—my safety handles, in case things got too slippery or slid in too far. I tossed a couple of extra-large condoms on the towel, in case too many kernels started smashing open when they squeezed through my asshole. I was ready for a night of lovin'.

I shucked out of my boots and clothes, tossing them in a pile by the door. The head of my dick was already poking free of my foreskin. I stroked it a few times, shivering at the feel of my hand gliding over my naked skin as I lowered myself to the bed. I scooted back until my ass was perched right on the edge, then I tipped back, lowering my head and shoulders until they were comfortably positioned on the pillow. My legs were bent so far back my knees were almost on my shoulders. My cock and balls fell forward, and my ass was wide open and accessible, just the way I wanted it to be. I grabbed the lube and squeezed a river of it onto my pucker, jumping as the cool gel ran down my crack and into the sheet.

Usually, I started out with a long, slow anal massage. Tonight, though, I wanted the first touch to be the bumpy eroticism of the corncob. I grabbed the littlest one, poured lube over it, and rubbed the tiny ridges over my asshole. I figured it didn't matter that I groaned out loud. Nobody was around to hear me but the barn cats and the cows downstairs. They didn't care if I got loud. I rubbed the little cob back and forth, flexing my asslips until they kissed upwards, quivering at the bumpy massage.

When I was almost frantic with the need for penetration, I set down the cob. With one hand, I pulled my asslips as far apart as I could. With the other hand, I picked up the lube. Taking a deep breath, I pressed the tip of the bottle to my sphincter, and I squeezed. The cool gel trickled down into my ass. I shivered hard, moaning as my cock jumped and my ass muscles instinctively clenched tight against each other. Then I picked up the starter cob again, getting a good grip on the base husks as the fingers of my other hand once more pulled my asslips open. I touched the tip of the cob to my hole, drilling back and forth with a firm, steady pressure. My asslips clenched frantically as the tip slid in. Then the bumpy rows were sliding through my sphincter. I gasped out loud as my muscles responded to the stretching burn, shuddering as my quivering asshole reached out and demanded more of the incredibly intense stimulation. Then my sphincter gave way. I groaned long and loud as the cob slid in deep.

"Fuck, man," I whispered, enjoying how the sound of the dirty words made my dick feel even stiffer. Though I routinely took good-sized ears of corn, I really liked the way my sphincter always kicked up a fit about that first, deep fuck. It was like my hole wanted to be seduced, but it was determined to be a bitch about it, every step of the way.

When the pain got more pronounced than the burn, I pulled my hand back and squeezed lube all over the cob and my hole again. And while my asshole was still throbbing, I drilled the littlest cob back in—faster this time, though still slow and gentle enough for it to be a thorough seduction. As usual, my cock had gone soft at this deeper penetration. But with my asshole still throbbing, I took my thick, heavy dickflesh in my hand and pulled my foreskin over my dickhead, stroking in time to my sphincter's squeeze around my corncob dildo. As my dick hardened, my hole gradually relaxed, like all the blood that had been filling it too tightly was rushing forward with the rest of the blood in my body to fill my dick.

I took things slowly, letting my body adjust to the sensations, shuddering at the hundreds of bumps gently teasing my hole open. When the little cob wasn't quite enough anymore, I set it aside and lubed up the next one. I'd done this so often, my hole knew not to tighten in the interim. I squeezed my dick a few times, rolling my balls around in my sac and rubbing my perineum, gradually stroking back to my hole again. When I touched the new cob to my pucker, my anal lips kissed it hello. And as I stretched my sphincter open again and started to press the tip in, my asslips kissed right up it until they were stretched over it just the way they'd been with the little cob. The tightening was more pronounced this time, but when I slid the cob back and forth, the friction of the bigger kernels felt so good I knew my asshole wanted more. I picked up the lube bottle, and holding it right next to my wide-stretched lips, I pulled the cob quickly out and squeezed lube in. This time, I didn't have to hold my sphincter open. The cool gel ran deep into my gaping hole. I shuddered, breathing deeply while the sensations surged back and forth between my cock and my asshole.

The cob squished when I slid it back in. By then, I was so relaxed and turned-on that my efforts immediately shifted into a hole-stretching fuck that had me daydreaming about Mr. Bartlett's chest and Mr. Perkins's dick, and then about Tuck's dick and how much I loved the deep growl of his voice when he praised me. I probably could have bypassed the next cob, but stretching my hole open just felt so damn good that I indulged myself, seducing my ass like it was a lover I'd been lusting after forever. The third cob was the biggest my ass was used to. It took me a while to relax enough to get into a really contented fuck. Pretty soon, though, my cock was oozing a steady stream from the pressure on my prostate, drops of precum occasionally running down my hip as my asslips fluttered against the kernels. With a series of long, slow strokes, I shuddered hard, my whole groin reminding me that this was the part where the serious fucking started.

With the third cob buried deep in my ass, I pulled the hybrid closer, caressing the huge bumps as I tried and failed to wrap my fingers around the widest part of the girth. I'd never had anything that big up my ass. I set the hybrid next to my hip and picked up the lube bottle. As I pulled the third cob out with one hand, I squeezed damn near a quarter of the bottle up my ass. My rectum contracted at the flood of lube gushing in, but I ignored it. I knew I'd have lube running out of me all night long, but I just didn't care. I tested the husks once more, making sure they were strong enough to pull the cob back out if necessary. Then I took a deep breath, lubed up my dream lover, spread my open hole as wide as my fingers would allow, and pressed the tip of the hybrid to my anal lips. The rippling bumps slid in the first couple of inches, up to where the cob was as wide around as the previous one. The sight of that huge cob sticking up out of my ass had me so fucking hot my dick drooled even though I wasn't hard at all anymore. Then I started pressing in.

The evening light was fading now, but I could still see the cob slowly moving down, disappearing into me as I felt my asshole stretching impossibly wider to take the huge, well-nubbed shaft. I lost track of time while I fucked the corncob slowly in and out, groaning at the relentless stretch and burn as my hybrid dick reached ever deeper into me, sliding over my anal nerves and my joyspot, massaging every inch of my ass with those bliss-inducing bumps, pressing the precum up out of me in rivers as I moaned and trembled and shook with the need to feel my asshole filled. It hurt just enough and so good I didn't want it to ever end.

My fingers touched up against my asshole. I froze, stunned to realize I'd taken the whole thing. As my stretched-out muscles tried and mostly failed to squeeze around the girth of the cob, I groaned long and loud, rubbing my fingertips over the well-stretched edges of my hypersensitive sphincter. It felt so good, tears trickled down the side of my face, dripping hot and wet onto my neck before they fell into my hair.

"Fuck me," I whispered, trembling as I slowly pulled the cob partway back out. "Stretch my hole and fuck me." I shook as I pressed back in. The bumps massaged my asslips, no longer really stretching or burning, just stroking in and out on a sea of sensation as my hole opened effortlessly to take that huge fucking corncob dick. "Fuck me so I know my hole's being used." My ass opened again as the words started rolling off my tongue. Once more, the sensation started boiling up inside my joyspot. "Oh, yeah. Fuck me so deep my balls can't help draining themselves," I moaned as the cob once more bottomed out in my ass. "Fuck me so hard I have to come."

My ravaged hole was too stretched to tighten any more. As my shaft filled, I started a long, slow, shallow rocking, keeping the cob mostly bottomed out in me, but fucking it back and forth just enough that my asshole was always aware of the bumpy kernels, so my ass was always being caressed, and my dick juice was being pressed out until I was shaking with the sensations. My other hand shook as I wrapped it around my dick and slowly pulled my foreskin over my dickhead.

The tremors started deep in my prostate, long and slow and so overpowering they almost tore my body apart. As the bone-deep waves washed over me, rivers of semen boiled up from my dick. I cried out, pulling the orgasm through my pulsing shaft until I was shaking so hard I was afraid I'd lose my grip on the husks. My hole was so slick and loose, my body seemed to be trying to suck the whole corncob into me. My shoulders rocked against the sheet and suddenly I was laughing and crying at the same time. Tears rolled down my cheeks as I leaned back into the bed. I was relaxed to my bones, covered in sticky cum, so contented I just lay there with that huge fucking corncob filling my ass.

I was so lost in the moment that, at first, I barely noticed that the stairs to the loft were squeaking. As the sound finally registered, I figured it was one of the barn cats, one that had been waiting near the top so it only had to go up the last few steps. When I opened my eyes, though, Tuck was standing inside the door. Even in the quickly dimming light, I could see the bulge in the front of his jeans was bigger than I'd ever seen it before. I was too blissed out to be embarrassed, and he looked so good and I wanted him so bad.

"I already came," I said quietly.

"Don't I know it, boy," he laughed. His voice was low and gravelly. "I've seen a lot of men come. But I've never seen anything as hot as you making love to your asshole." He slowly unhooked his overalls, stripping naked as I watched him bare every inch of his gray-haired, leathery skin. Then he was standing beside me, holding a monster cock in his gnarled old hands. His dick was as wide as a beer can and so long that even using both hands, he didn't cover the shaft. It was bigger than I'd ever imagined a dick could be. The exposed head was almost purple, precum running down thick and glistening. He stroked himself, shuddering as he pulled his dickskin up over the head.

"In all my life, I've met fewer than a half-dozen men who could take my cock, and none of them without shaking from pain." His eyes moved from mine to where my hand still gently rocked the corncob in my ass. Then he looked back at me, pure naked wanting in his eyes. I smiled at him and squeezed my cockhead, shivering as the last drops oozed out. Then I picked up the sticky bottle and held it out to him with my cum-covered fingers.

"I like lots of lube."

His blue eyes twinkled as he knelt down beside me. "That's a good way to be fucked, boy."

I hadn't had to use the condoms on the corncob. But when

I looked from the pile of rubbers on the sheet to Tuck's dick, I was suddenly aware that there was no way the latex was going to stretch that much. Tuck followed my gaze, then grinned and leaned over to pull a huge female condom from his pants pocket. He tore the package open, then knelt in front of me and moved my fingers from the corncob. As he pulled it free, I was certain I felt every bump moving slowly through my hole. Then his rough, calloused fingers were petting my ultrasensitive ass and I was trembling from head to foot.

"Your hole is beautiful, boy. Hot and loose and ready to be filled with dick." I shook as he slowly pushed the female condom up my ass. Then he squeezed lube into me, lots of lube. "I'm going to make you feel so good."

I smiled and reached up for him. He maneuvered me until we were lying in the center of the bed with my knees almost back to my shoulders. He touched the tip of his cock to my hole. Then he leaned into me. His huge, hot cock slid all the way in on a long, slow glide. My balls were dry, but I still shook like my whole body was orgasming. Tuck shuddered in my arms.

"Never, boy. Never, never, never...," he groaned, leaning forward and panting. He trembled like he was trying not to come, and I suddenly realized he was. When his eyes finally opened, his smile lit his whole face. "Not once has somebody just let me in." He pulled back, almost all the way out, then slowly thrust back in. "Your man-pussy fits me like work gloves, like it was broken in just for me." I cried out as his huge warm cock slid over my joyspot. "Like it was just waiting for me to slide in home."

Tuck fucked me long and slow and sweet. I'd figured I was too tired and oversensitized to squirt again. But when I started to shake once more, his husky voice growled in my ear, "I've waited my whole life for a hole like yours, boy. Let it happen."

I cried out, startled as my prostate contracted and a thin trickle of semen again oozed from my dick. Then I held him close, shaking as he grunted and gasped and his cock swelled even thicker as he finally emptied his load up my quivering, welcoming ass.

Tuck and I slept together like a couple of barn cats that night. When the lube ran out my hole so thick he had to hold a towel to my ass, he laughed so much I wasn't embarrassed. My muscles gradually tightened back into shape, just in time for him to work them loose and fuck me again in the morning. I'd never realized men could fall in love with each other, but Tuck was everything I'd ever dreamed of, and more.

That winter, my folks retired to Florida. Tuck and I took over running the farm together. Over the next couple of years, he showed me how to practice strengthening my ass muscles even more than I already had been. And when it was time to spread my cheeks, he worked me loose with corncobs, and later on with the butt plugs and dildos he bought for me. He even got a harness and laughed while I learned to work with the toys stretching my ass. I get hard every time he growls at me.

"Be ready for me, boy. Your ass is mine, now."

No matter how much I like the other toys, though, I'm farmer enough that corncobs will always be my favorites. Next summer, Tuck and I are growing some new hybrids that should be even bigger. I can't wait to try them out.

Positive
Andy Quan

Your skin is translucent, a thin layer of warm glass like the pane of a picture frame, the painting below of soft whites and pinks with constellations of beauty marks and freckles. The heat passing into me from my hands resting on your back. Perfect conduction of energy.

I never meet men in bars or at dance parties, though I've met hundreds of men who do. Finally, I break my never. A dance party in Sydney, a yearly fund-raiser for the state AIDS organization. There, chemically flying on ecstasy bumped up with hits of acid, I wandered through the crowd aimlessly, wearing a halo of lights and haze and spare vibrations from the dance track.

Did you see me first? Did I see you? All I know is that I stopped. Then joined in your swaying: unusual movements, your shoulders mostly up around your ears as if your whole body could disappear, melt, and be sucked into a hole in the middle of your chest.

"Well, aren't you cute?" Your voice somehow clear above

the music. You touch my arms above the elbows gently. A studded collar around your neck with spikes of fake danger, bare torso, shiny black pants that match your dark pupils. You lean in to kiss me and I fall and fall and fall.

When I come to, we're in another place in the dance hall.

"I'd like to take you home with me." Your voice has laughter in it. That and a melody, a tenor saxophone line in an upper octave, clear and precise, warm as coming on spring.

Nodding is all I do.

"But I want to tell you something first. I'm HIV positive. Have been for ten years, never been sick. I just wanted to make sure you're okay with that. Some people have a problem with it."

Positive, I think. "No problem." My blood is negative. My mind is positive. Yes. Yes. Yes. "Take me home."

We're awake and weary and tired and buzzed up when we fall across your white sheets. "Turn over," you command, and your hands are upon me, long and firm strokes of massage up and down the length of my back, shoulders and neck, scalp, and then lower, buttocks, thighs, calves, feet. "Now, the other side." My nipples hardening under the circles of your palms, my cock lifting up to touch your thighs as you kneel over me.

We're stripped naked. You're not a big man. You have a slim, sculpted muscularity and I would guess a fast metabolism. Also, the texture of an older man, skin moves easily below my fingers above a strength that has taken time to build.

Size is a nice surprise, and I'm astonished. Your cock is enormous. Dark and round and thick. Ecstasy takes away my hunger, but this makes me famished. I want to eat and drink for days at a banquet table fit for the king and queen of all those old countries that still hang on to royalty.

We make love for hours, and move between massage and

long kisses and my mouth on your cock and yours on my anus. I want to do the same to you, but you say, no, it's dangerous.

Neither of us can come with the drugs still coursing through our systems. For what seems like hours, I go through a stage of having to leave the bed every few minutes to urinate. But in the end, side by side, my head on your chest, hands on that astonishing skin, we come to a natural finish.

"It was amazing."

"I wanted to make sure that you felt you could do anything, and that we didn't have to fuck if you didn't want to."

"Well, maybe next time."

You look at me with a glint in your eyes.

Positive. Words repeat in my mind. Yes. Yes. Yes.

You become all of the positive lovers I have ever had and will ever have. What is unique to you, I revel in. I eroticize. I turn you into the letters of the word *desire*. I know it is perverse to do this. But is this not who we are, what we are, where our potential lies: the possibility of moving beyond borders, normality, the usual? Transcendence.

In fact, it's how we got here, crossing lines, sneaking past customs officers. Both of us countries on a map where the shorelines magically fit into each other, an isthmus into a bay.

Though I remain negative, I am becoming positive all the time—not in the cells of my blood or the hidden recesses of my brain, but in the way magnets change each other, the way electrical charges alter and become the same.

I celebrate masculinity. I saw a photo of your younger self and the face was round, like a boy's: the shapes of sun and moon and celestial bodies. Soft forms. Now the drugs have made your face gaunt, your cheekbones have risen like mornings, and your cheeks have strong lines carved into them. I say this to you: You look like a man. Your profile is an exaggerated model, a cartoon superhero, sleek and virile. And strong like seaside cliffs that weather wind and salt night and day and all of the middle hours. A few of my body parts fit perfectly into those crevices.

For a time, the Crixivan causes your stomach to protrude, and I know this makes you shy in public. Ignore the wondering eyes. I see a yin to the yang. The roundness here softens the angle in your face. Your belly protrudes and gives birth to new forms, to all of your hopes and fears, to petty victories and multiplying neuroses. I run my hands over it and it is the shape a belly should be, a shallow overturned bowl of the finest cracked porcelain, a dark shade of ivory, coveted by the museum that guards it.

This month, I am fascinated by your veins, the way they stand out, the rivers and streams on your arms in shades of blue, the color of sensitivity and communication. I can see the way your blood reaches your fingers, which are warm when you touch me.

When you changed the combination of therapy, you lost weight. Now, you worry how thin you have become, about taking on skeletal form. The drugs waste your muscles. Fat flies off of you. It hurts you to sit down for long periods because the bones in your buttocks are sharp. But look again in the mirror. Your body stretches up to the sky like a giraffe on the African plains, you are lean as a gazelle, this equatorial sun pleases you. Your flesh unencumbered is elegant, the body of dancers you have admired, and here you are free of practice and training and a hundred painful *jetés*.

I hold you, you are light in my arms. Like cradling the skull of a newborn, a chick in the palm of my hand, a crystal glass between thumb and forefinger. You are so heady and soft that

I drink you like champagne, or wine casked before the wars, so fine that it does not touch your throat on its way to your stomach.

How could I not want to make love to you? Like when the old down comforter split open under the rips of our passion and we had sex amidst feathers, a ghostly flock of ducks glad to bequeath us a backdrop. Our sweat and cum made the down stick together in soft clumps. Listen. If you were heavier, I would not have you. I have gotten use to this lack of gravity.

I love you for your vulnerability. Your body weak. From a cold made worse from a drug side effect, still the lingering cough? No, this time, it is the diarrhea, the river that doesn't stop, all of the insides pouring out and the drugs making you unable to hold in liquid or food. Out, it says. Expel.

I project a cradle around you to rock you into sleep, since I know you don't like to be touched when you feel like this. When I see you fragile, I remember recovering from the flu, sitting on a high stool in my grandmother's kitchen, sipping lemon and honey. I think of food that heals, and I want to dissolve into herbs for you to taste and be surprised that I am aphrodisiac as well as medicine. Savor me from head to toe and I will enter you. Spice of life.

Sometimes, it is when you are weak that you are the hardest. Like the shell of an egg. We marvel at it, how thin yet tough, the sandpaper finish, how gently it carries its secret sun within. I would lift you into my jaw and carry you farther to a safer place. But you would not let me. Instead you are as hard and sharp as that shell.

When you are that brutal, my cock strains against the inside fabric of my underwear, the outline appears through pants or trousers or shorts. Your bravado titillates me. Your knife-edge scares me. Shivers down my spine that reach down to the hairs between the cheeks of my buttocks.

Everyone fantasizes. Gay men are the best at it. As children, as a way to escape to someplace else, as adolescents, as a way to lose oneself en route to orgasm, as adults, as a habit. Gay men often fantasize about danger. The themes are leather, military, policemen, rough trade, construction workers, men who are powerful, who could overpower. Highway workers who hold up fluorescent yellow signs that say hazardous, warning, harmful materials, slow down, stop. For years I envisioned binding, tying, overpowering those who taunted me, those I believed would taunt me. They would fall, simply, beneath my magic strength, and I would have my way with them. Before I knew what sex was, I would simply envision them straining and sweating, the muscles tensing in and out of sharp relief.

We flirt with danger. Does it flirt back? Why not flirt with what is really dangerous? The disease. That which has destroyed, taken lives, ravaged nations. So strong and powerful. Sexier because we cannot see it, and must picture it in our minds. Everyone is talking about it these days. The ads on Internet chat lines: barebacking, skin on skin, no protection.

It is amazing the lengths to which we go. Bungee jumping, hang gliding, parachuting, roller coasters. The ground beneath us is gone, a sense of velocity that would usually equal injury or death but somehow, here and now, we escape it.

So the ultimate turn-on is not skin and sweat or the symmetry of nipples. A physical touch that reminds you of the shock of how sweet and rich are the finest Belgian truffles and at the same time of that dizzy, sharp edge of not eating for a full day. How hard kissing can be. A duet of tongues. Or how soft.

No, it's in the mind. An entire national library of the erotic. Here's the shelf on immortality, the invulnerability of the young or the want-to-be young. This is where you don't care. Where you do something that might kill you because the moment, or your imagination, or your just-fuck-it philosophy, takes over. Indifference to consequence can be the sweetest part of the body.

Some more shelves: suicidal tendencies. Here's a book on how growing up in a disapproving society gives you low self-esteem, and how you might think you're not worthy enough to protect yourself. Play with fire but get burned. We can have the most passionate of fuck-sessions and then feel wrong. So much unreconciled. Repression breeds heat, which may just explode into passion. Are the religious books here too, the ones that say joy must be paid for by penalty? It's all the same category. How many of us negotiate disaster because we feel we deserve it? Put an end to our pale, dreary lives? Gay men have always had a flair for drama.

The last stop on our tour, this section: sacrifice. The ultimate proof of love. I will do anything for you. There is nothing more powerful than to be inside you, for you to be inside me, to become each other. The model of twins rather than opposites attracting. I love you so much, I want you so much, I want to *be* you.

Of course, it manifests in a physical form. A shudder and semen in its pearly white case of saltwater glue. You finger paint with it until it dries. Dirty pictures on flesh. But it all starts somewhere else. From the electrical charges and bytes and synapses of the brain that let you know it's in charge. The mind, not the body, creating sex, allowing it to happen, rigid, not flaccid.

I'm safe. Always. According to my rules, which are con-doms and lube for fucking and being fucked. Oral okay. Rimming too, though only with the right asshole. But some-times, I fantasize about being as dangerous as other men. Fantasy is part of the fun.

Listen, when it comes down to it, I desire you because you are dying. Men are taught to be protectors. No matter how much I have bucked the trends of what masculinity is supposed to be, I still picture myself on the white horse, I gallop past and sweep you into my arms, and you are no maiden, no lithe willow. You are a man. I picture fairy-tale sex, tragic romances, those trashy movies about people dying of terminal illnesses, and I'm the star, I'm the one left behind, but before the big death scene, the passion is incredible, it makes everyone in the movie-house cry out from each sweat gland, they look like they're upset, but they're starting to writhe in sexual discomfort, or comfort, and when they reach out for the tissues, it's not just tears they're wiping away. We are having cinematic sex in Dolby sound and a clearer picture with more frames per second than ever before. The violins rise, fabrics billow, they've lit us so that the room is dark but you can see each part of our excited bodies. Close-ups: my gasping, open mouth; your hand on my nipple; the crack of your ass; my collarbone; your back, which looks like wings. The music gets louder and louder. The woman who wrote it will win an Oscar. We're approaching climax and in this film, the cameras don't pan away.

No, I lie. It is because you cheat death. Because you are stronger than me. Because these days, the drugs are working, the T-cell count is fine, thank-you-very-much, and the viral load is dropping, if you can count it at all. It's because you returned from that place, and when I catch you sometimes and you don't know I'm watching, you have this expression on your face that says you know a hell of a lot more than I do. You've glimpsed your own mortality and your eyes are lined, sometimes with dark patches beneath. Is this just some romance about those who have survived near-fatalities, not-so-terminal illnesses?

It is fact. You have taken stock to depths I can only guess at. You have prepared the true farewell speech, not some tragic teenage imagining *what would they do without me if...?* I am in awe of this. That you didn't turn to salt, or if you did, you became flesh again, pulled a few proteins and DNA out of thin air, and the blood started to flow once again. I desire you because you are surviving, you are proud, you are living with it and me, it's a *ménage à trois* that works.

No, I lie again. I rub my brass genie-in-a-bottle cock and grant myself not three wishes, but three untruths that when discarded and retrieved and pieced together and seen in a different light may just tell more truth than I want to let be known. When it comes down to it, it is because of you, dangerous and beautiful, swelling to fill my mouth, pushing out against soft pink membranes and yellow-white enamel, the tiny slit at the end of your cock like an eye searching its way down my throat.

The Bachelors
Douglas A. Martin

1. A Good Neighborhood

There were the men who'd just gotten off the train, men I'd
think later I should have followed, men I hoped would come
back, show me if they might want me, and then follow me off
this train, at my stop.

I take the F to Bergen.

Some say they don't usually do this, follow guys off the
train, talk to guys like this, give guys their phone numbers,
unlike the ones who must wander around there all day,
around the stations, from one to another, ones I would
sometimes begin following, next door to hotels, ones who
seemed to have only me as a standard, ones who stand under
their newspapers, smiling even in the rain, on the street out
toward the ends of my neighborhood.

There are friends I run into, and MTA workers, on
occasion, out here like this, where men pretend to be asking
for change for the subway, or one pretends he has hurt his
foot, and another walks over to the pay phone, making a
gesture with his mouth I can't mistake for anything else.

I follow one of these men into a bar.

Another asks politely if he can walk with me. Although I know I've somehow started all of this, I sometimes still say no. I know he might lose interest, but if he really wanted me, he'd follow me.

There are ones I lose, and then there's one I follow for blocks and blocks, even out toward the underpass, where he finally, unexpectedly, runs into friends. There would be another one like him, another night. I'd follow him all the way out toward the other highway, past the police cruisers, the local neighborhood station, the garbage men on their rounds, late at night, just doing their jobs.

He's been painting his apartment all day. It's an excuse I'd use to change my mind, to get away, once I didn't really want this anymore, after having had a little time to think, coming to my senses coming up the stairs, watching him walk up in front of me.

Maybe some other time. I think I might be allergic to the paint. Thanks, anyway.

I go back out into the night.

Another one of them finds me, takes me up the street, takes me up the stairs to his place. He doesn't have roommates, or his roommates are away. He takes me in and wants to know if I want to watch a tape, if I want to piss on him. I haven't done this, ever. He says I can do whatever I want, whatever. He wants to finish me off, says I have a good dick, spitting up behind me, on me, bending over the couch I don't lower my face into, before he begins to move in his tongue, just a bit, just a bit more.

He is cleaning around me.

Whatever. Whatever I want to do.

I'll leave them always and come back to my room. I'll have to do it to myself again, before I can sleep. I'm trying not to think of them, not to think of the guy who some nights stands naked in his window, all the lights in the room on behind him, as he motions over himself, up above a fish store on one of the main streets. Whoever is passing should come up.

I'm trying not to go back out there.

There are other men out there, ones I only watch from outside their gates, men holding on in front and behind themselves, one man I'd walk back by again and again, outside his place, noticing then another man across the street watching him, watching me, watching us.

We're being watched by the whole neighborhood.

There's the man who says to me maybe some other time. I've told him I have nowhere to go. I have roommates. I tell them all this. Some of them say the same thing, then wander off drunk, then come running back, don't want to lose me, ask if maybe they can just suck my dick, here in one alley I've started walking back by.

They follow me back there.

There are two more men by another alleyway I'd find another night. They hold me and kiss me. Something's not quite right with me. I'm not quite here. Another night, one of them will say fuck you to me, when I don't want him tonight, won't instantly open my pants for him.

Another asks me if I have a problem.

There are the two or three who give me their phone numbers I'd never call, as they stand there talking to me, looking down at me below my waist to see, and then up at my face.

Some of them don't see me the next days on their lunch breaks. I see them. I always see them. Wives must be back in the city by now. They'd push their strollers on Sunday afternoon, through our good neighborhood.

Tonight it would get dark again. Some of them want me again. I've seen them on the street, late at night, outside their real lives. There would be those who would turn around to follow me, when it looks like I might be lost. I must have lost someone.

There are the ones I'd like to forget, the ones with their odd tattoos over their pelvic bones, their symbols for men, and ones who must be costume designers, their apartments filled with mannequins, and ones who must be architects, their apartments filled with blueprints, ones who take me up to where the wives must be away, just for the night, or just for the day, or just off at work, who would maybe never suspect this, how their partners have been looking for someone just like me, on their lunch breaks.

There are the ones who pretend they are just going out for coffee, tell me again and again how this is a good neighborhood.

These might be just the ones on the street.

2. Men in Their Cars

He picks me up off the street, one night in the rain. I am wearing my slick blue coat, like some slut might wear. Perhaps this is indication enough, the way I am dressed. He slows down, rolls down the window toward me. I try to ask him for money, but he doesn't really give me any. He has to get gas, and I feel him, for a second, as we drive, feel him back, but that's it, as he says how he'll suck me, pulls up to the end of this dark street after the gas station.

He'll have me looking for this again. Maybe I'm not yet admitting to myself it's what I'm doing, not exactly. There's this schoolyard, late at night, and another night, when I still haven't found anyone, there's a man from inside this convenience store who will follow me. I just have to look back.

They've been with friends, or out partying, just not quite ready to go home yet, to leave this neighborhood, where one circles around me in his wrecker, where I lean over him in the front seat.

There's another one who says he knows where I live. He names the place. He does know. He'd take me there. Get in his car. Come on. He'll give me a ride. I should come by his work, sometime around lunchtime. No one's ever there. There's this quiet back room. He says he'll mend things for me for free, if there's ever anything I need mended.

He's a tailor.

I know the place.

There are those ones on those nights in the rain, those who have been working late. There are those who follow me down the street in their cars, ones I lead on, was letting follow me, ones who would have already given up by the next time they see me. They know I have nowhere to go.

I think some nights if I just find the right one of them, they just might keep me from this.

There are those out alongside the highway, once two of them there. They want me. I know I should have gone with them. I'd spend forever, all my stops after then, looking for them. They are my age. We're all still young. They're driving a truck, these workers, must be day laborers of some sort, perhaps painters.

They followed me, in their truck, down the highway, followed me from one exit to another. Then followed me, back onto the highway, and one of them would drive. They'd drive up alongside me, as I slowed down alongside them in the passing lane, keeping them in my sight, then looking back at the road, as the one in the passenger seat would arch, hitch his hips up into the air, so I could see past the one driving, pointing over to him for me to see what he's doing.

They motion toward another exit, simulating then, crudely, with large gestures that couldn't be missed, their wet tongues tenting inside their mouths, pushing out against the inside of their cheeks, those ones turned toward me, and then their fists up against their lips, too.

There's no mistaking what each one of them wants.

This was before I moved to the city and no longer had a car.

There's another I watch going from exit to exit, while I drive along behind him, all down the highway, after having somehow lost those first two in their truck. This must go on all over the country.

3. Boys in Buildings

There's one after I first graduated—it leads into that first long summer. There were all those times I went into those buildings for no other reason. I was never a boy when I was a boy.

I was looking for someone. I was looking for someone like him.

The first one I find is Asian, Japanese. It's the first real time in one of those buildings that there is what can be considered more of a real exchange. I touch him as he touches me, just as much. It's not like with the men in their cars, when sometimes I pretend to be looking for something else, money, and some of them would even humor me, give me a few bucks.

I don't know what's wrong with me this one night, the night I break down and just touch him, but he is waiting for me outside the door to my stall. He is waiting for me in front of a urinal, wants me to hit this specific target for him, come up high, there on the metal around the top, show him how I can control it, myself if I want, show him just how high I can shoot.

Then he wants me to watch him.

Watch.

Some of them wash their hands afterward.

The second is Asian, too, though I never see his face, just his movements, his back as he is leaving, after coming out of our separate stalls, the way his gait increased once upstairs. He reached under for me. He's getting away now.

They're the ones who stay around here, studying late into the night, these boys, these studious Asian boys.

He had some calls to return on his cell phone, and the lower level restroom goes all deserted. There were all those tentative, almost times. There were all those boys I wouldn't open my door to, those ones I only watched through my door. I was trying to decide if I really wanted this, always. There were all those boys. There were those who must have known I was there. There's one who has all of the shopping from the day still with him. We won't go that far, either. Maybe I touch his leg, like the one who is not really hard, even though I touch him.

They follow me.

There is one I follow repeatedly, one boy, because just once he turns and looks at me, a boy I never see anymore. I followed him for blocks through the city. Once, near Christmas, I stood near to try and overhear him while he talked to someone on a pay phone. I just wanted to know if he might want me.

This was part of it at first, just the walking. There's nothing in any of the stores for me. No men came by in cars.

Then it's just being out in these nights.

I could try to approach it, remember it all, by all the different places.

There are the boys who only go inside their homes, after I've followed them, out in the city, where they must live.

I think it must have really started when I began working those long days, those seemingly endless days in the city. There was nothing to keep them all separate. That's part of it. I'd see them some nights through their windows with others, that way. I am part of the night now.

They wouldn't know I was there, what I was there for, how I was scared some nights that this place was just too lonely for me.

I could only let myself go so far right now. Nobody would ever come to my front door like this. They'd ask me to please open my stall door. There were other voices besides just mine.

They'd watch me over the separations, some boys I'd never see again.

Some of them would ask me if I knew them, would say they want to know if I have some sort of problem, why I'm looking at them like I am then, what I want.

They are everywhere.

I'll not look up again for a while. There are those boys who I'll remember some days, how they've asked me if I'm lost, asked me if I need any help, asked me if I need any help with anything, anything.

There are those who somehow must have reassured me.

There are those who would come and watch me now with other boys there, how we were there, providing for each other and providing for ourselves. There are those I recognize by their arms, their hands, come to recognize by their shoes, those like me who are never whole, who always need more of ones like me.

There's never just one way to do this.

There are the ones who have waited for me for what must have been hours, make me feel as if I've already given in, just for even looking for them, that there's nothing else to do but just let myself go, let go of myself.

There are the ones whose backs to me are just enough, more than enough, all these I am now some part of, in all of this parting. There are the ones whose eyes I'm more curious about. I follow them because they sometimes look like someone else. Some speak to me, say how they saw me following them the other night. They bring back memories. Sometimes it's like starting a motorcycle wrong, a good and bad flooding, that can make me forget from time to time that it isn't my first try, the first grip, my mind blanking temporarily at present.

4. Shopping

Before I've just started doing it anywhere, whenever, there was this one Christmas, one of those times I've felt left all alone. The house was a strange place I am staying.

Part of it is this. The landscape is so alien at this time. There are all these places open twenty-four hours for the occasion, for shopping. Two of the boys there in the store have noticed me. I still can't do it yet, though it's always a question of how I define this accomplishment, whether or not I'm really going to be able to let part of myself just go with them.

It's the more-open one of the two, the less sensitive-looking, who finally speaks to me, as he holds me in the restroom. He describes his friend, the shy one, what he looks like without clothes, and then we scatter like birds whenever there is a noise, when someone is coming.

It's one of those conversations that take place in a restroom.

This might be what it means to be curious.

I say sometimes, sometimes. I say it depends. I am answering everything like this, still. I'm not so sure, still, so I get lost when I could have just followed the two of them out, should have, wherever they may have been going, after finishing their shopping, this night. They might be the real reason I keep going back there all over this Christmas, despite the weather, the snow, initially.

The streets will be all wet. I still trudge into public. I don't know if there is ever anyone there again, after this first time. I won't really remember.

There will be those who don't want me, because of the coat I am wearing, the way I am dressed, because of my shoes. Some nights they'd rather have each other, and I'll just be there, watching. There are all those opportunities suddenly ended. There are the schools I couldn't get into.

There are those houses I wish I could get into. There are

those days and nights to kill still somehow. There are all these empty hours in this city, when one has no money, no real home. I don't know if this is really a life or not.

There are these men and boys I'll never know, once they go home, one I will just want to get away from now, sometimes, now that they are more and more on to me, possibly. They've stood around just as long as me, in all these places where we are all alone, not part of these couples going by two by two.

I could tell by his baseball cap one of them might have been from South Carolina, almost like me. It could be just him and me. There are these boys like me who find ourselves here, repeating repeatedly. There are those who must have thought there was nothing wrong with me, that I'm fine. They bring me to this lower level, again and again. I'm just there to see, until I begin to truly attain, after that first one. There are the ones I think might take me over even more, might teach me even more, might want to take me up to one of the higher floors, one of the quieter places in these buildings.

There are ones I think I might know. There are ones who won't let me get away, back me up against a wall there, push me up into a corner.

There are those I'll never want to touch again. There are those I'd feel guilty for not being more there for, following me, asking me if I have a place to go.

There are those who thank me, ones whose hands I'd just allow myself to fall on, ones I'd ask to meet me somewhere else, please, later, whispering, ones I'd later just like to erase, ones who nod their heads in a quick yes, ones who motion over to others to just forget about me, ones I know by the looks we exchange will come with me if only I looked a little more hungry, a little more pleading, a little more pleasing.

If only I looked a little more gifted, a little more giving.

5. The Church at the End of Warren Street

I start taking them to the same place, this old church. Maybe it's still used for its original purpose during the day. It's not my destination, not at first, but I've just seen one, the clip of his walk, the direction he must have been coming from.

He's dressed nice, nice coat, glasses, still youngish looking. He's still probably in his late twenties. I don't know what it is about this time of my life. I like them looking more distinguished these days, and almost always now I want them to be closer to my age. It means they are in their late twenties, but still trying to get somewhere, and they need what I seem to need. We end up out by this old church.

It's toward the end of a street we have walked down for what must be about eight blocks. One can always go back and count. It's doubtful I'll ever see him there again, but I might see someone else.

Our walk slows with each other. He keeps looking at me, as much as I keep looking at him, over across from the other side of the street, every time I look at him.

He has one hand in his right pocket, is wearing tan slacks, these nice pants. I'm still dressed like no one special. He wears a long coat, like something I could never afford. There's my theory that if I could, I wouldn't be like this, almost always lost, so often, wandering around here.

Look where I've come.

It feels different, the way he kisses me there, in the middle of the street, there where the road ends, looking out of the corner of his eyes for any cars or passersby who might be coming down toward us, turning his head, looking to the side, while he begins feeling me through my pants. I don't stop him. It's not quite a smile, what he does, but something that means a feeling a little more relieved, a little released. Something thankful is being conveyed. He asks me my name. I can't remember what I say. I must still be lying.

Mostly he just seems to want to kiss me. We embrace more than I ever have on some street like this, out in this open, the late of this dark.

I think I come before him.

A gate to the side of the church opens down to some stairs, going down a level.

I keep kissing him while he keeps looking out, to separate us whenever there are these sounds, so we may act more like just some casual walkers, just talking to each other.

Maybe it's not until the end that he asks me my name.

Maybe I say the truth.

The next time I think I see him he tells me his name is something else, calls me partner, asks me if I have a name.

Maybe it's him I'm looking for when there's that other boy. He's walking down my street, but I then turn away from home. We walk slowly across from each other for all those blocks. There's another man we've lost in the process. I'm leading him to the old church. I know that then, of that place, if he will just follow me. Nothing is said, even when he stops off at the park, takes a seat on a bench, and I walk past him, walk down an alley. It opens out.

He's then there behind me, all the way down to the end of the street, around the corner. I can feel him, and then I look.

He's there.

The gate that leads to the metal stairs going down is open. I walk down and pee up against the wall of the church, and he comes down after me. I don't know his name yet, but he has the most beautiful eyes. He pulls his pants down. Like that, we press up against the bricks of the building's facade, lower. He turns around to me, talking to me now. We both talk to each other, tell each other. We both have roommates, but he seems reluctant to separate, to end this. It's our story, both of us. He wants me to fuck him, won't be surprised if I have something in my pocket. I don't. I don't have a condom.

I don't like him looking up from his knees with those eyes.

Back up against the wall, he says he wants to shoot, but we're still prolonging this night together for more and more minutes. Neither of us objects. There were cars, but they couldn't see us, not down here. There were people coming home in the dark across the street, but they don't look back over their shoulders at the church, see us there that level below the ground of it, off to the side.

Five a Day
Jaime Cortez

Artichoke

Artichoke is a flower, closely related to the thistle. If left unharvested, its coarse leaves unfold to reveal a gorgeous violet interior, the delight of bumblebees and a source of honey most superb. This is not evident to the casual viewer, because Artichoke cultivates extreme impassivity. The exterior is all spines and tough fiber armor, which demands a gingerly approach. You must insinuate yourself and coax away layer after layer of toughness. It is laborious at first, with scant rewards: a nibble of flesh here, a glimpse of pale, hidden skin there. At times, you wonder if there will be anything left under all that toughness, and throughout the process, Artichoke remains inscrutable, happy to let you labor on with no promise of success, seemingly indifferent that you've chosen to brave its barbed, bitter defenses. But eventually, you arrive at the heart. This is what it guarded with such green jealousy, this pale, tender heart. Yours to have now, the heart is doubly delicious for being so hard-earned.

Mango

Mango is the school slut and likes that just fine. Mango inhales its own scent and remarks, "I smell good." Turning around to admire its own sweetly rounded gold-and-red behind, Mango declares, "I look good." Noting the subtle indentations where admiring fingers have gently pressed, Mango purrs, "I feel niiiice. And my taste—well, don't even get me started." Mango sleeps in the nude and rarely alone. In the morning, Mango often wakes to find only the scent of the previous night's lover on the pillow, and it is never a problem. Mango takes four hours to watch Sophia Loren movies and frequently freeze-frames the video to take notes. More than anything else, Mango likes an oral lover, that is to say a lover who heaps praise upon its head. Details count. The worshipper who notes its seashell ears and exquisitely formed toes earns more points than clumsy devotees who admire obvious attributes. "My eyes are pretty? Thanks for telling me."

Asparagus

Asparagus is not a complicated sort of guy. He was born small and erect and eventually grew tall and erect, but that is the extent of his development. Asparagus is utterly without mystery. He is green and tastes green. There is no skin to peel, no surprising seeds to bite down on, and no distracting shape or color. Most anyone can have Asparagus, as long as they are ready to do it his way. His sexual modus operandi is based on the Patriot missile:

1. Determine your goal.
2. Locate your goal.
3. Pursue it relentlessly.

Asparagus cums in the style of porn stars or World Wrestling Federation champions, with much attendant noise-making, flailing about, and extravagant facial contortions. Once he has cum, Asparagus never stops to think about your orgasm. He washes off his pecker, slips on his action slacks, straightens his pointed green cap, and walks out with a wink that he fancies is most fetching. "I'll buzz ya', baby!" he calls over his shoulder. Even he doesn't believe that one.

Apple

Apple is the most sensible fuck in town. Apple is modest in appearance and rather brittle in her manner. She puts on perfunctory lipstick in red or green and provides consistency and friction. She is shocked, judgmental, and jealous of the flagrant, dribbling sensuality of Mango and the pornographic directness of Asparagus. Apple's greatest secret is that one thousand harvests ago, apples and roses shared a common ancestor. But a split occurred, with the apples playing down their blossom stage and devoting themselves to their plump, fruit state. In contrast, the roses channeled their energies into prolonging their blossom stage, their perfume and petals becoming ever more decadent, layered, and frivolous. Apple rejects all this, keeping on its pajamas when fucking, and stifling the urge to moan or drip, because of concern about what the Bartletts next door will think. Despite this, Apple eagerly awaits the day when some lover will hold her rounded sides and exclaim, "You know, I don't know why, but there's something about you that reminds me of roses."

Yam

No one ever fantasizes about Yam. It lies modestly under the soil, lamenting its turdy appearance and fantasizing about what life would be like if it only had Cherry's tempting color, Guava's scandalous scent, or Banana's riotous sense of humor. But Yam knows that no one will ever get past its appearance, so it works on inner beautification and masturbates well and often. On Friday nights, it is dateless, lounging about in the soil, its roots tangled all about it, uncombed. It curls up with its diary, a monocle on each of its squinty eyes. It writes arabesque love poems to the more gorgeous fruits, gets travel reports from passing worms, and formulates philosophy with tree roots. All the while it grows in size, wisdom, and richness, awaiting the day of its assumption, when it will be lifted bodily from the soil, cleansed of dust, released from its drab skin, and allowed to impart its nutritive, sun-colored riches with the gorgeous denizens of the bright world above.

Prolonged Exposure May Cause Dizziness
Sandip Roy

It's 12:25. He never comes in before 12:30, but I just wanted to be sure. Just in case, you know. The bench is hot on my bare butt and I wiggle around trying to avoid the nails. The sauna smells of stale towels and trapped air. Someone left a newspaper inside even though the sign explicitly says, "No newspapers." The pages have dried to a crisp. I glance at them—the sports pages, oh well. I spread my towel on the bench and sit down and wait. I have been watching him for days—from behind my book on the Lifecycle. It was very hard to concentrate on the book while he pounded away on one of those running machines next to me in his little butt-hugging blue satin shorts that showed off those sleek brown thighs. Once, after he had finished running, he pulled up his blue-ribbed tank top to wipe his forehead and I almost dropped my book as I was treated to a glimpse of his flat brown belly and I saw his belly button was pierced. I could even see the thin line of hair running from his belly button down into those satin shorts that looked as if they would just glide off him.

The other day I almost got him. Just as I was about to finish my shower, he came in. He glanced at me and then hung his towel on a hook and came to the stall right opposite mine. He turned on the water and jumped back with a start as the icy-cold spray hit him. He stood away from the stream of water, fiddling with the controls, while I feasted on his body. The slopes of his chest, the taut belly, and the sudden full-ness of his butt. His uncut dick. The neatly trimmed patch of pubic hair. Just above the hairline I could see a little tattoo. A dragon perhaps. Maybe that was his Chinese Zodiac sign. I could suddenly see myself between his thighs, my tongue flicking across that little dragon and around his sweet tight balls. And I wanted to see his throat tighten with pleasure as my tongue swirled around his balls and his dick swelled in anticipation of my mouth. And the water from the shower would be cascading down his back and chest and blinding me as I looked up. I could feel my dick stirring. I glanced over at him. He was looking at me in the shower. I turned around to face him and soaped myself in what I hoped was a languor-ous gesture. I took my time—pumping that liquid dispenser for all it was worth. I hated that evil-smelling pink liquid soap the gym provided. But I lathered myself with it for his pleasure. I ran my hands over my butt and let the water wash away the ringlets of foam, only to do it all over again. I filled my hands with soap and vigorously rubbed myself between the thighs, playing with my dick as I did so. I glanced over and saw his dick had lengthened. It was not hard but it definitely hung a little heavier. He glanced at me and then his gaze shyly darted away.

I turned off the shower and briskly rubbed my hair dry. Then I wrapped the towel carelessly around my waist, letting it slip down just a little, and walked over to the sauna. Just before I went in, I paused theatrically and glanced back. He looked away quickly, but he had been looking. After a while he followed me in. I casually touched myself, slung the towel around my neck, and smiled at him.

He adjusted his towel and sat down nervously, looking straight at the door. He was so heartbreakingly beautiful. The dark brown skin was still beaded with water from his shower. His black hair, glistening and tousled, and those full, perfect lips. Bee-stung, a friend of mine would call them. I preferred to think of them as ripe fruit, a plum perhaps, just waiting to be bitten gently. He had a plain gold chain around his neck. And that chest—firm and defined and naturally smooth, with the perkiest nipples you ever saw. I could just imagine my lips on those nipples, teasing them. I wondered how our bodies would look on each other—my brownness on his. My hairy legs entwined against his smooth, muscular ones. I smiled at him, trying to will him to drop the towel. He glanced at me. I smiled encouragingly. Did a flicker of a smile cross his face? It was hard to tell. His right hand casually brushed his left nipple. Then he leaned back and spread his legs a little more. A little more and the towel would slip off by itself. I wondered if I should say something. Something sexy and funny. A come-on line with a touch of flirtatiousness.

That was when the white guy came in. A thirtyish guy with blue eyes and bulging, gym-nurtured pecs. And the biggest dick I had ever seen. He was always parading around the locker room with a half-hard-on. He had shaved off all his pubic hair so that it looked like a big naked fleshy hosepipe dangling between his thighs. He usually did not even notice me. But that was okay. I much preferred this other boy with the nutmeg skin and slim, tight figure. And average-sized dick.

The white guy put his towel down and parked himself between us. We shrank into our corners and fell to examining our toes. I gave the white guy the "why-don't-you-leave-us-alone?" look. But he just glanced at us, leaned back, spread his legs, and started to stroke himself. I wondered what he would do if someone walked in. He wouldn't be able to hide that thing under his little white towel. Maybe he'd make a quick tent with the sports page. I gave my lover boy the "let's-ignore-this-monstrous-exhibition-and-do-our-boys-of-color-bonding" look. I wondered if it was polite to walk across this blatantly aroused man and make out with my man. It seemed kind of rude—and I just wasn't brought up to be like that. I stretched and walked to the door, ostensibly to look at the clock. Then I said to no one in particular, "Damn, it's hot in here," and stepped outside and got myself a drink of water from the cooler. Now I felt I could go and sit next to my guy instead of returning to my old spot. It wouldn't look so obvious. I opened the door and went back in and stopped short. He had moved closer to the white guy and was feeling his dick. I stopped, unsure of what to do. The object of my affection did not even glance at me. Forgetting all our telepathic messages in the shower, he started blowing the white guy with great gusto. His towel fell off his waist and puddled around his bare feet. I stood there, stranded, my towel in hand. I looked at his head bobbing up and down. At his smooth brown butt. His hand was pulling at his own dick as he sucked. I watched his dick grow hard. Then he put both hands on the white guy's waist as he tried to get that monster dick inside his mouth. The white guy stood up so that he could fuck his mouth better. He put his hands on my lover boy's head and slammed his cock into his mouth. The white guy closed his eyes and said in a throaty, bad-porn-star voice, "Yeah, baby, suck that big cock." That was so cheesy. I felt bad for my lover boy. He deserved better. But he just made a muffled choking noise and tried to open his mouth wider. I should have left right then. If I had, the white guy wouldn't have had the chance to open his eyes, look at me, and say, "Would you mind watching the door?"

But that was then. Today it will be different. My friends would say I'm pathetic. But I am willing to give him another chance. As one person of color to another. Also, I have checked— monster dick is not in today. And I'm horny. And determined. Afterward I will explain to him about racism in the gay community and why we boys of color must stick together.

I glance at the clock. 12:35—I start reading about college basketball. It's not very interesting but it's all I have. I glance around impatiently, get up, stretch, and walk up and down the sauna room before going back to my spot and sitting down.

12:45—the sauna is getting really hot. I rub the sweat across my chest. I casually arrange my towel over my lap and sit back and try to think sexy thoughts. Just to be ready.

12:47—my throat is parched. I should have brought some water. I walk toward the door and peer out. An old man in sagging blue trunks is taking a shower. He carefully wrings his trunks out. I can hear another shower going but cannot see who is in it.

12:52—I guess I could hop into the shower and come back. But what if he poked his head in right then and, seeing no one, left? But I am not sure how much longer I can last in here. After all, the sign outside does warn that prolonged exposure may cause dizziness.

12:55—getting hungry now. The old man comes in with his wet swimming trunks. I glare at him, trying to will him to leave. He stretches and hangs his wet swimming trunks over the coals to dry. I want to point out the sign that expressly forbids such activity but restrain myself. He sits down, coughing, and cracks his knuckles.

1:02—I am thinking about this Thai restaurant nearby that serves the best tom ka gai. And iced tea with sweet condensed milk—rich, tasty brown.

1:05—I am thinking basil and lemongrass and iced tea refills. My stomach grumbles. The old man coughs and picks his trunks up and leaves. Images of chicken pieces floating in lemony coconut-milk broth are clouding my vision.

1:10—I am starting to get dizzy from hunger and thirst. I try to will my dick to remain alert and playful but it is undoubtedly wilting. I am almost about to go when the door opens. I freeze. It is he. He pokes his head in. And seems startled to see me. I uncross my legs and look him in the eyes. He hangs his towel over the coals and hesitates. Then he quickly steps back out, shutting the door behind him. I wait, thinking maybe he was taking a quick shower before coming back. I wipe my brow and take a deep breath to try and calm my heart rate down.

1:15—he comes back, in his jeans and T-shirt, and picks up his towel. This time he does not look at me as he briskly walks out of the sauna. Now I feel like I can't even leave the sauna till he is gone from the gym. I don't want him to have the satisfaction of knowing I was waiting for him and him alone. I watch him outside, drying his hair.

I close my eyes and think of Thai food. I think of Combination Lunch Number 5. I wonder whether I'll get it with tofu, chicken, beef, or pork. Tofu would probably be healthiest. Fuck that. I am getting pork. And maybe some of that creamy coconut ice cream for dessert. And definitely fried rice instead of steamed rice.

He's still in the lobby when I leave. He's standing there, gym bag slung over his shoulder, talking to a blond man doing crunches. But I don't care. I walk past with my head held high. I smile. I can almost taste Combination Number 5.

Frantic Romantic
Alistair McCartney

1. When I'm Dissolving

I'm a very hot jock-boy. I live in a jock-house. With a red roof. Woof-woof! All fours. I need my butthole worked on: finger it suck it lick it or just fuck me until I shoot my huge load. All over the favorite part of your dog-eared copy of Tolstoy's *War and Peace*. The part that makes you cry, feel alive.

This is why I do it: sex is the only thing that makes me feel alive. I have my needs. The structure of my day is as follows: wake crave dream. When I'm bored I lick books, I like the taste of ink: a boy who licks books all day long is naturally called a book-licker. I love lockers, aging coaches, moldy jockstraps, boys who date cheerleaders. I don't brush my teeth. I don't have to. I have dentures. Dentures set you free. I take them out at night. If you sleep with me, you'll see. If you stay with me, you'll see how I take them out and place them in a clear glass of water. Will you stay the night? If you stay with me, let's cuddle like real lovers. Let's snore. I want to hear you grind your teeth as you grind your hips into me. Let's hold each other as if we're conjoined twins, fused at the hip. Let's love each other as if we share the same spine. Either we'll both die, which will be romantic in a *Wuthering Heights*-y, AIDS-y sort of way, or one of us will have to die to let the other one live a relatively normal life.

If you're kind enough to stay over, I won't be able to sleep, your presence will distract me, you're a distraction to me, but I'll guard your dreams. I'll wash the sheets as soon as you leave. I'll shoot anyone who tries to stop me from dreaming. Steps a foot on my property. Please, when you finger-fuck me: please keep your wedding ring on. Put your wedding ring in me. Please. I like the feel of diamonds up there. Cutting into me. I sparkle. You make me sparkle. With your fingers in me, I'll think of crabs, the rapidly disappearing art of ventriloquism, and a sideways movement: crab's shells are bright orange. My ass tastes like the rind of an orange. Sex is a rapid disappearing. I'll resent you if you don't make me dissolve. I want a veil. I want a wedding cake. I want a knife to cut the cake. Will you take me to the hospital if you burst me? If you split me? If you rupture me? Will you order an ambulance for me? Will you ride with me in the ambulance? Will you make sure they have the siren wailing? Will you flirt with the hospital orderlies, who are always hot and sexy? That's my ideal man: a hospital orderly. Will you hold my hand while they stitch me up like a dress? I won't mind if you cut off your tongue and place it in me. I won't get angry. Will it feel rough or slippery?

In Sierra Leone, teenage boys high on cocaine hack off the limbs of men women children babies everybody as a warning, for diamonds. They sew diamonds beneath their skin to get them out of the country, diamonds scar differently, diamonds make for strange scars. If they can why can't we? I'm your warning to you. But don't worry. I'm not only a good fuck a god fuck. I'm easygoing. I like to kick back. I enjoy baseball canoeing and roller-blading at the beach. I shoot like a fire hose. You can reap the rewards. You get to keep all the gold you mine from me. I like the feel of felt. Fire engines and fire hats and sex all have one thing in common: they are all red. I'll wail when you fuck me. I'm 6 feet tall, 180 pounds, all-American boy with a great body, washboard abs, like they used to wash clothes on in the olden days, prior to washing machines: What is America? What is all of America? Why do we desire what we desire? What is a boy?

My body is splendid and plentiful but my face got burned in a fire. It used to be pretty: now it's scarred. Scar-red. Scars like little red ribbons. Scars like little red ribbons that little boys lust for. I can't afford plastic surgery. My ex-boyfriend set fire to my house to get back at me. For betraying him. All my treasured possessions were burned, all my original copies of nineteenth century novels, all my porn tapes—pre-AIDS—in the nineteenth century they had social realism; in the twentieth century we had pornography. Yes, everything got burned, but only halfway, singed sort of, at the edges, so they're still usable, I can still read my copy of *Madame Bovary*. I wish I had ovaries so that I could have your babbling babies. I'd make the best jock-momma. But I wish everything had burned down until it was nothing but ash so soft and black that I could trace my finger through it. Write love letters to you in it, you my little burned-down house. You my red lacquered thing. Love is a singeing, many-scarred thing.

Oh, by the way, I also love sucking and gagging on cock, I love coke, and I like it when I can't speak. I like old Charlton Heston movies, Charlotte Brontë, men in tunics, mad love, brunettes, bluntness, thighs, fakery, making you shoot, or just getting your fat cock ready for my hot pink satin hole, satiny and pink as a pink satin-lined hatbox your mother kept her pink foamy hat in, the horrible one she only wore on special occasions. It lurked in the box like a shy animal. Think of me as the bright snare that sits in a forest waiting for unsuspecting creatures. I'm waiting for you pink and wet and dripping like the world after it's been raining. God started the flood so that the world would forget the meaning of the word *dry*. I'm wet thinking of the idea of you. My hole's twitching like an eye, like we've all got something to be nervous about.

God started a flood, so why can't I?

2. The Frozen Spaces

I'll find you. Stay still. Your staying still will help me find you. At the end of breath you'll always find a boy. I'm looking for one sincere young man, eighteen–thirty, who wants to learn about gay sex from an older, fifty-nine-year-old more experienced man. I was born during the war; my father died in the war, a bomb explosion, I love to shatter grammar with a hammer, how horny is a large body of men organized for warfare? How horny? During World War II, all the men had great upper bodies, but their legs were spindly like pipe cleaners. I'll teach you about the war. I'll teach you all sorts of interesting things. You youngsters don't know anything.

My hair is red, like Lucille Ball's. I have a sense of humor. Though in actual fact my hair is orange, to call it red is inaccurate, but we go on calling it red. Tongues are a habit. My hair is curly too. I can teach you to shave: we'll stand together in front of the mirror in our wife-beaters. I have a lovely wife and three lovely children. All estranged from me. We'll shave with no pants on. Snicker-snicker. Wakey-wakey, hands off snakey. Going to sleep is infinitely more sexy than waking up. We'll both have silver razors. I'll make the first swipe over my skin, and you'll follow, and if you cut yourself, I'll put a little piece of toilet paper on the cut, that'll stem the blood flow; maybe later when I know you better I'll taste your blood. But we'll save that up for later.

I'll teach you to drive too, if you don't know how. Instead of screaming at you when you make a mistake, I'll fuck you. In your car, in the parking lot behind that Jack in the Box where they beat that boy senseless the other night, carving FAG into his back with a Swiss army knife. I'll teach you to swim. I'll teach you roman numerals and all about the birds and their detachable wings and the bees and their little black stings that look like the letter I I I...this is a beehive we're in. I'll shovel my honey into you. If you get stung, I'll try not to push the sting further into you. Desire is a complex, honeycombed structure. Many-stinging thing. I'm clawing my way out of my own lined gravity-flying skin in my search to find you. It's as if you're one of those cute boys who were in that plane crash, that plane that crashed into the pointy icy tip of a mountain, icy like my heart, pointy like my dick. I need a boy to melt me. For the frozen spaces in me. There was a movie about it, but it was real, they were soccer players, boys on soccer fields at night are illuminated. I see halos above the heads of pretty boys. The halos are fashioned from pipe cleaners.

We'll take it at your own pace. Real slow, as a snail: did you know a snail could crawl across a razor without harming itself? Wouldn't it be fun to be able to do that? Maybe when we're together, our love will make such razor miracles pos- sible. You're the kind of young man who wears shirts with collars and buttons: you button the buttons to your throat. That's nice and polite: it shows you've been raised properly. But you do this to hide the hickeys from your family. The hickeys that I'm going to give you. On your neck in your car. I'll fuck you and make you claw at the fake upholstery. You'll suck on the silver door handles. I'm a kind man; I'll be very kind to you. I'm the kind of man who counts the hickeys on your neck, and writes down the number of hickeys and the day the hickeys were imprinted by me into you, in a little exer- cise book. In a separate column I write down whether there were clouds in the sky that day. I'm a kind-as-kind man. I'm kindness in the shape of an old man, don't listen to what they

say. When I'm inside you it's raining, it's pouring. I'll trans-
port you. We'll arrive we'll arrive we'll arrive. I'm the kind of
man who will tear off the buttons on your shirts while you're
sleeping, drooling over your pillow, all that dream drool, I
love it, I love it, I love it, I'll lick up your dream drool, I'll
bottle it in old jam jars and sell it at church fetes to widowers
and spinsters. I'll tear off your buttons just so that I can show
you that I know how to sew on buttons. How kind I am.

You'll come to my house, which is located in a very nice
part of the San Fernando Valley. I'll give you clear directions.
It'll be easy to get to. You won't get lost unless I want you to.
I can roll up a map real tight with an elastic band and fuck
you if you like, a map-fuck, you'll have geography inside you.
I happen to live right next door to the house where that poor
boy got raped by at least six other boys; a friend found him
unconscious in his bedroom, lying on his bed with the pink
frilly polyester bedspread, your asshole will be pink and frilly
like the edge of your mother's nightgown, by the time I'm
done with you, that highly flammable one she wore, it'll be
Elizabethan, it'll be nostalgic, his airbrushed posters of horses
all over the walls.

Sex is like being at sea and not wanting to go back to
shore. The poor boy was the kind of boy who loves horses.
There are many such boys. Freud was particularly interested
in, that is attracted to, these boys. Freud wanted to fuck
every one of his patients. Freud's therapy sessions were like
phone sex, but more intimate. Confession without the screen.
Alfred Hitchcock was also interested in boys who dug horses.
Hitching boys to horses. His fat belly rubbed against boys.

From my kitchen window I can see right into that particular bedroom. I've peered often into that bedroom. Especially at
night, about nine o'clock, after I've eaten my meal, while I am
washing the dishes. There'll be no more of that, once you're
here, you'll be responsible for the dishes, for the suds and the

silver and the china. I like the sight of a boy, his hands hidden in suds. I used to enjoy watching that boy in his bedroom, on sultry nights, his sulky silhouette, just a slip of a thing slipping out of his tight dresses that revealed every boy curve and his slutty short-short skirts with the slits and the boob tubes with glittery strips and lacy panties and his bra. Made me feel all slurry. Thinking wouldn't it be nice to have been born a boy? When his friend found him he wasn't sure if the boy was dead or dreaming. He didn't move him because he knew that you're not meant to disturb a dreaming body. It's dangerous to disturb a dreaming boy. The boy had been raped and sodomized by at least six other boys. All the boys were members of a graffiti tag team. The boy's body was covered with their tags, bruises, cuts, abrasions, and bites of various shapes and sizes. Despite himself, the boy's friend got aroused at the sight of his dead or dreaming friend.

Every year it takes more and more to arouse us. He considered for a moment also raping him, what's one more, they wouldn't notice one more, but then he decided against it and paged the boy's mother. He had a page-boy haircut; all the other boys' heads were shaved. Baldies. Fucking is going against the I, derailing identity; I love boy's spines, pale pale train-lines, time-lines without the numbers. Sex goes tearing into time.

Apart from the smog and that incident, the street I live on is relatively peaceful. It's real quiet. You can even hear birds if you listen hard. Can I drag a bird's beak down your spine? We'll talk and relax and get to know each other over a drink of coffee or milk or Coke or some other sort of soda. If we both want to proceed to explore a sexual relationship, we'll take it one step at a time, itty-bitty baby steps, babies gurgle and fall over; we won't do anything we don't both enjoy. You can be my kitty. I'll take little bites out of you. You can be my kitty boy. You can be. No hurry no rush no hassle. If one of us is unhappy with the way things are going, we'll be honest about it. If we can't resolve a problem we can part company with no hard feelings. Or, we could haggle over the issue. I could take you to market. I could always drill a hole in your head and pour soda pop in it. Enough of you, now, for me. I have to tell you: I have thinning hair. I am almost completely bald.

I cannot tell a lie: I'll chop down that cherry tree of yours, boy. Boys in period clothes are a plus. Those lovely red curls aren't mine. It's actually a wig, a toupee that I wear on special occasions. I'll wear it when you first come over, but gradually you'll grow to love the real me. I love showering. I don't usually get into anal stuff, like running your tongue along a gutter, silver, and fear of waste is at the base of desire, but I have been a top in the past. I appreciate all races, white, black, but especially Asians, Latinos, Mexicans, and Germans. The Nazis judged the desirability and durability of people on the shapes of their skulls. I won't do that to you, but I'd expect that you would shower right before stopping by my lovely home, I'd expect that of any idiot and any boy, I would be doing the same. If you liked, we could have another shower together when you arrived. I could wash you thoroughly, scrape away at the surface of desire and tell you what I see. I could wash between your toes so that you don't develop fungus, and behind your ears so that you don't get pimples there although I have a weakness for pimples, delicate volcanoes. I could wash your ass until there is nothing to remind me that you are human.

For anyone who is interested in exploring this idea of sane, safe intimacy, please respond to me.

Immediately.

Wake the King Up Right
Mike Newman

On the road from Baton Rouge to San Francisco, April, 1970

Kevin opened his eyes in the dim early light to find a man's face startlingly close on the next pillow. His fuzzy mind woke up in sections, like the windows of a dark house lighting sequentially as someone moves from room to room. He remembered Jerry getting into his car, he remembered Jerry's naked body in the shower, he remembered Jerry's cock going up his ass. There was a sunset over the Grand Canyon back there somewhere, and a campfire, and a fistfight. And Jerry's cock up his ass.

Asleep, his hitchhiker seemed younger than before, closer to Kevin's age, even boyish, with his dark eyelashes innocently knitted together and his lips parted slightly, showing the white of his front teeth. Kevin's morning erection stiffened. He felt like a spy, staring so intently at the unguarded face of a stranger he had picked up only two days before, now dozing inches from his eyes.

For the first time he noticed a slight asymmetry to Jerry's

face, a subtle mismatch of cheekbones that made one side look friendly and the other side seem stern, even cruel. One black eyebrow arched a bit more than the other. An off-center dimple marred an otherwise perfectly square chin. But it was mostly the eyes. Jerry's features shifted between angelic and crude as Kevin searched from one closed eyelid to the other. His hard-on throbbed.

Fucking mesomorph. You guys have all the luck. Your face is lopsided and you're still sexy. How could anyone be horny for a girl when a man is so…achingly…*male?*

The stubble Jerry had grown during their short time together dotted his jawline and spread down his throat. Kevin tensed his cock until it hurt. He wanted to lick the coarse, black bristles sprouting from the protruding Adam's apple.

I don't just want to fuck with you. I want to *be* you.

Kevin sighed. Trying not to jiggle the bed, he slipped from under the covers and padded, nude, to the bathroom, flipping on the wall heater as he passed it, watching his hard-on wag with each step. A window behind the plastic shower curtain let morning light into the room, making the old claw-foot tub and the checkered tile floor glow blue.

Squinting groggily, he stood at the toilet and pushed his erection down to aim at the bowl. It insisted on pointing out and up instead. Twisting it to the side only made it impossible to let anything out through the rigid tube. He moved to the bathtub and stood with his hands on his hips, cock high, waiting for the valve inside him to unlock from the night's sleep.

He yawned. He shifted his weight from one foot to the other.

He stared at the dimpled clot of his semen still clinging to the shower curtain, below the gap where he had torn the plastic loose from the curtain rod while Jerry fucked him up against the wall. His asshole tightened and his hard-on reared at the thought. He let a blip of gas pass, and took pleasure in the vibration. When his urine first stung at the base of his dick, he liked that, too. Crossing his arms and hugging his bare nipples, he brought back the image of the two of them pissing into the Grand Canyon side by side. Interior parts functioned, his most personal muscles loosened, fluid trickled inside him. He farted again, loudly, and forced out his first burst. A physical pleasure like a minor orgasm sent a shudder through him.

"Ah-h-h," he sighed, relaxing and flowing freely, playing with his private little golden arch, twisting his hips to sweep the stream up and down the tub. "My piss pistol," he whispered, repeating Jerry's name for it as he held it down level and squeezed off three strong shots that made satisfying splatters against the shower curtain across the tub. He shuddered again, farted once more, shook himself off, and laughed at his wickedness.

When he turned around he saw another streak of his cum across the mirror above the sink, trailing runny drips now congealed on the glass.

God, how many times did he fuck me? It's a wonder I can fart without leaking.

He used toilet paper to blow his nose and wipe his butt, which was clean and sore—properly sore, he thought, for a piece of personal equipment he had finally used right for the first time in all his twenty-one years.

Back at the ticking wall heater, he turned his behind to the warmth and cupped himself. His pouch had shriveled like a prune in the cold air but his erection still strained toward his navel. As the flame growled behind him and the backs of his legs baked, he surveyed the cabin.

Thick, dark curtains drawn over the front window blocked out most of the daylight, leaving only a halo around the edges that softly lit the rest of the room. Jerry's blue jeans lay wadded on the carpet by the table, then some balled-up socks, then Kevin's briefs next to Jerry's white boxers. He liked that, the trail of his first real night of debauchery leading to a bed with a naked man still sleeping in it. Kevin bent forward slightly to push his bare buttocks closer to the heater. His balls sagged in his hand.

Under the faded color photograph of the Grand Canyon, Jerry lay on his back with one arm crooked to his hairy chest, holding a corner of the sheet part way over his belly and hips. One muscled leg stuck out from under the tousled green chenille spread that half fell off the bed. Slowly pulling on his cock, Kevin watched the expansion of Jerry's chest as he snored.

My sexy sailor in the desert. I wish I could see you in your Navy uniform.

Even from across the room, Kevin could smell the cigarette butts that spilled from ashtrays on both bed tables, and stale whiskey, and suntan oil. The lampshade tilted up, exposing the lightbulb left the way Jerry had turned it while they watched themselves dog-fuck in the dresser mirror. The empty Jack Daniels bottle lay on the floor below Jerry's foot, next to the motel towel with the brown smudge where Jerry had wiped Kevin's ass.

And Kevin gloried in it all. He lifted his elbow and took a long sniff of his armpit, the way Jerry had done while jacking off on the toilet the night before. He spit on his fingers and wet a patch of dried cum on his belly, then put it to his nose and smelled his own reconstituted semen. Gripping his hard-on, he closed his eyes and inhaled deeply.

"Me!" he whispered to himself. "Mine! This is what I want! Cock and cum and asshole sex with another man. This is what turns me on."

He longed to scoop Jerry into his arms, lift him up naked with the sheets and their dried cum and their undershorts and all the smells and all the booze and all the sweating and sucking and fucking and shooting off together, gather up the whole room and the night, and drag it with him all the way to California, and never let go of any of it forever.

He stepped through their scattered clothes and carefully settled onto the bed.

Fuck. I want to kiss you so fucking bad. His cock twitched in his hand. No, don't risk it. He'd be pissed again. He leaned over his hitchhiker's big chest. Has he got a hard-on under the blanket? He considered pulling the draped cloth away from Jerry's hand. No. I don't want to wake him up yet. This is too good.

The way Jerry had his elbow crooked over his body showed his black panther tattoo slinking down the outside of his thick arm, and on the inside a tuft of dark hair sprouted between the bulge of his muscle and his chest. The memory of that arm lashing out at his jaw made Kevin's heart thump nervously as he moved closer, getting his face back into an intimate proximity forbidden with another male. He bent down and put his nose and lips right up to the cleft where the underarm hairs curled out, and sniffed the acrid odor of his sleeping giant.

His dick stiffened in his fist. He whimpered out loud, "Muhhh!"

Jerry stirred. The big arm muscle bulged up and down as he twisted his forearm with his fist tightened. The glowering cat's paws moved. "Pant'er onna prowl," he croaked, with his eyes still closed. Kevin's hard-on grew slick in his hand. He kissed the tattoo.

"Mmm, yeah," Jerry sighed. "Turns me on." He flexed his arm again. "Lick all over it."

Kevin lapped his tongue across the cat and then sucked at the smooth skin. The mattress bounced as he masturbated shamelessly. Jerry raised his head and peered down. "You jerking off, man?" He laughed and coughed at the same time.

"Over me?"

"Uh-huh," Kevin said, sitting back on his heels and display-
ing his erection to Jerry. "I've been watching you sleep. You
aren't mad, are you?"

"Naw, I don't mind." Jerry yawned, distorting his words.
"Nah affer—eeeeYUH—las' night. You beat off over my sorry
bod all you want." He took a deep breath, put his fists to his
shoulders, and raised his elbows up high. "Rub my belly," he
grunted, arching his back.

Kevin put his hand under the blanket and made circles
on the warm, hairy skin. Jerry squinted his eyes and twisted
against the sheets. His abdomen hardened and then vibrated.
Kevin laughed. "I can feel it in your stomach when you fart,"
he said.

Jerry grinned and squeezed out another. "You know, if I
was king," he said, cupping Kevin's balls with his hand, "I'd
put you on the payroll to be my own personal wake-up boy."
His palm warmed Kevin's nuts. "Be your official assignment,"
he purred, tugging and fingering softly between Kevin's legs.
"Jump in the sack with me every morning sportin' a big ol'
boner like that, and then wake the king up right."

"You don't have to pay me," Kevin said. "Just tell me what
to do."

"Okay." Boosting himself up with his elbows, Jerry punched his pillow behind his neck and looked down at the lump
in the blanket. "First thing the king needs is a good scrotum
scratch," he said, spreading his knees apart and making a tent.
"King's always got itchy nuts first thing in the morning."

Kevin reached lower under the bedclothes and found Jerry's
hairy bag, hanging down loose and warm and slightly damp.
"Like this?" He nudged the soft pouch up with the back of
his thumb and dragged his fingernails underneath, watching
Jerry's face for approval.

"Yeah, like 'at," his king said, raising his arms and locking his fingers behind his head. The sour smell of his sweat blossomed in Kevin's face. "Get the right one now," he commanded, eyes narrowed to slits. Kevin fingered Jerry's right testicle with his nails. "Uh-huh. Now get upside the left one some more. Mmm-hmm. Now come right up the middle between the two of 'em. Yeah, right there."

Kevin's cock flamed in his fist as he felt another man's bare balls flopping about in his scrambling fingers. "Feels so fine," Jerry said, flexing his muscles and turning his face to sniff his underarm.

Kevin groaned. He leaned forward. He licked Jerry's open armpit, tasting salt on the fine hairs.

Jerry laughed. "King's wake-up boy is really throwing himself into his work," he said, twisting to reach for his cigarettes. "King likes that. Enthusiasm in the troops is a good thing."

"Muh!" Kevin moaned. "I'm so queer for your body it just makes me crazy," he said, running his hand back up the trail of hairs to Jerry's navel, inserting a fingertip into the knotty hole in his belly.

"Yeah, you got the main qualification for this job covered, I do believe." Jerry lit up and inhaled. "Play with my tits some," he said, blowing out through his nose as he dropped his lighter on the table.

With the sweet first puff of tobacco smoke filling the air, Kevin spread his hands over Jerry's chest and massaged the solid muscles. "I still can't believe you let me touch you like this," he said, circling his fingertips through the curls around the nipples. "It's so sexy that you're just kicking back and smoking while I feel up your body."

"You like that, huh?" Jerry put his free hand under the blanket. "Pull on my tits," he said, narrowing his eyes.

Kevin pinched Jerry's nipples and tugged at them.

"Harder," Jerry said. The blanket lifted and fell. "Harder."

Kevin got a better grip and stretched them out a full inch. "Doesn't that hurt?"

Jerry squinted his eyes. "Uh-huh," he nodded. "'Specially when you do it for me. Two things I like to do when I beat my meat, is to suck on my tat and pull on my tits." He smiled shyly. "Gets me going real good when you do it for me." He took a puff and threw his head back to blow smoke straight up. "Harder," he breathed, tensing his chest.

Panting shallowly, Kevin pulled until Jerry stiffened and groaned, muscles bulging. He grimaced so alarmingly that Kevin slacked off the pressure, and Jerry slumped back against the pillow, grinning with his eyes closed. Kevin toyed with the two stubs, now red and elongated. "Your nipples get hard like little dicks."

Jerry looked down his chest. "Uh-huh. You got 'em sticking up like two little baby boners, huh. Standing tall." He licked his lips. "Just like the big guy down between my legs." The lump in the blanket rose and fell.

Kevin ran his palm down Jerry's chest, touching the bruise over his rib. He noticed a three-inch scar below it on Jerry's belly. Tracing it with a fingertip, he imagined Jerry in a hospital with a doctor slicing around inside his abdomen, taking out his appendix. He hesitated, envious that another man had touched a part of Jerry's interior that Kevin could never reach. He pushed the bedcovers down a few more inches, to the bare skin where Jerry's pubic hair began to bush out. "Can I see him now?" he whispered. "Can I see the big guy?"

Jerry pulled his hand from under the blanket and hooked his wrist behind his neck again. "You gonna be a good wake-up boy?" He took a slow draw on his cigarette. "Gonna treat the king's cock right?" He held the smoke out, butt end first.

"Oh, yeah." Kevin put his lips to it and took a puff. "I'm gonna be a real good boy."

"Okay. Head on down south and show me how good."

Kevin lifted the crumpled sheet and blanket.

Jerry's pale hard-on sprang up from the shock of black hair between his hips, standing tall indeed, robed and regal. Kevin scooted down by Jerry's side, kicking the blankets off the foot of the bed. His hitchhiker's manhood swayed proudly in front of his nose, smelling of Coppertone.

He touched a swollen blue vein. "This is the real king," he whispered. "Down here." The shape of the head showed through the foreskin. Kevin slipped it back until a circle opened and the tip peeked out, pink and glistening at the slit. "That's what you've got between your legs. The king of cocks."

"Think so?" Jerry held his cigarette down to Kevin's face again. "The king we all obey, huh." Kevin nodded and took a puff.

"Okay, whyn't you get all the way down there between my knees," Jerry said, stubbing out his smoke. He spread his legs apart. "Lemme teach you a trick with my dick."

Kevin curled up between Jerry's thighs, propped on one elbow. "Tell me what to do," he said, locking his legs around Jerry's calf.

"Can you suck your own cock?"

Kevin looked up from aligning his erection against Jerry's leg. "No," he said, and shrugged. "I used to try, but I can't quite get to it. Can you?"

"Nah. Used to be able to touch my tongue to it, back when I was skinny like you." He toyed with his nipples. "We'd all suck ourselves off if we could, huh?"

Kevin grinned. "I sure would."

"Okay, I'm gonna train you how I'd give myself a blow job, if I could get my mouth down there to it."

"This is so queer," Kevin said, humping Jerry's calf. "We keep getting better at it."

"Yeah, champ, I'm working on that," Jerry said. "Here's the deal. Pull my foreskin up. All the way up over the head."

The fine skin rolled up in Kevin's hand and formed a pucker at the tip. Beyond it he could see Jerry staring down at it as he tugged his nipples out.

"Keep the hood up until I tell you, okay?"

He cupped Jerry's balls with his other hand, fascinated by their softly rolling heft, as Jerry's voice floated down to him. "Now open your mouth wide and put it as far down on it as you can go."

Looking up Jerry's belly and into his blue eyes, Kevin lowered his gaping mouth.

"Yeah," Jerry said, nodding and twirling his nipples. "Uh-huh, like 'at. Now close your mouth on it and give it a good suck. Get it good and wet."

Kevin engulfed it, an alien thing yet quite recognizable, a creature with a life of its own, vaguely reptilian, as strange in his mouth as a frog but familiar as a million secret orgasms in his hand. He wrapped himself around it.

"Ah-h-h, yeah-h-h," Jerry breathed. "Now, hold your mouth still and start pulling the hood down real slow, while you're sucking on it. Uh-huh, I wanna feel it roll back inside your mouth." Kevin obeyed, slipping his finger and thumb around the base and retracting the thin sheath through his lips.

Jerry sounded distant. "Go real slow, buddy, re-e-e-al slow. Mmmh! Quarter inch at a time. Peel it back. Eighth of an inch at a time. Fuck, sixteenth of an inch, oh yeah real slow."

Kevin could feel the foreskin withdrawing past his tongue, dilating around the head of Jerry's cock. When the knob popped free, Jerry groaned and put his hand on Kevin's neck. "Now!" he whispered, pushing down until the rounded head probed the back of Kevin's throat. He choked at first, but he held fast until he had to back off to breathe.

"Do it again, man," Jerry urged. Kevin obliged, running the foreskin up to loose folds between his lips, mouthing the whole thing, drawing the moveable skin down until it released the cockhead, then lunging forward to make it jab at his throat. He sputtered, his eyes watered, and Jerry's encouragement enthralled him.

"Get all over it, buddy," Jerry ordered, and he did. "Show me how much you love it," he whispered, and Kevin's erection burned against Jerry's leg. Kevin added flourishes, discovering he could retract the foreskin by pulling down on Jerry's balls, twisting his other fist around it on the upstroke, repeating, repeating, humping Jerry's hairy calf, knees clamped around him like a horny dog as he felt a slick spot spreading under his own dick.

The world receded. Kevin sucked grateful obscenities out of his sailor, teased him into helpless, plaintive cries, made him groan, "Yeah, Kev, buddy, oh fuck yeah like that!" then backed off to make Jerry collapse into breathless, trembling gasps of "More, man. More, buddy. C'mon, Kev, make me cum."

Cock connection. This is what I want. Complete connection with another guy's hard dick.

Knock knock knock.

Jerry jerked in his hands and hissed, "Shit!"

No! No! Not now! Kevin closed his eyes tight and pressed his face into Jerry's pubic hair.

"Room cleaning," a woman's voice came from outside.

Jerry cleared his throat and whispered, "I locked it last night."

"Nuh!" Kevin squealed through his nose. *Go away! He's mine! Leave us alone!*

But keys tinkled, the lock clicked, and the door swung open, just as Kevin raised his head and let Jerry's hard-on pop from his mouth. Sunlight glared around a girl carrying a stack of towels. She stepped inside, calling, "Hello?" Her brown face peered in past the white cloth. Her eyes locked with Kevin's.

"Oh!" she said.

Kevin stared back, too dismayed to speak. He realized that a strand of cum stretched from his lower lip to the tip of Jerry's dick, silver in the light, trembling with each thud of his heart.

"Oh!" the girl repeated. Then her voice lowered in comprehension, "Oh." Backing up, she bowed and mumbled, "Excuse, por favor, excuse, please." She bumped her elbow on the door and a towel fell on the floor before she disappeared.

Raised to be a polite Southern boy, Kevin considered briefly if he should pick it up for her. But her hand reappeared and snatched it up as she sang out, "Check-out time is eleven o'clock!"

The door slammed and the light dimmed again.

"Shit fucking almighty," Jerry muttered. "I know I threw that goddamn dead bolt last night."

Kevin wiped his lower lip, hesitated, and then licked his finger. Jerry rolled away and reached for the bed table. He squinted at his watch. "Fuck, man. It's after one o'clock. No wonder she's pissed." He got up and yanked the curtain open. "God damn it, she's heading straight for the office. She's gonna tell that old fart she caught us sucking cock. Shit!"

Kevin blinked in the light. "She's probably just going to tell him she can't get in to clean the room. Come back! I want to finish!"

"Did that bastard take my number down last night?" Jerry turned to him. "I showed him my Navy ID, remember? Did he write it down?"

"I don't think so." Kevin frowned. "I think he just looked at it." In the bright window light, he could see that Jerry's cock had gone completely soft.

"If that fucker calls the shore patrol, my ass is grass."

Kevin shook his head. "Jerry, we're in fucking Arizona. There's no shore patrol at the Grand Canyon. I mean, for what, canoes? Come on back."

"Okay, the highway patrol. What if he calls them?"

Kevin remembered the cold stare the greasy old man had given him. "Oh, shit. He did write down my license plate number. And I know he caught on that I'm queer."

"Damn it! Now I can be blackmailed."

"What?"

"My security clearance. I told you, I work for the fucking admiral."

"So?" As Kevin stared at him, Jerry's neck and cheeks slowly reddened. "You're blushing," Kevin blurted.

"I'm brainwashed," Jerry muttered. He balled up his fist and smacked it into his palm. "Fuck! Now I'm a security risk, see? If anybody's tailing me, all they gotta do is talk to her." He bent over suddenly and grabbed their underwear from the floor. "Come on," he said, throwing Kevin's briefs to him. "We gotta get out of this dump."

Kevin wiped himself dry with his BVDs, watching dazedly as Jerry pulled clean shorts from his seabag and stepped into them. When Jerry's cock and balls disappeared behind white cloth, Kevin heard himself whimper. It was over. He sighed. His hairy animal now looked civilized.

"Jer," he began, but he didn't know what to say. Jerry looked up, stopping with one furry leg into his jeans. Kevin asked, "Can I, uh, borrow some of your underwear?"

Jerry pulled on his pants and tossed a second pair of his boxers onto the bed.

They dressed quickly, stuffing their things away unfolded, Kevin into his cardboard box, Jerry into his seabag. "Check for roaches in the ashtrays," Jerry told him, zipping his bag. While Jerry loaded the car, Kevin picked through the cigarette butts and then dumped everything into the trash. In the bathroom he swiped at the mirror and ran the water in the bathtub to rinse away the yellow puddle. He straightened the lamp in the main room, heaped the covers back onto the bed, kicked the dirty towel underneath it, and dropped the empty whiskey bottle into the can on top of the ashes.

Jerry came in and slapped the room key onto the dresser with a five-dollar bill under it. "That's, like, a week's pay in Mexico," he said, slipping on his aviator sunglasses. "Let's go."

At the door Kevin hesitated, looking back at the bed. He adjusted himself inside Jerry's loose-fitting boxer shorts. He flexed his asshole. He took a deep breath, smiled, and followed his new buddy out to the VW.

I'm a Top
Otto Coca

The Basics
Location: Chelsea NYC USA
Age: 29 and holding
Body type: Muscle-bound
Physical description: Tall, good looking, smooth, perfect teeth
Height/weight proportion: Perfect. 12% body fat
Outness: Everyone but my family
Relationship looking for? Long-term/Short-term/Sex/Hiking

Tastes
Favorite movie: *Titanic!* I've seen it 7 times! Really!
Favorite music: Everything! All types of disco, techno, and house. If it's got a diva wailing over it, I love it!
Music I hate: Country, Metal, and Rap
Favorite book: Anything I can learn from and gay romance novels.
Favorite vacation spot: In a k-hole
Favorite food: Met-Rx peanut butter and banana bars. 28 slamming grams of high-quality protein! Excellent!

Personality
Scene: Activist, Circuit boy, Military
Butch/Femme: Butch
Morning/Night? Um…both?
Preferred place to live? Big City/Gay Mecca

The Rest
Religion: Buddhist. Me, Edwina Monsoon & Tina Turner!
Job: Personal Trainer/Pharmaceutical Researcher
Alcohol use: Socially
Drug use: Socially
Piercing: So 1998!
Tattoos: A snake on my hip and a huge rainbow flag with stars on my left 18" bicep. (But I'm thinking of getting it covered up with something more tasteful.)
In my free time: I help gay youth with their workout routines. It's never too early to start looking good, but for some it's already too late.

Hello to everyone from MuscleStud99X!

Thanks, all of you, for responding to my personal ad.

I have never placed an Internet ad before, but since the Web has been so effective getting me laid, why can't it find me love too! I'm really serious about finding my "Special Guy" for the Summer 2002 season and I sincerely hope that you, <- enter name -> make the finals. It's amazing that based only on my tastefully nude picture and the sentence, "I'm a top," that I would get so much action. I got over a 100 responses and that was after cutting out all the guys who live more than 30 minutes away from 23rd and Eighth. I've now narrowed my search for true love down to you special 58 guys. You all either have hot bodies and large cocks or you seem to share my passions and interests while having hot bodies and large cocks. Now that I have chosen you, I think it's only fair that you get to know a little more about me. Please forgive the impersonal nature of this form letter but I just can't respond to you each individually or I would never get to the gym.

Okay, down to business!

First things first: yes, I am really a top. And no, I've never really been fucked. I mean, don't get me wrong, I like some attention in the downtown area, and if my "Special Guy" wants to kiss and cuddle my bronze Bat Cave of Love, I'm certainly not going to be as selfish a lover like my last boyfriend. (BTW, he goes by the screen name Bigmonster88. Be on the lookout all you runners-up!) But other than a rim job and maybe a well-manicured finger or two, my butt is strictly "Exit Only."

And yes, BigPapiMan64, there have been a few times when I came close to losing my hard-earned "Exclusive Top" status. Like when I was at the Black Party last year some nasty Daddy-type guy started rubbing my tits and stuff and trying to get some backdoor action with me. I was just standing in the orgy room (the one on the second floor, not the sleazy one in the basement) minding my own business when I suddenly felt a hand on my bare ass and then this rush of electricity run through my body. It's so unlike me, really, I don't know if it was the music, the smell of his leather gloves, or the GBH, but the next thing I know I'm bent over a vinyl sawhorse and I'm enjoying the attention of his pecker against my poopchute. The funny thing was that he was totally NOT my type! He had this hairy chest and way too much dangling jewelry in places where you should really only have studs or a simple ring. I think he might have been a skinhead but it's hard to tell nowadays since the Nazi look isn't so hot anymore. His moves were so smooth that if it wasn't for the 3-gauge ring in his cockhead, I might have never felt a thing. Fortunately, my best friend Donny (who weighs more than I and is eight months older) was witness to the entire event and at just the right moment, he slurred, "I always knew you were a dick-hungry man-bitch. Take Daddy's cock deep, and moan like the girly slut you are!" Well, that set me straight, so to speak. At the magic words "man-bitch" I popped right up, adjusted my thong and headed for the bar. Donny came over sheepishly and I bought him a Bud Light for literally saving my ass. The next day, when I realized how close I came to losing my reputation as an "Exclusive Top," I actually cried. But I think it might have just been the aftereffects of the X.

That brings me to the fact that I'm only looking for smart guys, like my best friend Donny. He has a rule that he will only date doctors, or others in the medical-type professions. I admire that eye-of-the-tiger attitude, but once Donny tossed off a perfectly good lawyer for a plain looking psychiatrist who was two cans shy of a six-pack (abdominally, not mentally, of course). When I asked Donny why, he gave me his sweet glazed-over stare and said, "Musclestud, I always choose prescriptions over penetration." And knowing the way Donny likes penetration, that must have been love.

Okay, enough about my asshole. What about yours? When I was reading the questionnaires that I asked you all to fill out, I was amazed by the amazing variety of positions and places that guys like to get it from behind in. I think some of you can teach me a thing or two. Like for instance, ButtBanquet29, how did you ever think of using buttermilk and sangria for an enema? Are you Mexican? Do you pit the fruit first? Also, while your picture settles all doubts, I still can't believe that anyone would want to do that with a jalapeno no matter how much you enjoy the "tingle." I think I want to meet you but I'm gonna pass on the dinner invite. Don't get me wrong, I like a good meal but to keep a body like this, a guy's gotta watch what he puts in his mouth.

And speaking of eating, food is very important to me. Seriously. I like really excellent meals, the kind of meals that someone like Emeril or those fat chicks on Food TV can make. (But not that Iron Chef stuff 'cause eel and crap is fatty and gross.) I think food is so important that I insist that my "Special Guy" also like food too. You know what I mean? Don't be emailing me if you don't like good meals 'cause I can tell. If we're at a nice restaurant of my choosing and I catch you eating an overdone steak, or pasta that's not al dente, well, you're out. I won't put up with that. When I say rare, I want it rare, not medium. (Private to AllyMcbeallOver75, I admire your willpower, but I insist that all food stay down at least 45 minutes to count as "dinner.") I love Italian food. I'm Italian on my Mom's side and if you think some Prego sauce on noodles is good eating, then you're not my soul mate. And that's what I'm looking for, a soul mate that appreciates my cultural style. Even when I'm training, I take the time out to have at least one meal of solid food a week and then it's a night out at the Olive Garden. I just don't let myself fill up on the breadsticks even if they are "all-you-can-eat." When you're riding with me, my little anal vice, it's class all the way. I want to drink my Moët with strawberries just like Richard Gere in *Pretty Woman,* pour Hennessey down the small of your back like an early LL Cool J video (obviously, hairy backboys need not apply), and smear your smooth, round pecs with some sort of nonfat whipped cream substitute. If this sounds like you, then you want me. I've spent a lot of time in the gym getting right with myself and working out my issues. I know that I'm worth the man who is a perfect reflection of me. And only that person should respond. All others, let's not waste each other's time! I can't help it. These are the little details that separate us from the apes.

Other things I love? I love adventure! I'm totally the sort of guy that likes to go on safaris or travel through the outback like on *Survivor* and shit. That is totally me. But I want to do it with food and a 4X4 or something 'cause rice is gonna fuck up my diet. If you have a 4X4 and have a copy of *Let's Go: Outback,* that's a definite plus! And when I meet the guy that wants to do stuff like that, and is really hot and well-hung, I'm going to do it. You can't hold me back. I'm burning, man. Touch my fire. Think about it: you, me, and our big-dicked sunburned blond Aussie guide named Sven or Hans. Traveling the outback, hunting for dingoes, and petting the kangaroos and stuff. Sven/Hans would have just gotten out of high school where he was a star soccer player. Football, soccer, whatever, either way he wouldn't be shy about hanging out naked in front of two butch numbers like us. From the moment we hit the road, he would be shirtless with his nipples brown and hard from the sun with his smooth chest just filling out as his boyish frame transitions to manhood. His thick tanned thighs covered with a soft layer of invisible sun-bleached hairs that disappear into his tiny khaki shorts that bunch up so tight in the crotch when he squats. And he squats a lot. He ends our first day on the road by taking us to a secret spot that isn't even in a *Lonely Planet* guide, a sexy waterfall where he and his friends come to get drunk on the weekends. "Ay," says Sven/Hans, "me and my mates come out here and bring our 'birds.'" In Australian "bird" means girls, but I'll give him that look that says, "Yeah, right, buddy. I got your bird right here." You'll be unpacking the tent or something.

Sven/Hans will then strip off his boots and shorts, "Ay, mates, we don't need no stinking swimsuits in Oz!" You and I will smile and watch as this lanky hunk of teenage boy lust hits the water and does a slow back float at the surface, his uncut cock poking into the air like a fuck snorkel. We both dive in seconds later, naked and sporting hard-ons that Sven/Hans notices but laughs off, "Ay, yeah, ain't Australia beautiful? Really gets your blood up, don't it?" After an hour or so of good-natured splashing around and a semi-obscene game of Marco Polo, we lie back on the rocks and let the sun warm us.

As you and I lay together, deep in the rapture of our love, we watch as naked Sven/Hans goes off to some bushes where he squats and pulls at some leaves. I grab your nipple as we both stare into Sven/Han's peach-fuzzy anus and watch his pink pucker tense and release with every tug on the leaves. You laugh shyly as I call to him, "Sven! (or Hans!) Stand up straight, your dick is getting dirty!" Sven/Hans turns quickly, and grabs at his cloaked cockhead that has been resting on the ground since he squatted. He shakes his dick at me as if I should be insulted; instead we both pop wood that neither of us tries to hide as he returns.

"Ay, mates, this is traditional Aussie sunblock I got out of the Ogga-Booga plant over there. My grandpa taught me this trick when I was a boy. Want me to show you how to put it on?" The sun is behind Sven/Hans and we squint to see him. His silhouette is perfect and casting an erotic shadow over our touching bodies. I can't help but notice that his shadow cock is dangling right over your firm tan-line-less ass. Sven/Hans crouches over me with his slick manroot balm and when his soft, fat pink prick accidentally slaps against my upper thigh, I throw all caution to the wind and grab his turgid ballsac. Minutes later, Sven/Hans's ass is our lunch-box and we both help ourselves to a Vegemite sandwich. I'm so turned on right this second that I swear I can hear Olivia Newton-John singing "Xanadu."

Which brings me to my other love: music. I love music. All kinds. From Hi-NRG to disco classics and everything in between. I have every CD that my gym has and then some. I love to party and dance, but sometimes, I like to just chill with some old skool Swing Out Sister or Sade. I also like classical. I'm totally a believer that not all music needs words. I go to the clubs a lot, but I'm strictly there for the music. The X and blow jobs are merely a side benefit to me.

When you respond to this letter with your 3 pictures (remember, one full-body!) and your twenty-dollar processing fee, tell me what kind of music you like. I can act really interested in anything you like. I have a lot of experience with relationships. But let me tell you right now that don't even think you're getting with me if you don't hate rap, metal, and country. I wouldn't be caught dead with a guy who liked that shit. I know that I'm going out on a limb with that one and I'm probably damning myself to a life of muscle-bound celibacy, but this is not something I'm gonna back down on. I gotta be true to myself. I can deal with anything else. Prefer Tori over Fionia? Fine. Personally, I can't tell the fucking difference. They both sound like they have their heads buried in Kate Bush's snatch if you ask me. I mean really, where do they find these chicks? Is Warner Brothers trolling some teenage rehab somewhere looking for the most supremely disturbed inmates? Why don't they just donate a thousand guitars to bulimia clinics all over the country and put out a boxed set? Whatever, but I'm not the type of guy who is going to dictate my views on people. You should be independent and possess your own wisdom of Free Will, as long as you agree with me.

And what do I do with my free time? I go to the gym 3X or 4X a week. That's deeply relevant to my psyche but I'm not sure why. Hopefully, I will meet a guy who likes good meals and hates rap, country, and metal, and he'll explain it to me.

One last thing: body types. This may sound kinky and unusual, but I really get off on a guy with a lanky swimmer's-build type. Someone who's hairless, preferably blond, and has nice white teeth. Sorry, you Orthodontic Donnas, but no brown-toothed trolls for me! Also guys who are over 30 and yet still refer to themselves as a "boy." What a turn-on! Please, when we meet, wear a baseball cap so you look youthful and "collegiate." Wear it turned backwards and I just might cum on the spot! You ever notice that a guy could be 40 or so, and yet, in a baseball cap and baggy pants, he's a sexy 25 all over again? It's a gay miracle. When I was in the asylum, um, I mean, on vacation, I did it with this guy who thought he was Napoleon, so I love role-play! If you would call yourself a "boi"—even better! I'll play along!

Sometimes, living in this bubble of CK1 and attitude, I wish silently to myself so no one will know (unless they are reading my lips, which I move unconsciously) that more than anything else, I want to have the man that will make all my friends drool. It's not for me, you understand. I can put my ego aside, see. It's not like I want to be the best-looking, most handsome guy in the room, I just want the best-looking, most handsome guy in the room to *want me*. Is that asking too much?

Finalists will be notified by email within two weeks. In case of a tie, the top five finalists will be invited to a private party where they will be put through a 45-minute Tae Bo routine while rectally clenching a Jeff Stryker super-realistic dildo with moveable balls. Light snacks and poppers will be provided. Please bring a clean towel.

Huh?

Ron Winterstein

Sorry, still didn't catch that.... *Ooooh,* I thought you said, Do you wanna *get* high? Okay, hi. Just out for some air cuz I *(hee hee hee)* quit breathing somehow. And you...? Well, nice night for it, huh? Did you see the moon...? Here, I'll show you. Uh, right *theeerrre* through that tree blowing around.... A silvery scythe? Now *that's* poetic *(hee hee hee).* I'd say, glowing toenail. Uh, you live around here...? I used to live there, *buuut* I had to move.... Well, cuz my roommates were kinda freaks? Let's just say sometimes I peed in jars cuz I didn't wanna leave my room *(hee hee hee)....* What...? Oh. Kenny. And you...? Hey, my best friend's name is Andrew too.... Yeah, really. He moved to New York to be a model? So I don't hear from him anymore.... *Hmmm,* yeah, people say that, but I don't have the confidence for it.... Well, I'm in school.... Don't really know yet? But I think graphic design eventually. Hafta get all these bullshit classes out of the way first.... Um, twenty. People say I look younger. I have this fake ID, but I'm sick of the clubs anyway. How old are *you?*—Why are you laughing? *Right* on. You don't *look* that old. I had this boyfriend, Robert? He was kinda your age…. Well, he said he fell out of love with me, but really I think it's cuz of Jared, this boy that'd just graduated from high school and moved here…. Naw. Don't have time for a boyfriend currently. Sure is a nice night…. *Hmmm…?* Oh. *Wellll?* Actually, just down the block—um—would you like to stop by? Just for a bit…. Yeah, three roommates…. Uh-huh, we get along great, and they're never home…. Okay, cool. This way. You'll hafta pretend there's no mess, though *(hee hee hee)*. People always say that, huh? So, what do you do…? Cool. That's like a stockbroker, right? Guess I should start learning about investments, huh? *(hee hee hee)*. My parents give me money, they're kinda loaded. But I work too, part-time, cuz I like to feel, um, independent…? Javarama. You know it? It's okay, but when it's real quiet after work? My ears still ring from the espresso machine *(hee hee hee)*. Check it out! There's this one dude who comes in, like, always? He wants me to, like, marry him!…*Yeah*. He brings me these what he calls *tokens of affection,* which are really just kind of, um, suggestive? You know, toys 'n stuff. I don't even know him, but he's always dicking around, asking questions. And I know he watches my ass when I go to the fridge to get the latte milk. I put everything on the top shelf now. I mean, he's really gorgeous 'n all? But it creeps me out, y'know? He's started following me after work, so I hafta, um, detour, pretend I'm going home. Trippy shit…. Oh. Yeah, they're cool. Especially my mom. She even bought me these slinky cocktail dresses 'n stuff from Nordstrom's? But I'm not really into drag. Before she returned them she made me try them on, took some Polaroids *(hee hee hee)*. After that, when I'd come in the door? Dad started pulling me into these real tight hugs…. Yeah, they're cool. Only thing was I don't think they approved of Robert, cuz like, he was their age? Oh, here we are—Hmmm. *This* key, I think, um, can you tell I just moved here?—After you. Okay, follow ME—OH. BOBBY,

THIS IS, UM...YEAH, ANDREW. ANDREW, THIS IS BOBBY—OKAY, RIGHT THIS WAY—SORry about that. Bobby and his music. I like some of that downtempo stuff? But you really gotta be on a dance floor.... *Wellll,* um, he's kind of a tweaker? Actually, major that. Which means either (a) he's distracted and rude, or (b) plain rude—Here we are. Sorry about all the clothes. It's about me and decisions *(hee hee hee).* Lemme just...Yeah, aren't they funny? That's actually a vintage Pet Shop Boys poster. Hey, how 'bout some music? Let's *seeee...*Oh, it's this trip-hop CD my friend Jordy got me? He says I need to pull my head outta the '80s' ass. But I *like* retro. Is this too loud...? Oh, that *(hee hee hee).* Yeah, scanned that off the net. Sorta beautiful, huh? But then, I'm kind of into, *ummm,* assholes *(hee hee hee)*...I mean, anatomical ones.... Now, that's *(hee hee hee)* the inside of a piano.... Uh-huh. It's kind of ridiculous and heavy and, um, rusty. When I lived with Robert? He found that on the street, put it in the garden outside my window facing, um, west? So when the wind blew the wires would start to, uh, sing.... Yeah. *Verrry* soft. Kinda spooky. But beautiful at the same time. *Hmmm.* Now it just sits there all quiet, unless there's a draft.... Oh, yeah, I was studying. But the walls started closing in, y'know? That calculus textbook is the heaviest yet, in more ways than one *(hee hee hee)....* Ah! Don't let him freak you out. That's Baxter. He's a hedgehog.... Yeah, *really.* My friend Sol/r gave him to me for my birthday. I think they're illegal to have as pets. He's named after an old boyfriend. It's a joke. Something about *(hee hee hee)* burrowing mammals.... Yeah, he seems happy in there. Sol/r, that's his Fairy name, his real name is Jon, he knows lots about weird animals and stuff. You should see *his* apartment—Um. You want some water or something? Or—Whaaat? Um, don't mean to sound dopey? But your eyes and mouth work well together—Uh, would you like to pet Baxt*eruhmphmmmmmmmmMMMM*

MMMMMMMMMmmmmmmmmmmmmm—hmmmmmm. That was *nicemmmmmmmmmmmmmmmm.* Um. You know? I *mmmmmmmmmmmmmmmmmmmmmmmmmmmmmmmmmmmmMMMM-MMMmmuhermmmmm!* Um…I uh… This is great 'n all,—Oh! Nothing's wrong. But…Hmmm. Could we just do this, you know, kiss, make out? For now? I mean, you're *totally* cute, don't get me wrong. You just seem like, uh—really nice. Like maybe we should put it off for now? Unless, there'll be no "now" in the future. I mean, can I just hold you or somethi*mmmmmmmmmmmmmmmmmmmmmmmmmm* um. *mmmmmm-mmMMMMMMMMMMMMMMMMMMMMMMMMMM Mmmm (hee hee hee)*—Let me *uhmmmmmmmmmmmm-mmm*…Let me close the door—Hey. Cool boxers. Are they designer…? *Right* on. Maybe I should try boxers. Robert wore them, you know, too—*This* I hafta hang up. It wrinkles if you even breathe *(hee hee hee)*…. Oh. You like it…? Yeah, well, it was a ritual scarification? The spiral represents *going into the vortex.* It was done on the solar plexus cuz that's where I was holding? Sheryl, this cool dyke who did it? Said it was a direct route, spiraling inward to confront inner, you know, stuff…. *Wellll?* Early sexual abuse and stuff? We've probably all had it…. Yeah it hurt, but—*Ah-ooo,* uh, careful. It's still sorta—Um *(hee hee HEE)* that's tender in a whole dif-ferent *wuh—waaaaaaaaaaooooooooooooooooooooooooooooo ooohOH.* Oh! Muh-my dickhead is kinda sensiti—*mmmmm mmmmmmmmmmmmmmmmmmmmmmmmmm.* Oh! *MMMM MMM MmmmmMMMMMMMMmmmmmmooooooooooooooooooo ohhhhhhhhhhhheeeeeeeeehhhhhhhhhh haaaaaaaaaaaaaauuuu uhhhhhhhhooooooooooooooooohhhhhhooooooohhhhhh-hhhu uuummmmmmmmmmmmmmmmMMMM…*that feels *grrreeaaat! Mmmmaaaaaaaahhhhhhhhhh hhhuhhh* Huh? Oh, well, I get a limpy sometimes. Nothing personal—I think I hafta pee*peeeeeeeeeeeehhhhhhhhhheeeeeeeeeeeeeehhh-hhhuhhhhhhHHHHHHHHHHHHHHHHH*…Ah! Ah!…Oof.

Ow! *(hee hee hee)* I'm smushing Pooh Bear. I
I *waaaaaaaahhhhhhhaaaaaaahhhhhhhh...Er.
rrrr-RRRRRrrrrrrrrrrrrrrrrrrrrrrrrrrrhuuuuuuu
hhhhhuuuuuuuuuhhhhhhhhhhuuuuuuuu*—He,
okay...? No, raw... *Yeah*, I'm sure. Lube's *riiiight* —
here—*Wow*, I'm hot. You have fab pecs.... *Okay uuuuu
uhhhuuuhhhhhhhhhuuuuuugggggggghh*...Ow!   Sorry!
*(hee   hee   hee)...uuuuuuuhhhhhhhhhhhhhUUUUUHHH
H   O   O   O   O   O   W   W   W   W   W
aaaaaaaaaaaaaaaaahhhhhhhhhhhhhaaaaaa...uh uh uh...uh
uh uh uh uhuhuh...OOOHHH...FFFUCKK UH UH
UH UH UH UH...UHUH UHUH UHUH...UHUHUH
UHUHUHUHUHUH...OHOHOHOH...PUHPUH...
PLEEEEEEEEEEEZ...OH OH OH OH OH OH. WOW!*
...I think I... Are you*uUUUUUU...HUHUHUHUHUHU
HUH UH UH UH UH UH UH UH OOOOOOOOOO
OOOOOOOOOMMMMMMMmmmnnmmm—Woooh.*
Phew! That was *soooo* hot—Um. Are you okay...? It's cool,
really. Robert used to fuck me without... Yeah, I know you're
not. You sorta remind me of him, is all. *Hmmmm*—Oh,
sorry, I tranced out there—*Heeey*, you know, you don't hafta
go. I mean, you can stay as long as you want. Really. Well,
unless you totally *have* to—Oh. Sure. I forget people have
real jobs. I should actually study for that midterm anyway,
since it's tomorrow 'n all...Huh? Oh, I think they're—*Here*
they are. If you forget anything you know where I live *(hee
hee hee)*—Hey. You wanna see these pictures my friend Drew
took of me?? They're kinda nasty *(hee hee hee)*.... Yeah. It *is*
late, huh?—Hey. Can I, like, give you my phone number...?
Cool. Do you like movies? I like to dance. You like that...?
Yeah, well, the clubs are tired anyway—Here. Um. I'll walk
you out—So, you CAN CALL ANYTIME...I SAID—Phew,
that's better. That's another thing I need to talk to Bobby
about—Wow. Is the moon gone already? Pretty quiet now,

huh? Except—hear that? My favorite sound is leaves in the gutter. I think I'll just sit out here for a while. You know, fresh air *(hee hee hee)*. Yeah, so, thanks—I mean, see ya? Nice meeting you.... Okay, bye—Huh? Oh *(hee hee hee)*. I thought you said something.... Okay—Walk safe———

—Hi. Pretty good... No, sorry, I don't smoke... Huh?

Losing It
John Orcutt

I'm lying on my stomach on the bed with a pillow tucked under my chin. He's slowly parting my asscheeks and very slowly, very gently lapping at my tight hole. I moan just a little bit. "You like that?" he asks. I nod vigorously and he licks one of his fingers and presses it against the opening until I give way. He slowly fucks me with the one finger and then he spits on a second and pushes them both against my ass. "A good lover will take his time to make you feel comfortable, work up to it," he instructs. "How does this make you feel?" Just like a therapist. Okay, yeah, I'm in bed with my therapist. It's a long story.

Considering how amazingly rounded my heels are from circling the block for the better part of two decades, I am still what is commonly referred to as vanilla. I try not to couple with anyone who requires paraphernalia or special outfits in order to have sex. I have never understood the lure of leather and am still waiting for the gay community to eroticize cotton. Like most people I have very specific things I like to do, and don't like to do, sexually. I don't like to go home with people. Quick and uncomplicated has been a formula that's worked for me for years. "Do 'em where you find 'em" is my motto. I also hate talkers. Chatter during sex should only consist of directions, updates, and forecasts. I am not your boy and, at a boyish thirty-five, I am certainly not your Daddy. Say "daddy" in any context and images of my father mowing the lawn appear instantly, dooming any mood approaching horny. Preferences? I had a tonsillectomy as an adult, which I like to think of as the only gay cosmetic surgery I'll ever need.

Despite these limitations, I do get plenty of action. I'm a standard five foot eleven inches, I have jet black hair and the kind of ice-blue eyes one generally finds on Alaskan huskies pulling sleds. I don't have a gym body but swim and practice yoga on a regular basis. I guess I'm just not that good at fantasy play and role-playing and verbalizing. How many times have I been perfectly happy down on my knees sucking off some hottie when he insists, "You want that dick, doncha," pulling it out of my mouth and slapping me across the face with it and actually expecting an answer to his ill-timed and highly rhetorical query? "Yes, I want it. That's why I just sat in a smoky, dark bar through four beers, half a pack of cigarettes, and your boring life story, so that I could wrap my lips around your big fatty despite the fact that I'm going to have to walk home at sunrise while it's raining out. However, now that you're caning me with it I'm a little less enthusiastic."

Despite years of frequenting video booths, parks, sex clubs, bathhouses, warehouse districts, back rooms, and the apartments of numerous strangers, I'm still a virgin. No, it's true. In the strictest sense of the term I *am* a virgin. Please keep it under your hat as it could obviously ruin my standing in many social circles. It really is amazing that an attractive, sexually active gay man in his thirties can say this. Even the butchest top men have been fucked at least once.

Why? I'm not sure. Maybe I'm saving it. Maybe it has never

truly appealed to me. Maybe I've got some sort of hang-up. But it seems like something I should know how to do in a pinch. It's like working for AAA and not knowing how to change a tire. I think I figured that when Mr. Right came along, I'd bite the bullet (and pillow) and learn to love being sodomized. However, after hundreds of Mr. Right Nows, Mr. Wrongs, and Mr. What-the-Fucks, I started sizing up my friends like women assessing potential sperm donors. I had chosen a handful of potential candidates on whom to bestow the honor of busting my cherry if I still had it by the age of thirty.

That was half a decade ago. It's cute and somewhat flirty when you're a teen or in your twenties to let your curious date know you've never been fucked. When you're thirty-five and you've been sexually active for nineteen years, it's downright creepy. It's not that I haven't gotten any offers. I got a lot. And a lot more once they discovered it was untrodden territory, which is why I started to act like a stone-cold top, when I'm not. In fact, I'm the most passive top in the universe. It takes an extremely bossy bottom to launch me into action. Generally, I only fuck tricks when they are screamers. It is the equivalent of stuffing a sock in their mouth. Also, I'm uncut, and I think safe sex is important, and, well…perhaps other uncut guys will understand, but it's kinda like trying to put on pantyhose over a pantsuit—just not that comfortable.

So, until this year when asked, "Do you get fucked?" I always said, "No" in such a way that my trick du jour knew it was nonnegotiable. They never pursued the subject.

Rich didn't do that. On our very first date, six months ago, when he asked if I ever had been, I had to answer honestly. He didn't seem to care why, and I think he saw a challenge—and I saw salvation from my ass becoming the Miss Havisham of the gay world. Because he used to be a whore (opposites do attract—I've always given it away free), I figured he was a trained professional and would be the perfect candidate.

My first task was, of course, to get ready. I'm a regular Girl Scout when it comes to a project. I am also the kind of person who has to clean the *entire* house before anyone visits. Here's a question "Dear Abby" doesn't get that often: is it less shaming to buy one personal hygiene item but make several such trips than to buy a whole lot of personal hygiene items at once? I was asking myself this as I sized up the aloof staff at my local drugstore. I was trying to determine the fastest, most unobservant clerk and whether I wanted to save ten cents on a generic brand versus the tried and true. Sidling up to the checkout carrying a half-dozen enemas with a line of people behind you including two of New York's finest is embarrassing. Finding yourself on your elbows with your face pressed against your (very clean) cold tile bathroom floor staring at the underside of your toilet while squeezing a small plastic bottle filled with god-knows-what into your ass like the little man on the box is mortifying.

Assuming everything needed to be clean and trouble free inside *and* out, I tried to sandwich my butt waxing somewhere among a manicure, a pedicure, and a haircut. If you're wondering what butt waxing feels like, don't ask your straight female friends. However, when they tell you to go to a Russian lady, listen to them. Svetlana was a dear. I assumed this would occur on all fours, but she kept me lying face down and the pain was minimal—I mean, I'm not Sasquatch. There was a tricky moment when she asked, "You vant zee eenside, too?" "Ah, um, yeah," I mumbled, as if the idea had never occurred to me. "Vell, I veell need you to help me," she instructed. The image of me prone pulling my asscheeks apart with both hands while a large (yet gentle) Russian woman holding a pot of hot wax pulls strips of hair off my ass is not one I'll soon forget.

These weren't the only problems. Rich's was not what one would consider a "starter dick." If it were a mobile home it would easily be a double-wide. I decided to have several dates with what the package referred to as "The Love Club," chosen for its tapered effect, allowing one to, well, loosen up, a bit at a time. After all this preparation, both mental and physical, you can imagine how I felt when Rich spit on the head of his dick and rammed it against my lubeless ass. "How'd everything go?" asked my informed and expectant roommates later, much like a group of Third World women waiting for me to produce the bloodied sheet. "Fine," I answered. "He said, 'Am I hurting you?' and I said, 'duh' and smacked him."

After several such failed attempts, Rich dumped me. I can only assume it was because my asshole didn't slam open after one glass of wine and a Johnny Mathis album. Though my virginity was still intact, my interest in keeping it so no longer was. I decided my problem was in my head, and, like any college graduate, I decided to seek therapy. My first therapist, an elderly, myopic Jewish man in a badly frayed cardigan, insisted this was due to my father grabbing me by the scruff of the neck and kicking me in the ass when I was a child. It turns out that my ass will open like "a flower in the springtime" once my father passes away. After using my eighty-eight-year-old living grandfather as a standard, and some quick math, I decided I didn't want my asshole blooming when I was in my sixties. My second therapist, an environmentally ill lesbian who insisted that I not wear deodorant, concluded I was not just a control queen but *the* ultimate control queen. Who else could maintain such a "hypervigilance over the barbarians crashing my gates for so long"? My third therapist, a straight woman who had never been told that home perms are never an answer and needed the term "rimming" defined, determined that I was an overprotective mother and my ass was my child, and that I didn't want to expose it to the harsh realities of life.

Shortly after my final session, my roommate and I were meandering through the meatpacking district on our way to a party. We overheard a shlumpy businessman on his cell phone explaining, "She's a therapist…a sex surrogate," to some befuddled friend or family member. Trust me when I tell you that finding a hot gay sex therapist who will actually fuck you isn't that easy. It took a lot of talking to people and much trial and error. This is like my eighth session with him—the first five were all talk and no play. The sixth was all show and no touch, and the last session was pretty much foreplay and chat about the fact that this one would be the big fuck.

Roger, the therapist, is thin and tight with ropy muscles. His hair is brown and a little too long with a sprinkle of gray here and there. He seemed like a good therapist, but I wasn't sure he'd be a good lover. After the fifth session where I finally saw him naked, I didn't really care. He has one of those cocks that inspire porn directors. It's proportionally too thick for his thin frame, with two veins on either side that run up and down from base to head like the Yangtze and the Volta. When he gets really excited the head turns a dark purple as if it's going to explode. His balls are chunky and hang low as if he had his ballsac professionally stretched to just the right length. Hair-wise, he has a light sprinkling around his nipples and on his ass and balls, and that perfect *V* from his navel to his pubic hair.

That's why I'm lying facedown getting ready to give it the old college try while Roger lubes up his third finger. I realize that there really isn't any reason for me to remain a virgin. I'm not saving myself for anyone in particular, as if there *were* anyone in particular. I actually am not here anymore to lose my cherry. I'm here because I want Roger to fuck me. I want his fat, veiny cock inside me. He's fucking me with three fingers and I'm rocking like a crazed three-year-old on a hobbyhorse. Jesus, I'm so glad that I'm here and I'm going to get fucked. I want him to ram it in me. I feel him start to place the head against my ass.

"Yeah, stick it in me," I say.

I can't believe I'm not only saying it, but meaning it. I want Roger to split me right in two with his donger. I want him to tear me open. I want to sit and spin on that thing Thai-style. They could lower me in a basket from the ceiling so that my asshole could swallow his cock whole, and then I'll pound against his pubic bone until he's black and blue.

"Yeah, fuck me. Fuck me hard!" I scream.

"I'm afraid our time is up for this week."

Neighbors
Trebor Healey

I'm horny and José's not here. So I'm washing a week's dirty dishes, wondering when he'll be home. Dating a hustler can suck. This morning he wouldn't let himself cum. We were getting it on hard, too, and I could see he was close. I had him nearly doing a headstand, I was fucking him so hard.

"I've got three clients today, Sid, I can't cum," he shouted, holding his cock firmly as if it would explode once he let go. I stopped in midthrust.

"Gee, José, maybe I should start paying you too. Then I could see some of that white stuff…just cum! The check's in the mail," and I went back at it.

"No, Sid, I can't!" I pulled my cock out with a pop.

"Don't do me any favors, José." I hopped up to take a shower.

"Shit. You know we should never fool around in the morning. This always happens," he shouted at my back.

" 'This' being nothing," I replied, disgusted.

"Whatever." He moped. Now I was supposed to feel sorry for him. I grabbed a new bar of soap and lathered up, reigniting my cock, which was still hungry for José's sweet ass. I started jacking it with the bar, wondering as I did how we might find a solution to this little problem that kept coming up. Maybe José could get stuntman packets like they use in movies for blood, only his would shoot cum. Or maybe he could have some kind of surgical procedure so that he could shoot at will ten times a day. He was twenty, for chrissakes—I could cum five times a day when I was twenty.

I've got it good and hard when I notice him, through the curtain, standing at the door. He's got that puppy-dog look in his eyes and he's stroking himself. He's so beautiful, with his thick little uncut Indian cock, his big blue-gray balls, a sweet black trail of fuzz running down his tummy. I pull back the curtain. "Come here." He lights up, smiling, hopping into the warm water and locking his mouth on mine as I grab hold of our cocks together in my fist and jack us both to grunting, furrowed-brow ecstasy.

"Shit," he says, not a second afterward, looking at his dick.

"Sorry," I offer insouciantly.

He cracks a quick smile, letting me know he's not blaming me. His mind has moved on to the day's itinerary.

"Go look at some porn, you'll get motivated."

"Yeah, all your fucking Latin porn—fat chance." He was busy getting dressed, while I cranked up the coffee.

"When you coming home, José?"

"I don't know, page me."

"You know I hate that fucking thing, and I hate how you always call from a client's so I have to listen to some john cooing at your shoulder. Ain't gonna do it, man."

"I'll call you around seven. Wait, I gotta meet my friend for that paper I gotta do."

"Paper on what?"

"*Huck Finn.*"

"Fuck him." I smiled. "All right, I'll see you late, then."

We locked our mouths up one more time, tongued each other hard, licked each other's stubbled chins. I hate bourgeois kisses. "Adios."

"Bye."

It was never a question of monogamy, since half the time José was withholding cum, and besides, he was fucking his brains out with twenty different men a week. He only asked that I not get emotionally involved. Happily—or sadly, as the case may be—that was the easy part.

But mostly I was too busy. I was going to nursing school, putting in volunteer hours at a clinic. And I was thirty. I'd long ago lost the energy to go out hunting for it. I'd been relying on the YMCA for months now, which is where I'd met José, but even that wasn't an option nowadays, what with the volunteer job. It wasn't a problem, though—José was keeping me satisfied. Enough, anyway.

Then again, if it was thrown in my face… I turned to put a dish in the rack and saw him in my peripheral vision. Out my window and up two stories to a window on the third floor of the hideous behemoth of an apartment building across the fence, a guy had his shirt halfway up his torso and over his face as he pulled it off. I stared; he got the shirt up and over his head; he tossed it on the bed or somewhere behind him. He hadn't noticed me. The drama queen in me wanted to drop the plate I was holding and let it shatter at my feet. The poor student in me wouldn't allow it, so I placed it gingerly in the drying rack, never taking my eyes off the vision hovering above me like a saint in a Mexican *retablo* painting.

He was standing there, gazing out the window. I started praying and pleading to childhood angels that he'd look down and see me. It was an odd habit I couldn't shake. I'd always say Our Fathers and Hail Marys when I saw a cute boy at the gym, bargain with a God I hadn't believed in for fifteen years. Catholicism dies hard, or it doesn't at all. I thought it was sort of cute when I caught myself doing it. It made me feel young and eager.

Then he looked.

I smiled.

He smiled.

I kept looking.

He unsnapped his Levi's top button.

I yanked my shirt off hurriedly to catch up. He was beautiful and I hoped he was seeing the same in me. He was close to my age: maybe six foot, lean and brown. His jeans dropped to reveal white boxers. I snapped my jeans apart speedily, letting them fall, realizing too late that I'd put no underwear on after the shower with José.

He smiled enormously, bent forward, and removed his white shorts, first lifting one leg, then the other. His cock bobbed, half-hard and handsome. Damn.

We were both stroking it now, playing with our tits and balls, posing for each other. It occurred to me I'd never be able to cum after having just done so with José an hour ago. And José thought *he* had problems!

I yanked the window open and leaned out, looking around to see if anyone was watching us. He struggled with his own window, got it open with a jarring screech. We both said at the same time: "Wanna come over?" And answered together, too: "Yeah!"

"What's your address?" I asked quickly, pressing my desire to go to his place. He told me and I threw on my clothes and raced over, my heart beating like fear.

He buzzed me in and I hurried to his door, which opened as my fist rose to knock. He put out his tongue and licked my knuckles.

"Fuck," I said lustily, and pushed my way in. He was back

in his boxers and he tore doggedly at my clothes to get them off quickly as he led me, walking backward, tripping, toward his room. Then he pulled me on top of him as we fell together onto his bed, kissing sloppily and smearing saliva across each other's mouths. I rolled him over on top of me and pulled off his shorts as he arched his back up to assist. Having checked my conscious reason at the door, I was following my own lead and found myself scooted down and sucking on first one big ball and then the next as he straddled me. Then he grabbed his crooked shaft and cock-whipped my face while I darted my tongue out, trying to lick it.

Things moved fast. My legs were on his shoulders, his cock sliding across my asshole, popping up with each thrust to run across my balls before rising into view. I was jacking off furiously as we kissed, moaning and knocking our teeth. He growled deeply once, twice, and then I felt his tongue push far back into my mouth as his warm semen plopped up onto my chest, one, two, three, four globs, before trickling across my skin. He lifted himself up straight-armed and looked down at my cock as I bucked and shot onto his smooth, brown chest. He muttered: "Yeah, yeah."

Then we both started laughing hysterically.

"So, who the fuck are you?" We said that at the same time too, and laughed again. "No, go ahead, you first," we both said, chiming in at the same time—again. We laughed some more. "Well, we're both fags, and we're neighbors. We know that much."

"How long have you lived here?" I asked him, with an expression that said, *I've never seen you before.*

"At least a year," he said disarmingly, as if I should have noticed him by now.

"Well, I'm Sid," I introduced myself.

Grinning, he replied, "Nice to meet you, Sid," and put out his hand. I grabbed his softening cock instead, getting another laugh out of him, as he answered: "I'm Victor."

"So, Victor, I hate to rush out of here, but I gotta go." He was nodding, half-disappointed, but as if he expected as much.

"I've got a class, Victor. I also have a boyfriend, just so you know, but I'd love to do this again." And I grinned.

"Well, anytime," he answered, sighing.

"See you at the window," I coyly cracked as I left.

"Yeah," and he lit up. "That'd be cool. See ya."

To tell or not to tell…. I debated that all day. Because Victor wasn't just some anonymous trick; he was our neighbor.

"Never shit where you eat," Kenny offered his words of wisdom after physiology class. I looked at him quizzically.

"That's a fucking stretch, Kenny. Where'd you come up with that?"

"No, I'm not kidding. I never fuck anybody within a five-block radius of my house."

"And you live in the Castro?"

"Yeah, don't you think it's possible?"

"Well, it's a pretty small neighborhood, Kenny. That sounds like a better policy for the Avenues or something. I mean, if I had that policy, I'd live as far away from all the fags as I could."

"Yeah, well, I'm not some slut." Kenny got on his high horse. "I can control myself."

"You're looking for a relationship, blah, blah, I know," I patronized him. "And a little distance too, it sounds like. Intimacy issues? How close can your boyfriend come?" I chided him. "A block, two, twenty feet?"

"Save it, Sid. You know I have rules and you know they work. And that's why you bring this stuff up with me."

"Oh, brother," I sighed. Kenny prided himself on his long-term relationships. He considered himself well-adjusted. He'd had years of therapy, plenty of abusive boyfriends, but oh, he made it work, boasting two-year—and even three-year—averages to my usual fling of two weeks, give or take. For Kenny, it wasn't about being happy of course, it was about being successful. Or something like that, as ironic as it may sound.

"You'll never make it work with José if you start slutting around, mark my words." She was out of the gate and there was no catching her now. I stifled a laugh. If he only knew. And he didn't. I didn't dare subject José's choice of a livelihood to Kenny's moral compass.

Eventually he shut up, but not before I got in the last word: "Kenny, you live exactly seven blocks from me," I said enthusiastically. "Let's fuck."

"That's not funny, Sid."

No, but things were getting funny in my life. When I arrived home, the gate to my building was tied open with a string and all the signs of someone moving in were evident: strewn boxes, the wide-open door up the stairs, voices discussing logistics in that particular tone people use when searching for wall sockets or commenting on cupboard space.

They arrived in tandem, loping down the stairs: my new neighbors. The woman was a rambunctious, blue-haired, pierced-up baby dyke with a loud voice and a twinkle in her eye. Her roommate was fucking devastating. He looked Dutch-Indonesian with all the advantages of both sides of the globe. I hoped they were a couple: a ridiculous notion. In fact, it was beyond unlikely and even comic to consider. But he was way too cute for me. I wouldn't have to worry about him.

His hello smile was awfully seductive, though. I stammered out an introduction—she said that she was Tammy, he was Karl—and shook their hands. "Well, hope you like the place," I said in parting, almost throwing in—"if you need anything, just..."—but I didn't allow myself.

I feel as if I'd been hit by a train, not once, but twice. So when José comes home and casually asks what I've done all day, I draw a blank.

"I survived," I finally reply.

"You all right?"

"Yeah, yeah, I'm fine. How are things with you?"

"Well, my last client canceled; I finished my Fuck Finn paper and now...."

"You're horny, right?"

He laughs out loud, slightly embarrassed. Was I like this when I was twenty? I suppose so, just more repressed. I had affairs with bathroom sinks and socks, so it's hard to remember just how often I had to take care of that need. In other words, there are no faces to remember, and without faces...well, you've only got so much room in your head, you can't waste precious space on erotically charged bathroom mirrors and stiffening, threadbare argyle socks.

I fall into him, smiling. "How many times today, José?" I ask him sarcastically.

"Five," he proudly states like a little boy. Since I'm heading into number three, I really shouldn't be mocking his youthful exuberance.

I get my hands under his shirt and feel his chest and belly as we kiss. We have this common ritual we follow that I never seem to tire of: I love pulling off his shirt and my own and rubbing our chests together as we stand there pecking each other with our lips. We grind our cocks together through our pants and breathe harder and faster. It's so wonderful to discover his body over and over again. The image in my mind—though sometimes more idealized—can never achieve the visceral, pungent, warm, heavy, hard, soft earthiness of physical sex. That's why porn is doomed to fail us all. We all need fucking sex! So I lick his neck and face. We smile and passionately kiss—sloppy-wet so that our chins shine—as our hands go to each other's belts. Then to the problematic shoes. We fall into each other, rolling. Shirts and pants going, we drag out the underwear part. There's something amazing when we're naked together, and we always stop to marvel at whatever that feeling is as we play a little tender swordfight.

Then we attack each other. I like José's wantonness, his lack of modesty. Sometimes his pager throbs from across the room, because he has the kind that vibrates. When our roiling nebula of pleasure ends, he'll reach for it as we disappear back into ourselves, but right now we don't care about anything but smothering each other like gravy. We end up rabidly 69ing, until I hear him groaning and I pull my mouth off his cock with a slurp, his lower back arching up as I jack him, watching his blue-gray balls bounce and shake, until the white shot slaps across my Adam's apple, and he's got two fingers so far up my butt that I shoot across his belly before any of his cum even runs off my neck.

We sleep quietly that night, two well-spent boys. But I dream of Karl. And that's not the only time I dream of him, either. It's not some wild sex orgy, though. I keep following him up the steps into an apartment I've never seen and it always turns out to be different, huge places. One time it's a movie house and we sit eating popcorn, watching the two of us making out on the screen. Another time, it's like a corporate office, and everyone's walking around naked except us and it's bugging me that we can't seem to get nude, as if our clothes are glued to our bodies.

I ran into him the next afternoon.

He asked me for a cup of sugar. No, not really. He needed an extension cord. I debated whether to say "be right back," or "come with me." He saw me hesitate and shyly grinned. I sighed and laughed with embarrassment. Oh, shit, is he coming on to me? What, am I gonna resist this guy?

"Uh, do you wanna come back to my place and help me look for it?" I smiled sheepishly. It was lame, but it wasn't meant to be otherwise. I wanted to find out if he was feeling what I thought he was, and I was too anxious to have to wait until our next meeting. I don't know why. The dreams, I guess. It didn't matter what stupid invitation I came up with. I'd likely get my answer; I knew that much.

"Come on," he answered directly and seriously, without any hesitation. He knew what he wanted and didn't need an invitation to get it. Fine by me. I couldn't believe this was happening. Just yesterday, I'd concluded he was way out of my league, and now I was about to make him. Well, let's not get ahead of ourselves.

We walked around to the back of the building, where I lived. I unlocked the door, put down my backpack, realizing, as I did, that I'd be missing that class—if I was lucky. I pretended to look for the cord, but I knew I didn't have one. I was leaning down, looking in a kitchen cupboard, faking it, when I felt his hands—both of them, one on each cheek. Then I felt his hardening dick through his pants as he pressed it against my butt. I pushed my butt back at him and we did that for a while. Then I heard him unbuckle his belt and before you could say, "Let me see your cock," he had his out and was rubbing it bare against my pants. That was too much and I dropped to my knees and turned, taking his thin, bent cock into my mouth in a greedy gulp.

I heard him say flatly, "I wanna fuck you."

And I pulled off his cock, long enough to reply, "Then I won't have to beg," before going back to work on it. A moment later, he pulled out and pistol-whipped my face a few times, all the while smiling broadly.

I got up and we both pulled off our shirts quickly, stripping everything else off in a hurry and tumbling naked together onto the bed. He just as quickly wrestled his way on top, reaching under my knees firmly with both arms, while I clumsily fumbled for a condom on the headboard behind my head, never taking my eyes off his beautiful lithe, brown body. I found one and handed it to him. This boy liked to be in control and he could have it. I lay back and relaxed, and he drove that sweet crooked branch into me with gusto, banging me while I held onto his biceps for dear life. "Damn, damn, damn, damn, damn!" he gasped and his face screwed up so that I knew it was time. And we went white together.

It was turning into a strange week. And it was only Tuesday.

"Your boyfriend's really cute," Karl threw in as we said good-bye. "We should do a threesome sometime." And off he went, not waiting for a reply.

Things were getting ahead of themselves, to say the least. I was still debating how and whether to tell José about Victor and now I'd added Karl to the mix, and on top of that, Karl was interested in doing us both! Calling Kenny for advice was out of the question, but considering what had been happening lately, perhaps fucking him wasn't.

To calm myself, I made some tea. I always got great comfort out of a whistling teakettle, and I always filled it up because I loved to watch the water sputtering out the top—like a dick cumming. I watched it spurt and sputter briefly before turning off the range, grabbing a cup and teabag. And then…it was *déjà vu* time: Victor, shirtless, through the side window. I looked. He touched his nipple; he smiled; he laughed and bent over as if he was really cracking up. Then he disappeared.

"Whatever," was all my tired mind could come up with, as I moseyed over to my big reading chair to drink my tea in peace and sort things out.

But it wasn't to be. The doorbell rang. I hated that because since I lived in the back and the gate was way up front, there was no way I could ever know who was there. But it was a weekday and the Jehovah's Witnesses only came out on Saturdays around here. No Mormons ever showed their white shirts and name-tag-clad, bicycling ignorance in these parts. But fund-raisers and political causes were constantly blanketing the neighborhood with solicitors, who bored me so much that I gave them my money and refused the raffle tickets promising exotic vacations that would spare me a few weeks of their harassment. But I was too tired to fight it today, so I buzzed whoever it was in, and left the door open a crack as I sat back down. A moment later came a knock, and Victor's head poked around the door.

"Victor!" I said with surprise. I didn't think he had the nerve. I'd told him I had a boyfriend.

"Hey, I hope I'm not bothering you," he offered politely.

"Uh, no, no...you want some tea?" I got up to make him a cup, offering him my chair, which he flopped into.

When I returned with the tea, he grinned and thanked me, taking it carefully so as not to burn himself.

We both said, "So..." simultaneously and nervously, and laughed.

"I guess we just aren't meant to talk to each other," I joked.

"You wanna do something else?"

"I wanna try, but I'm really tired, Victor." I didn't want him to think I didn't want to do him again, but I'd just shot a major load and I didn't see another in the foreseeable future. Then again, it wouldn't be the first time I didn't see something coming.

"That's cool. I'm happy to sit here and drink tea with you," he offered. I smiled, relieved. And we talked and talked. About his job—working with retarded kids at a day center; about HIV and the drugs and acupuncture and homeopathy and shamanic healing. He told me about Vacaville and the redneck white boys who hated him doubly for being a beaner *and* a pussy. And he told me about his first time, about Kendrick, a big black boy from West Sacramento he met at the Interstate 80 rest stop, who fucked him so good, so good-naturedly, smiling and praising his beauty and taking him home for the weekend to fuck some more. I thought, What a lucky first time that was. I myself had been plowed silly by my seventeen-year-old cousin, who called me a *faggot sissy* as he filled me with his big uncut weenie jizz. He told me he was just too virile to only fuck women, and besides I was a fag so he couldn't be gay since he hadn't fucked a real boy. "Well, you got a real nice cock," was all I'd thought to respond. And he cuffed me hard on the shoulder for it.

Victor was for falling in love with—I could see that. With our stories out like that, and the day's classes forgotten, I was in his arms kissing him, breaking all the rules I'd agreed to with José. No matter, I thought, I can explain everything. Besides, the best fuck is a love fuck, and I'm feeling love for this boy and his boy's story and I can't see how there's anything wrong in it. There isn't.

And so we kissed and stripped, and quietly, softly touched each other and licked one another's arms and legs and armpits and knees and Adam's apples and ears and feet. Me all lanky and pale and pink; him all jet-black-haired and cinnamon. We fondled for hours, our cocks bouncing about and colliding from time to time. But it wasn't sex about orgasm, it was sex about all of it, so our dicks could wait.

That didn't mean José would, though. My heart leaped when I heard the lock click from a key in the door. I dumbly raised my face from Victor's wet, wrinkly, plump scrotum, half-panicked and half-resigned. I was busted.

Or was I? I saw José's face, saw the crease deepen between his eyes. Then the grin, and as the door swung open—Victor up on his elbows now and looking disoriented—Karl following right on José's heels. "Well, he's here, all right!" José exclaimed, and he let out a laugh as Karl grinned widely.

"Uh, José, uh...could you, um, give us a minute?" I pleaded.

"Why?" he laughed. "Karl wants to have a threesome— why not make it four?" I relaxed, seeing José was in a playful mood, the one thing on his mind I feared was separating us about to bring us together in a whole new way.

"Close the door and get in here!" I commanded, smiling. Victor and I were both up, tugging at their clothes as I awkwardly introduced everyone, without stopping my lusty pursuits. "Victor, this is Karl, and José, my boyfriend. Karl, Victor." Karl and Victor greeted with a tongue-tying kiss as José asked me nervously, "Is this cool with you?"

"This is fucking better than cool. It's fucking ice-hard cock," I answered, grabbing his crotch. In no time we were all naked and playing a sort of random, accidental twister—flexed flanks and free-swinging balls, male energy roiling like cock stew with a cum stock. Victor had Karl's asscheeks spread with his hands while his cock bobbed at the back of the stud's knobby brown knees. Standing there, Karl was a god with his big prick in his hand and José and I on our knees, kissing wildly with Karl's cock floating on our tongues between us as he pistol-whipped our cheeks a ruddy red. It was beyond hot. I'd never been in a group scene where everyone was so hot for everyone else. There was cock hunger all around, enthusiastic assholes and wanton tongues.

But most of all, it was the friendliness of it that touched me and aroused me beyond anything else. We ended up all four of us on our knees in a huge four-way jack off, with everyone's hands on different cocks and our tongues wrapped together and slithering around like anxious snakes in a soaked cage. And then we all got free. Like fireworks, one, two, three, four. The "ah—, ah—, ah—, ah—" as we each exploded, all uniquely. José, head back—"Fuck!"; Karl, watching his direct hit on my belly—"Damn!"; Victor, grinning—"Yeaaaah," and shooting an X on my flank. I yanked my waist in a half-circle as I shot, muttering, "Cock-fucking-love," splashing it across them all.

Victor started, and then we all laughed. Fell back onto the bed and laughed; tangled; played; rolled. And eventually reminisced, telling each other stories of our old neighborhoods when we were just boys.

"There were no cute boys in my neighborhood," Victor lamented.

"There were *too* many cute boys in mine—with guns!" Karl remembered. "It sucked."

I offered a description of my exhibitionist cousin's enormous schlong.

José's was best: every Christmas, a piñata and all the boys swinging ragingly at it, until one little guy busted it wide open and they all went "ah!"

"Right on," Karl said, nodding his head. "Right on."

And we smiled at each other. Then giggled. And then laughed again. Neighbors.

Straight Boy
James Williams

Back in the bad old days, when rubber was what your Corvette laid in its five-second skid from zero to sixty, I used to get my kicks at the Eiffel Baths in San Francisco. Things were so loose for a while in that town that the place even ran suggestive ads in the big city dailies, and now and again some Bette Midler impersonator made a local splash singing a run of "boy" songs: "Water Boy," "Drummer Boy," "Danny Boy," and the like. Since I kept up with the music scene, the bathhouse concerts and the bathhouse itself became part of my Sunday Supplement consciousness.

The Eye-full, as it was known on the street, was also famous for its raunchy help—attendants were rumored to be routinely found with their ankles behind their ears amidst the sheets they were supposed to be changing—and because it was reputed to be the only fuck-bathhouse in history that admitted women. As a consequence, a number of straight guys came there looking to hit on the females they figured would be swinging from the chandeliers. Also as a consequence, since very few straight women actually ever did show up, house policy provided perfect cover for a straight boy to learn that the smell and feel and taste of cock could make him pant and sweat and squirm just like any other faggot.

That straight boy—that was me. Among my regular buddies I was just another regular buddy: I worked my nine-to-five, kicked back on weekends, and went through women like a hot tongue through soft ice cream.

But what none of my good buddies ever guessed was that some nights, around the time the bars shut down, I got a peculiar tightness in my nuts that tingled like electricity. It felt different from wanting to fuck my number one girl and different from wanting to fuck some other girl, and it was more than just wanting to get my rocks off or I could have hobbled home to Mrs. Hand and her five daughters. It was urgent and overwhelming, like the sudden need to pee little kids have that makes them dance and clutch their crotches and come away with wet hands.

On those nights I'd pretend I didn't feel a thing and start to head for home. But then, curious, hopeful, frightened, and so excited my hands were sweaty and my mouth was dry, I'd find myself motoring over south of Market Street as if someone else were doing the driving. Soon I passed through those disco doorways where fifty or a hundred or two hundred men groped down dark warrens with thin trick towels tucked around their waists or draped like leis around their necks.

By that time my head was hot with anxiety and a fear bred of sheer dumb ignorance. Never quite knowing or admitting to myself what I was doing there, I descended the wide redwood stairs and let my eyeballs do the walking, scoping out the game room, the TV lounge, the snack bar, the indoor hot tub. I went to my little cell and stripped, and then, with my own towel split up my thigh like a fan-dancer's banner, my heart gushing in my throat like some fountain of youth, and my head prickling as if I had brain fever, I checked the outdoor tub, the sauna, and the fantasy dungeon. After a shower and some heat to calm myself down, I stopped pretending I'd come looking for quim. That's when I really relaxed.

Roving up the halls and down the halls, pacing myself around the stations of the maze, I loved the ritual of cruising: that flicker of the eye, that twist of a finger, that tiny movement of the towel that said *Yes*. Lingering kisses with strangers in the shower. Butts for touching and butts for looking only. Coy jokes and promises to get together later, if something better didn't work out.

The first time I passed Kelly, I got so confused I fled back to my private cot in the dark red light. If he had been a woman, I told myself, I'd have known just what to do. But the way he shot his skinny hip out to block off half the aisle; the crew cut, the arrogant face with its wide lips and its arching nose like a condor's beak; even I could tell that he was not just going to be a man, he was going to be a man in charge, and I didn't understand exactly why my legs began to tremble and my heart to pound all over again.

When I passed Kelly the second time he had a boy with a Nautilus body pinned against the wall outside a group room. Kelly gripped the boy's wrists above his head with one enormous hand, while with his other hand he gently traced the outline of the boy's face: jaw to chin, lips, forehead all at once, then the eyes. I had time to watch him lift his knee precisely underneath the boy's big balls and slowly press them up between his thighs. The balls spread apart and straddled Kelly's knee. He jigged his leg once and both balls fell to the left. His dick made his towel billow like a tent. He caught the boy's whole sac between his knee and the boy's own thick thigh. The boy's eyes opened wider and wider while Kelly looked straight back and deep, as if he were looking through the irises and into the meat and memory of the boy's brain.

Kelly's hamstring stood out taut against the flesh of his back leg, the toes of his floor-bound foot dug down for traction, his bent knee pushed up harder against the root of the boy's hot cock, and his hand still soft as a lover's breath lay calm upon the twisted face as the boy gasped and groaned and shot so hard his own mouth and Kelly's both got wet.

Gradually, Kelly let the boy's hands go. His head fell onto Kelly's shoulder, and Kelly put his arms around the boy and held him close. Finally he kissed the boy and wiped his face. He turned around and looked directly at me. Then he walked away.

I saw Kelly the third time when I'd already decided this was not my night. I was headed for my closet, planning to dress and go home, when I almost stepped on Kelly's foot. He held out one arm as if to stop me and his fingers grazed my belly. I was hard before my foot hit the floor.

"I saw you watching me," he said.

"What?"

"Third time's the charm."

Kelly was as tall as I am, a good six feet or more, but very wiry, while I used to be thought of as a hunk. He pushed me backwards gently. My towel fell off my hips and a curtain parted behind me. I kept walking backwards, propelled by his three fingers resting just below my navel. My cock was dripping sticky webs that trailed from his forearm where I kept bumping him.

"What happens in here?" I asked, abrupt anxiety making me stupid as a virgin.

Kelly didn't buy my innocence for a moment. He pinched his lips together and then said, "I fuck you in here, just like you've been wanting me to do all night."

I stammered in protest, but my cock was so hard it hurt all the way up to my heart, my balls were screaming tight, and for the first time in my life I felt neither straight nor bi: right then I was a gay man, and Kelly's dick was all I wanted in the world.

The backs of my legs bumped against a mattress and Kelly's fingers pushed me down onto it. I lay back and opened up my legs and arms. He opened his towel and tossed it on the bed, showing a long, thick, hard dick glistening at its single eye. He settled down on top of me with his cock against my cock, and my joint and asshole twitched as if I were going to come.

"Uh-uh," he said, squeezing the tip of my cock with a thumb and finger. "Don't you dare."

I swallowed and took a couple of deep breaths, holding back until I calmed down some.

"Better," he said, nodding. "I want you hard when I fuck you."

He kissed me, and slid up my body till his cock was at my mouth. For the first time I understood cock-hunger, and reached for his with my tongue and lips and my whole head, but he wouldn't let me touch it. He didn't even tease. He just waited, holding himself above me on his hands and knees, watching me intently. Then, when I was just about to beg, he pushed his cock deep into my mouth and let me suck him while his balls in their soft skin hung beneath my chin down toward my neck.

He slid out of my face when I started to gag.

"Breathe," he said.

I sucked in air, then his cock was down my throat again. Out. "Breathe." In. Out. "Breathe." In.

"Turn over."

"No, please. Fuck me from the front. I want to see you."

One corner of his mouth ticked up a fraction of an inch. Kelly was smiling. He knelt between my legs and I hiked myself up, holding the backs of my thighs in my hands. He spit in his palm and lubed my ass, then brought his cock up against me.

"You a straight boy?" he asked. "You're so tight you must be really scared. Hmm?"

I nodded.

"Too bad," he said, and pushed his way in.

I felt as if my whole body were being torn apart. The pain was like a burn that seared me from my asshole to my gut. My face must have shown a series of emotions because Kelly finally laughed out loud. He braced himself on the backs of my thighs, and then as he pumped me full of himself I felt my asshole open up, my stomach open up, my heart and face and head open up. I felt complete and full. I threw back my arms and head and howled.

In the bad old days relationships didn't blossom out of chance encounters at the baths. Fuckbuddies might meet up there from time to time, and regulars had familiar faces. Friends might even come and go together, but the whole idea was to have happy, dirty, mindless, guiltless, anonymous sex in surroundings that were more sensuous and comfortable than glory holes, back alleys, or the parks.

After Kelly wiped his cock I figured we were over. The gay stud had had his straight boy, and the straight boy had had his limits and his asshole stretched for good. So I was surprised when he wiped me down as well, and said, "Why don't you come over to brunch tomorrow?"

I was even more surprised when I heard myself reply, "Where? What time?"

Kelly told me his name then, and gave me an address in the heart of the Castro, a couple of blocks from what was in those days called the Elephant Walk. "Show up at one or two," he said. "No one will be up till then anyway." Then he picked up his towel and walked back out through the curtains.

It must have taken me a quarter of an hour to get myself mobile. I had been most righteously swived, and my body was relaxed to the point of indolence. More important, my mind had been thoroughly fucked as well. In my lethargy I pictured Kelly's cock in front of me, and felt my own cock swell. I wondered what had made me think that I was straight.

Another man peered into the room and eyed my hard-on as I lay there on the wet, chilly sheet. I gave him a faint smile and shook my head; he shrugged and went away. I got up on shaky legs and headed for the shower. There, as I cleaned up, I looked at the other men who joked with one another, or displayed themselves self-consciously, or hurried through their ritual ablutions. I could see no difference between us, nor could they.

Someone began to soap my back.

"That feels good," I told him over my slippery shoulder, "but I'm through for the night."

He paused for a moment, then put the soap in my hand. "You do me, then. I'm just beginning."

And so I soaped his back and leaned around to soap his chest, playing with his nipples till they stood out hard. I soaped down his arms to where his hands rested below his hips. I soaped his hips and his ass, working my hands between his thighs to soap one of his legs all the way down to his foot, then I soaped the other leg all the way up to his crotch. I soaped his cock and balls until his cock was stiff, and after I helped him get rinsed off I knelt on the public shower floor and sucked him till his breathing started to heat up.

I stood up and gave him a quick kiss. "That's to get your evening off to a good start," I said, and I went back to my little cubicle and dressed and walked out into the dawn.

Just for curiosity's sake I drove to the address Kelly had given me and parked across the street with the engine idling and the city birds chirruping all around. I had no idea why I was there, miles across town from my own apartment at five o'clock on a Saturday morning. I was vaguely troubled by what

I had done at the Eiffel, and confused by what I was feeling now that I was outside in the tired, slanting, early light.

The door to Kelly's place opened and a beautiful young man dressed all in white stepped onto the sidewalk, closing the door discreetly behind him. He stretched like a cat, looked up and down the block, looked at me sitting in my car, and turned to walk away toward Castro Street.

Somehow he was the sign that I'd been waiting for. I was still worried about what I had done, but I was no longer confused about what I was feeling. I wanted to see Kelly again. I wanted to feel him lying in my arms, and I wanted to feel his dick up my ass. Now I knew that I would come to brunch, and see what other lessons Kelly had to teach me. My cock got hard as if I hadn't come all night, and I felt my nuts start tingling all over again. I put my car in gear and turned myself toward home. I was grinning as if I'd drunk too much caffeine. I didn't know if I could wait till one. I opened a couple of buttons on my jeans and wrapped two fingers around my pulsing cock, glad my current number one girl had taught me to wear no underpants.

For Hire: A Date with John

Sean Meriwether

Shiloh: The Other Size Queen

The door opens and he comes into your apartment. He is very tall and looks like a famous actor, though you can't remember which one. You tell a joke because you're nervous and you've never done this before, at least not with him. He laughs, a deep rumbling that puts you at ease. He follows you to your bedroom and takes off his boots. His long feet are sculptures of flesh. You feel tiny next to him, but that's what makes him erotic; this is why you requested him. He will posses you, molest you as if you were a teenager. The proportions are correct. He smiles patiently when you attempt to tell him your requirements. He removes his clothes and folds them over the chair next to the bed. You take off your clothes and join him. You lie next to him and run your hands over his long legs. They are soft and warm. He says, What do you want to do? You tell him you want to be bent over his knee and spanked as punishment. He complies. You get hard as his meaty hand slaps your ass. He asks if you want him to fuck you. You do, but you wish he had just done it. He slips on a condom as you bury your face in the pillows, like when you were fifteen and your older friends took turns with you. He is gentle, but you want him to be harder. You moan when he speeds up and you bite the sheet beneath your head. You relive the erotic torments of those older boys from your youth and splash the sheets with semen. The tall man behind you grunts and fills his condom. He rolls off your sweaty back. You watch him get dressed and slip the money into the pocket of his jeans. You show him to the door, absorbed in the odor of memory.

Aaron: The Suburban Hustler

The door opens and he comes into your home. This is the third time this month the two of you have gotten together. You joke that you must be supporting him by yourself. He laughs like a boy, with a blush and a dimple. You can't help but like him; he is someone who listens to you, who understands that you love your no-good boyfriend even if he doesn't want to have sex anymore. This boy says men need sex, it is true to their nature. He follows you to the bedroom and you take each other's clothes off. It is like the beginning of a relationship when the first thing you want to do is have sex, then talk. His hands are guided along your body as if he were reading your mind. He kisses you at all the right moments. You don't have to think or worry about anything, just your pleasure and his. It is all so easy and you think, This is how it is supposed to be. He is hung and this time you attempt to take it all. It hurts, but you feel more complete with him inside. Afterward, you lie in his arms, your boy-man, your lover, but the void remains. You want to explain this emptiness inside but you can't find the right words. You cuddle with him instead. He makes you feel like a horny teenager, that your desires are legitimate and should be addressed. You want your boyfriend to understand this, but you know he won't listen. The boy in your arms understands; he cares about you and wants you to forget your problems. He is very sweet and intelligent and hung, and you can picture the two of you playing house together. You make an appointment for next week and miss him before he even leaves. You stand at the door and wave like a war bride as he drives away.

Bino: The Classic Eros

The door opens and he comes into your apartment. You assume he is of legal age but he looks like a boy, a mature boy. His hair is golden and you run your fingers through his long curls. He looks like a Renaissance painting done in warm oils. You pull him to you and hug him. He has a slight accent and it bewitches you because you can't place it. On impulse you pick him up in your arms and carry him to your bed. He laughs uncertainly. You put him down, strip off his clothes, and admire the androgynous beauty of his tight body. His chest is hard and developed, his ass is compact, each globe the right size for your hands. He falls onto your bed and rolls around, giving an occasional glimpse of his growing erection. His uncut cock makes you think of naked Greeks in the Olympics. He seems very comfortable in your sheets and you want to bind him up and keep him forever. You undress and lie in bed next to him. You roll him onto his stomach and massage his back. You wet your finger and slide it up into him. He moans in appreciation. When you screw him, he groans beneath you. He tells you to fuck him harder, but you are afraid of crushing him into the mattress. Too soon you are beyond worrying as you explode into him. You fall to the side, too exhausted to move. He stands next to the bed and looks like an angel with his tanned skin glowing, his halo of golden hair. He looks stronger than when he came in, more solid. When he leaves, with a handsome tip, you can't help but think you've seen him before and then you remember Donatello's statue of David. You agree that he too should be in a museum—your own.

Iseha: The Video Fantasy

The door opens and he comes into your living room. He is built and as graceful as a dancer. His lean body is carefully sculpted into curves and lines, a perfect specimen of man. You lick your lips and lead him to the couch. His voice is familiar and you remember him from that video you bought. You ask if that's him and he smiles. You compliment him on his capabilities, the way he used his body in particular shots. You have been watching a lot of black and Hispanic boy movies and now you have your fantasy in the room next to you. You ask him to top you, to order you around. He laughs a moment and you think you've said something wrong. Then he strips out of his tight pants and shirt. He wears nothing but a jock. He shoves his crotch into your face and orders you to suck it. He is loud while being pleasured and you worry about the neighbors, but his comments make you so excited you're afraid he'll stop. He tells you to take off your clothes. He puts on a condom and works a long finger up into you before replacing it with something much larger. You think of gang-boy gang bangs as he plows you. He stops. He says he doesn't normally do this, but would you like to have him? He says, How can I be a good top without being a good bottom? You are confused. He lies on his back and stretches his long, lean legs up into the air. You are distracted by what he offers you. You do him for a few minutes, but you don't feel quite right. You ask him to switch places. He finishes the job quickly. When he leaves, you pop in *Love for Sale* and watch the scene he is in three times. You think, he was just here, and you can't wait to tell your friends. They will be so jealous.

Jonathan: The Tourist Trap

The door opens and he comes into your hotel room. He is a little taller than you expected, but he is attractive in a bookish way. Even though you are horny, you can't get it up. You are nervous that the man at the front desk knows why this boy is here and you double-check the hall to make sure it's empty. He sits down on the bed, his long legs slanting away from his body. You ask him to do a striptease for you. He dances methodically, removing each article of clothing in timed display. He rolls his hips; your eyes scan the mobile mound in his shorts. Finally nude, he approaches and asks if you would like anything special. You tell him you want to suck him, but you mean to say you want to fuck him. He seems to know this, but it will not happen yet, not with forty-five minutes still on the clock. You bury yourself in a trimmed nest of pubic hair as he stands next to you, arms at his sides. Your ministrations wake his cock and it swells between your lips. When both of you are hard, you don't know how to ask him for what you want. You thought he would do whatever you wanted; that was why you invited him over. You think, he must be familiar with the unspoken needs of middle-aged men like yourself. The idea of other men's hands touching his young body excites you and you redouble your efforts to get him up to your level. You'd swear you are doing him better than anyone else who has come before because he tells you so. Maybe he will give you a discount. You finally penetrate him, with fifteen minutes left to the date. You blow your wad in five and it makes you feel sated and guilty. Keeping this secret from your wife makes you desperately hard again and you ask for another hour. He tells you he has another appointment, but can meet again tomorrow. You clear your schedule.

Johnny: The New New Yorker

The door opens and he comes into your foyer. You have to look up to meet his gentle eyes. He is well over six feet tall and thin like a boy should be. His height excites you in a way you did not expect. His voice is gentle and soft and you have to ask him to repeat himself because you keep missing what he says. He has a beautiful smile with even, white teeth. You take his surprisingly small hand and lead him to your bed and lay him across it. He doesn't fit; his long feet dangle over the edge. You remove his shoes and socks. Stripping away his clothes reveals that he wears no underwear, and you sniff the crotch of his jeans without a second thought. You blush. He reminds you of a Walton, innocent in a way that you have not seen in other men you have worked with. As he becomes erect, your attention is drawn to the massive column of flesh that stretches out across his tight stomach. Only a third of it fits in your mouth, but you give it your all. You want it to fill you up, but you are afraid it may break you in half. Take it slow, you tell him, as you lower yourself onto his shaft. Once it breaks the surface you absorb it inch by inch. It never stops. You can feel it in your throat. Your legs spread open as he burrows into you. The pain is exquisite and you see stars swim before your eyes. Then it draws back slowly. You thank god. As the pace increases you are equally full and empty and you can't even beat off because all your attention is on your overstimulated posterior. The boy beneath you flushes red as he pulls out and covers his body in white spurts. He pants as he jerks you off onto his stomach. You shoot across the room. You stare at his massive erection as it subsides and you cannot believe it was ever inside of you. You feel madly proud that you were able to take it. You kiss him tenderly as if you shared something significant and spend the rest of the hour marveling at the enormity the thin boy holds between his legs.

Niko: The New Economy

The door opens and he comes into your apartment. When he speaks he sounds slightly breathless, as if he ran to meet you. It fits in with your fantasy. He is wearing a business suit as requested. You have conquered Wall Street all day at work; now it's time to conquer it at home. You spend every waking moment in the testosterone swirl of the Financial District but are unable to act out your aggression with those co-suited men. Now you can bend down on your knees and bury your face in his wool-blend crotch. You tear open his zipper and pull his dick out and absorb it into your mouth. You picture the two of you doing this on the trading floor and all the other traders stopping to watch. You slip out of your pants and finger yourself. He tells you how good it feels, how hot you are. His sextalk makes you hotter. You bend over the back of your couch and tell him to fuck you with the suit on. He slips on a condom and fucks you with the frantic pace of the Dow. In your mind you are standing on the platform above the trading floor, ringing the closing bell for all it is worth. The men beneath you are naked, sucking and fucking in true bacchanalian fashion. You stop and change positions. On your back you can replace the sweaty face above you with those of the men who work side by side with you. Each one of them screwing you in succession. Oh, yeah, the man says, banging you with the dicks of a hundred men. You blow your wad and it splatters the coat of the man between your legs. You laugh gratefully and toss him a towel to wipe off. That was hot, he says. He tucks his jacket into his bag of toys and leaves you reeling from the ride. God bless the stock market.

Snow
Jameson Currier

Outside the window, the snow obliterated the view of the highway, but since Tyler was less than a mile from the airport there wasn't much to see except ramps and lanes and traffic. The snow had started that morning when he had landed in the city for his meeting: small, enchanting, romantic flurries. By the time he had hailed a cab in the afternoon, four inches were already on the ground and flights were being delayed. He'd gotten one of the last rooms at the hotel, just as everyone—the receptionist, the cab driver, the airline reservations clerk—had started to mouth the word *blizzard* to him, or, rather, started to mouth *two* words, *big blizzard,* as if the description *blizzard* was not an adequate enough weather forecast to instill a sense of urgency to get some place and stay there for a while. Now, in Tyler's fourth floor hotel room, the snow was so fierce it drained the color from everything, the dark green bedspread, the hunting print above the bed, the cherry wood of the desk and chair. Even the air in the room seemed as if it had been washed away, or, rather, had been sucked into a clear bottle and frozen, waiting to be thawed.

Tyler, stripped of all his clothes, pressed himself close to the windowpane, the stale coolness seeping through the glass like an undetected gas leak. His shoulder felt sore so he rotated his arm, then rubbed his dry hand across his drier skin. Winter, he thought. Aches. Arthritis.

Tyler stood at the window with his back to a young man named Brad or Chad or Tad or something like that. Tyler didn't care anymore what the guy called himself. He had cared the night before, when Tad had arrived, but for the last twelve hours he hadn't cared at all. Any sense of intimacy Tyler had felt for Brad or Chad had evaporated long ago. Tyler was bothered by his growing callousness—wasn't this what he had always wanted? Time alone with a young man? They had stayed up late drinking a bottle of wine, snuggling against each other, and watching television till Tad, or Brad, fell asleep. Tyler had absorbed the alcohol quickly, the wine fading into a headache and insomnia. Tyler had held whatever-his-name-was in his arms until he felt himself sweating, then pushed the young man away so that he slept on his side.

But by morning Tyler had been seized by a weighty restlessness. At the window, Tyler rubbed his hand along the fine hair of his own chest and realized he might be attracted to Brad if he had been someone else. *Another* Brad. Maybe a *Chad,* he said to himself with a laugh. I've had Brad, he thought. Now give me Chad. Glancing down, Tyler watched with bored interest as his testicles shrank the closer he moved to the window. If anyone were in the parking lot looking up at his window, Tyler knew they would be unable to see him up there, striped by the blinds, with freezing nuts and a painful shoulder.

Todd—it was Todd, Tyler decided—lay on the floor wearing only his red flannel boxer shorts, an item of clothing he had sexily revealed with a flourish the evening before. Todd was young and lean, a handsome brunet with a nose too big for his face. Now he was busy touching his knee to his nose doing stomach exercises and shooting annoying breaths out of his mouth as if he were about to hurl a spitball. He'd been doing this senseless thing for almost an hour.

"Let's go down to the fitness room," Todd said. "Mr. Tyler?"

His voice, in this air, stayed even after the meaning was gone from his words. The room remained full of his voice—dropped into corners like packed snow on the roadside in spring. "I'm sure the fitness room is more like a fitness *closet,*" Tyler said. The edge in his voice was easily detectable. "And it's not 'Mr. Tyler.' It's just 'Tyler.' " He didn't bother to look back at Todd. He had studied and studied the body till it no longer excited him. Todd had finely carved abs like the cuts of a diamond, and it was a magnificent display watching them flex and twist and breathe. But what was the purpose, Tyler wondered? He had seen them and now they were ancient history. He wanted something else. But even more, he wanted to be *somewhere* else.

"At least the electricity works," Todd said. "Last year we lost power."

"How long did it last?" Tyler asked.

"Three days," Todd said. He held his knee to his nose. "Can you see anything?" he asked.

Tyler didn't respond. He couldn't see anything beyond the white wall of snow. When he arrived at the airport yesterday he had been delighted to hear that the flight had been canceled, not from the snow—snow was always expected in this region—but because of the wind gusts. The airport closing gave him a legitimate reason to stay overnight, a bona fide expense report item to submit, a chance to have some fun before returning back to the closeted grind of corporate meetings and lunches and lectures and conference calls. Tyler had seized the opportunity to order room service and a hustler. Todd had arrived quicker than the food. By the time they had finished, though, there were already four more inches of snow, frozen granules mixed in with the lighter stuff—and the television said bus service had been suspended until the roads could be cleared and sanded. And Tyler hadn't been so eager to see Todd disappear.

"Everybody's always in a hurry to get somewhere," Todd said.

Tyler didn't answer.

"Do you like my stomach?" Todd asked.

It was only the thousandth time he had asked Tyler that question. He heard the insecurity creeping into Todd's voice and if he could placate Todd without using too much energy, he decided he would. So he nodded. He could have easily turned Todd out into the snow last night. Wham, bang, here's your money, so long, don't hurry back even though you are gorgeous and it was incredible sex. But it was late and dangerous outside and early on Todd had tapped into that warm fuzzy paternal spot Tyler always felt for the young and pretty boys who looked put upon. Now, Todd's company had worn thin. Tyler turned and took a long look at Todd's stomach and managed to work up a grin, trying not to be one of those sour old businessmen, who, well, float into town and hire hustlers. "What's not to like? You should do movies."

Todd stretched both legs out in front of him and pointed his toes, then sat up straight at the waist, a perfect right angle, sure of himself. "I guess," he said, then smiled at himself. "Best abs in Hollywood."

Tyler started to turn back to the window, wondering why he was the one now doing the pampering. Wasn't Todd supposed to be indulging *him?*

"I was in a commercial once," Todd said. "I did an internship at a television station my sophomore year. One of the camera guys was filming a diet commercial. I got to be the 'after' guy. Did you know that it's not the same person? I always believed that they could lose the weight."

Tyler did not react. Too much chatter, he thought, and he tried to tune Todd out.

"Wanna play around?" Todd said, dropping his voice into that low whispery octave that had so excited Tyler last night. "No charge since you're letting me stay."

"Too beat," Tyler said, and looked back at the window, weary and bored.

"I'm going to go downstairs," Todd said, making it sound like a threat, though Tyler couldn't imagine what kind of threat it could be.

"Better put something on first," Tyler replied.

Todd didn't move from the rigid shape he'd got himself into. With the lamp on inside the room, Tyler could see Todd's reflection in the window and he studied that—the reflection—squinting to see if he could detect the definition of Todd's abs in the snow.

Then he looked beyond the reflection, back into the snow. It swirled and curled and danced in front of his eyes like a busy computer screen saver. The warmth of the room was pulled up through the window and sucked off into the snow. He looked down at the parking lot and thought he could detect someone racing into the snow, his hands pumping together as if clapping, probably to keep the circulation going.

At the window he looked deeper into the snow, believing for a minute he saw thousands of men clapping their mittened hands together. They were sure they were going to freeze if they remained motionless, never to arrive someplace warm. Then they disappeared.

"Tyler?" Todd asked.

Tyler ran his hand down to his groin, running his hand across his cock. He was aware of Todd looking at him.

"Is it still hard?"

"Sure," Tyler answered, playing the suggestive innuendo game but unable to mask the cynical tone in his voice.

"How much longer?" Todd asked.

That raspy voice again. How much longer snowing? Tyler thought, or in this room? Or in this room *with him?*

"What's your hurry? Am I such unpleasant company?"

"Of course not," Todd said. He pouted in a boyishly self-absorbed manner.

"It's just that the snow's making me cranky," Tyler said.

"Let's play some more," Todd said. He stretched out his body and cupped his balls.

"Aren't you worn out?" Tyler asked.

"No," Todd said, his grin taking on a fake, impish quality. "Are you?"

"Yes," Tyler said. "You're too much for me."

"So let's just neck some more."

Tyler didn't really want to be unkind to him, though he knew he was being hustled now. "Neither of us has shaved."

"Want me to shave you?"

Years ago he would have been delighted with the offer. *Hours* ago he would have been delighted. "I'm not twenty anymore, though I wish I were, sometimes." Tyler turned and looked at Todd. "Or I wish I was twenty and knew what I know now."

Todd smirked. Tyler turned and faced the window again. As he did he caught sight of his own reflection this time, his white hair crossing against the currents of snow. Everything would be all right again soon. All he had to do was wait.

"Tyler?"

"Huh?"

"Wanna shower together?"

"Hmmm."

"Or soak in a bath?"

"My joints are damp enough," Tyler said.

Todd went into the bathroom. Tyler heard him take a leak and flush the toilet. Then he turned the water on. Then he heard the shower begin and the sound of the water change as Todd stepped into the flow. Tyler stayed at the window and ran a hand over his chest and pinched the slackness at his hips. He was still there when Todd came back into the room, dripping onto the carpet.

"Tyler?"

"Huh?'

"I'm going crazy in this room."

"Put something on. You're going to get a cold."

Todd put his boxers back on and a T-shirt and ran the towel through his hair. Tyler watched the process in the reflections of the window, momentarily imagining Todd was a soccer player, toweling off after a game. The image burst apart in another flurry of snow and Tyler again felt old and vulnerable in his sagging flesh.

"Wanna get something to eat?" Todd asked.

"If you want."

"Room service?" Todd asked.

"Sure."

Behind him, Tyler heard Todd pad across the carpeted floor and sit at the desk, thumbing through the hotel journal till he reached the room service menu.

"What do you want?" Todd asked.

Tyler smirked at the loaded irony of the question. I want to be out of this room, in an airport, on my way home, away from you, on my way to someone else. For a moment he thought about running out like a lunatic—racing down the hall and into the lobby with nothing on. At least he might be arrested. At least it would take him to jail. *Somewhere else.*

"Nothing heavy," he answered.

"How about some ice cream?" Todd asked. "Or a milk-shake?"

"Coffee," Tyler said. "I'd like something warmer."

The ice cream and the coffee came ten minutes later. Todd's spoon clinked against the glass at an annoying speed. Tyler sat in a chair facing the window, a cup in his hands.

"That killed a half-hour," Tyler said when he had finished his coffee. Tyler finally pulled himself away from the window and sat on the edge of the bed and turned on the television. Todd curled up into a fetal position on the bed, a pillow crammed between his legs, as if waiting to be petted.

"Wanna watch a movie?" Todd asked. "They have a movie selection here."

"Let's check the news first," Tyler replied. He flipped the channel, wondering if God would give him a respite with the snow. Even a little one. He shook his head to clear it.

"Something the matter?" Todd asked.

Tyler shook his head to indicate *no*. The moving images on the screen made his vision blur. He lay down, exhausted from the anxiety of trying to decide how long he might have to stay. He thought that maybe he couldn't last—that he'd have to cancel his appointments for tomorrow as well. The snow had become his business now. Something tugged at his inner ear. A rumble that seemed to shake the foundation of the building. He lay still and quiet and then felt it again. "What?" he asked.

"I didn't say anything."

"Are you sure?"

"Yes."

Maybe it was Todd's voice again, stirring in the room from some dead sentence. It tugged again, and Tyler realized it was a sound outside the room, far off. "Hear that?"

"I don't hear anything."

"It was the parking lot. Someone's leaving." Tyler felt his pulse quicken and, as he lifted himself off the bed, he struggled to overcome a dizziness. He padded across the carpet and looked out of the window again.

"Maybe they're salting the highway."

"No, listen," Tyler said. In another minute he heard it again, barely above the blood beating in his ears. Todd joined him at the window. Tyler smelled the soap Todd had used. He was aware of Todd's heat and the hairs on his leg stood up, warning him.

"It's lighter," Tyler said, looking out through the snow, the tone of his voice brighter, breezier.

"Sure is," Todd added.

While they were watching the snow, a man walked through the parking lot beneath them. Tyler's eyes followed him, watching the man's mittened hands clap together. The snow swirled in thinner gusts now, flaking against the window before melting.

Tyler walked to the phone and dialed. "Are they back on schedule?" Tyler asked. As the receptionist explained that flights were now leaving, Tyler thought that his giddiness would give him a heart attack, his blood now a roar in his ears. He hung up the phone, smiling.

Tyler packed hurriedly and with a determination he had not possessed since he had arrived in the city. He kept looking outside as he packed, watching the flurries thin out. He could now see the sharp line on the horizon where the highway was.

Todd was dressed in his jeans and coat in a matter of seconds. Tyler waited for him to ask for more money, but as Tyler lifted his suitcase off the bed and moved toward the door there was nothing. Impulsively Tyler stopped and kissed Todd abruptly on the lips with a passion he hadn't shown the boy since he'd first arrived in the room. Todd slipped his arms under Tyler's jacket and returned the kiss. Suddenly they were all hot and bothered at the idea of losing each other. "I'm here often," Tyler said. "Could I see you again?"

Todd nodded and Tyler knew that if he wanted more he would have to pay the price of it. In the elevator he felt relaxed. Peace, he thought, and studied Todd with his clothes on, finding himself mentally undressing him and growing hard at the thought of the young man.

By the time Tyler reached the airport he was as exuberant as the sun, the light bouncing so brightly off the snowdrifts he paused only to search for his sunglasses.

A Bedtime Story
Jay Neal

"Come over here. Lie down so that I can groom your chest fur."

"Mmm. That's good. Now tell me a story."

"What kind of story?"

"A bedtime story, of course."

"Once upon a time, far, far away…. Ouch!"

"No! Not that kind of story. A proper bedtime story."

"…far, far away, there lived a handsome prince at the edge of an enchanted forest."

"Was he a bear?"

"He certainly was. A big, beautiful prince with a big, beautiful brown beard and a big, beautiful belly all covered with fur. You see, he lived in an ancient time when all the beautiful and important people were husky and hairy."

"What was his name?"

"His name was Orsino. Now, Prince Orsino was a good prince, much beloved of his subjects. He had the most beautiful smile, too, and whenever he smiled the sun would shine all day long and the people would be happy and dance merrily.

But lately the villagers had begun to worry. Prince Orsino had not smiled in many, many months; he just moped around his castle all the time looking sad. Because of this, it had been cloudy and rainy every day for many, many months and the people were getting tired of it since it meant that instead of spending their time dancing merrily they had to stay inside and do paperwork.

"They started gathering in the rain outside the castle to shake their heads at the sad spectacle and whisper about the situation. Soon there were so many people gathered that their whispering grew very loud and Prince Orsino came to the portcullis to see what was going on.

"When they saw him, the people cried out, 'Oh, most beloved Prince Orsino, why are you so sad all the time? Please smile so that the sun will shine and we can dance merrily instead of having to do this paperwork crap.'

"The Prince addressed his people. 'People, although I love each of you with all my heart, I cannot smile for I am very sad.' The people nodded their heads and made sympathetic noises. 'As you know,' the Prince continued, 'I am of an age when the people of our land take a mate to live with them and work at their side. Alas, I have found no mate with whom I might form a loving relationship, and because of this I am sad.'

"After the Prince went back inside out of the rain, the people discussed this turn of events. They convinced themselves that the problem with their Prince was basically a lack of sex, so they came up with a plan to correct that. Certain that there would be sunshine the next day, they slept peacefully, despite the sound of heavy rain on their cottage roofs.

"The next morning the village cooper arrived at the castle with his oldest son, John, and knocked at the portcullis. When the Prince appeared, Mr. Cooper presented his son.

" 'Beloved Prince, this is my oldest son John. As ye can

see, he is a healthy, robust boy with a broad, hairy chest and strong, muscled arms from working the iron bands for our barrels. Beneath his full, black beard he has most of his teeth, but his mouth is large enough that they don't scrape. Aye, as any in the village will tell ye, John here is his father's pride and the best cocksucker for many days' walk. Sire, accept his willingness to serve ye. Enjoy his welcoming mouth and skillful tongue so that the sun might shine again.'

"Prince Orsino was touched by Mr. Cooper's gesture on behalf of the village. He felt sure that John Cooper's talent would not lift the cloud casting its shadow over his heart, but the young man was attractive and a good blow job couldn't hurt anything, so he welcomed the young cooper into the castle.

"John Cooper was eager to please and in no time he had taken off his homespun clothes and stood naked before the Prince. Orsino ran his hands over Cooper's thick arm muscles and down his broad, hairy chest. He was about to admire Cooper's large balls and already stiff dick, but before he had a chance Cooper had removed the Prince's codpiece and buried his bearded face in the Prince's crotch.

"Cooper's talented tongue, wet lips, and warm, receptive mouth entertained the Prince's dick while his beard tickled and caressed the Prince's balls. Orsino succumbed to Cooper's ministrations, drawn along by the sight, sound, and sensation of the tongue bath his dick was receiving. Cooper held on tightly to Orsino's butt and increased the pace of his oral therapy. Soon the Prince felt a rising urgency within him and he exploded in a gushing climax.

"Some moments passed, and when he was able to breathe again and collect his thoughts, Orsino looked down at John Cooper's smiling face. As Mr. Cooper had promised, the young man was a very talented cocksucker. Indeed, this was the best blow job the Prince had ever had. But still his heart was heavy: his lasting happiness was not to be found here. He was grateful and thanked young Cooper for his sincere efforts, but regretfully sent him home.

"The entire village was disappointed to see John Cooper return among them. He related his tale, and the villagers all agreed that he had given his best blow job ever. But still the problem remained. Oh, what to do! Many of the villagers stayed up all night trying to think of something that might cause the Prince to smile again.

"The next morning the village miller arrived at the castle with his twin sons and knocked at the portcullis. When the Prince appeared, Mr. Miller presented them.

" 'Beloved Prince, these are my sons, good men both. As ye can see, they are finely furred with beautiful asses that they get from working with the milling stones. Please overlook their misfortune of being born twins with identical appearance. Unfortunately, both have fiery-red hair from the top of their heads to their very toes, but this does not prevent their having the finest assholes for fucking in the entire village. Sire, accept their willingness to serve you. Enjoy their asses so that the sun might shine again.'

"Prince Orsino was touched by Mr. Miller's gesture on behalf of the village. It still seemed unlikely that the Miller Twins could lift his heart's burden, but they did have the most beautifully shaped asses, and a good fuck couldn't hurt anything, so he welcomed them into the castle.

"The Miller Twins were very eager to please and in no time had removed each other's clothing and stood naked before the Prince. Orsino admired their firm, round asses, and agreed with Mr. Miller that the fiery-red hair covering every part of their bodies was no detriment. Orsino was about to express his appreciation of their rigidly identical dicks when he found his codpiece removed and the Miller Twins bending over before him, presenting their hairy, hidden treasures for him to plunder.

"Momentarily burdened by feelings of *noblesse oblige,* the Prince was nevertheless aroused by the inviting sight before him, and his dick grew hard. He slowly pushed it into the asshole of the first twin and enjoyed the warm, firm stimulation as he moved in and out. After a few minutes he turned his attention to the asshole of the second twin and was a bit surprised that the Miller Twins felt as identical on the inside as they looked on the outside.

"While he worked the asshole of one twin with his dick, he worked the asshole of the other with his finger so that they might enjoy the experience equally. As he increased the pace of his fucking, both twins seemed to breathe faster and moan louder, all the while pushing their asses to meet his increasingly rapid thrusts. It wasn't much longer before Orsino felt the irrepressible rising urgency within him, and his explosive climax was met with loud grunts and simultaneous ejaculations from the Miller Twins.

"After he was able to breathe again and collect his thoughts, Orsino looked with melancholy at the red-furred asses of the twins and pulled both men up to face him. As Mr. Miller had promised they were remarkable fucks, undoubtedly the best in the village, despite their being twins. And yet—and yet the Prince's heart felt empty and cold; he knew that his true and lasting happiness lay elsewhere. He was grateful to the Miller Twins and thanked them for their sincere efforts and then sent them home."

"I must be the Prince in this story. I'm husky, I'm hairy, and I get to fuck all the men in the village, right?"

"We'll see about that. Anyway, since the village had high hopes for the Miller Twins, they were doubly disappointed to see the twins return. The twins told their tale, and all agreed that they had given the Prince the best fuck ever, but still it rained. The people were starting to feel desperate for they were running out of ideas to try. They thought, and thought, and thought, and still it rained.

"So it was that three days had passed when the Miller Twins again arrived at the castle with their father, the miller, and knocked at the portcullis. When the Prince appeared, the Miller Twins presented their father to him.

" 'Beloved Prince, this is our father, a loyal servant of yours despite his deviant sexual tastes. Although he is now aged beyond forty years and his beard and hair have mostly turned white, he remains the kinkiest man in the village. Sire, please accept our father's willingness to serve you. Tie him up, whip him, piss on him, pierce his skin, and perform unspeakable acts with his naked body so that the sun might shine again.'

"Prince Orsino was touched by the Miller Twins' gesture on behalf of their village, but he was beginning to feel that enough might be enough. He felt certain that Mr. Miller's total submission wouldn't do much to lift his own spirits. However, since the silvery hair that seemed to cover Mr. Miller's entire body aroused his curiosity, he welcomed him into the castle. He called for servants to take Mr. Miller to the dungeon, where they were to chain him naked to its damp, cold stone walls.

"The Prince was about to change into his leathers and fetch his whip when he was suddenly overcome by weariness at the futility of his search for a companion. Although he felt guilty at neglecting his responsibilities, he called again for his servants and instructed them to go to Mr. Miller in the dungeon, to whip him, piss on him, pierce his skin, and perform unspeakable acts upon his hairy, naked body. Meanwhile, the Prince would go for a walk in the enchanted forest and consider his plight.

"The Prince walked and walked, lost in thought, when he encountered a one-armed woodcutter in a clearing, cutting wood. The woodcutter was big and husky with bulging muscles from a lifetime of cutting wood, and like the wild man he was he had long, wild hair and a long, wild beard, and his whole body was covered with hair, and he had an enormous dick.”

"How could you tell how big his dick was?"

“Because it was an enchanted forest and he was completely naked. So anyway, the woodcutter worked, swinging his axe while his enormous, rock-hard dick and equally enormous balls swung in rhythm. This attracted the attention of the Prince, who stopped to talk. ‘Greetings, naked, hairy woodcutter. How goes your work?’

“The woodcutter paused and leaned on his axe. ‘The wood cutting goes well enough for such a pointless activity, but it never stops raining and my mood is as gloomy as the weather because I can’t give myself a proper hand job with just one arm.’

“The Prince asked how he lost his arm and the woodcutter answered, ‘I once met a creature who asked a riddle I could not answer: what walks on three legs in its youth, four legs in its maturity, and two legs in its old age?’

“After a bit of thought, Orsino agreed that it was, indeed, a difficult riddle, then he turned to walk away. The woodcutter yelled, ‘Halt!’ and raised high his axe. ‘Now that you have heard the riddle, you must answer it or forfeit your head to a deft swing of my axe, unless you’d rather give me a blow job.’

“The Prince considered his options, first looking at the woodcutter’s enormous axe, then at the woodcutter’s enormous dick. He dropped to his knees, grabbed the hard dick in front of his face, and held it up against the man’s hairy belly so that he might admire the beautiful pair of balls in front of his nose. These he licked and sucked with delight until the woodcutter began to squirm. Unable to subdue his appetite any longer, Orsino began licking and sucking the woodcutter’s dick with frenzied abandon.

"Just then, while Orsino was fully absorbed in his cocksucking, and the woodcutter was distracted by his approaching orgasm, a knight rode into the clearing on his giant stallion. Sir Butch, for that was his name, wore strange armor that resembled leather chaps, a harness, and a studded leather codpiece. When he recognized the figure of the Prince, he became indignant at the degradation that Orsino had been forced to suffer. In his fury, Sir Butch drew his sword and with one stroke sliced off the woodcutter's head, just as the woodcutter began to shoot cum all over Orsino's face.

"Surprised at this development, the Prince looked up at the Knight. 'Good Knight, I thank you for your assistance in my time of need, but whence your haste? Now I shall never know the answer to the woodcutter's riddle.'

"The Knight dismounted and bowed before the Prince. 'Good Prince, I am Sir Butch, of the neighboring realm.

'I chanced upon your dreadful predicament and, seeing the humiliation you were forced to suffer, I was filled with rage and determined to punish the woodcutter on the spot.'

"Orsino stood back and looked the Knight over with growing interest. Certainly, the leather armor was appealing, and the way that Sir's chest hair poked out around his harness was provocative. A thought came to mind. 'Sir Butch, I appreciate your candor and your bravery, and I find your aspect most pleasant to look upon, particularly the chest hair that pokes out around your harness. I, myself, am looking for a mate to share my life. Are you already spoken for?'

"Looking upon the Prince's big, beautiful brown beard and big, beautiful belly undoubtedly all covered with fur, the Knight wanted to accept, but he couldn't. 'Alas, my Prince, it cannot be. I am strictly a Top and, since you are the Prince and therefore could not be a Bottom, we would face a lifetime of frustration.'

"The look of confusion on Orsino's face masked his deep

disappointment. 'I do not see any obstacle. Pray, Sir, what is this Top and Bottom you speak of?'

"Sir Butch was startled by this deficit in the Prince's knowledge. 'When I make love with the man of my choice, I put my dick into his mouth for him to suck and into his asshole for me to fuck. I am the Top, and he is the Bottom.'

"The Prince reflected on the Knight's words, and saw a glimmer of hope. He explained to Sir that although he was forced to suck the woodcutter's cock, he had rather enjoyed it, only he didn't smile because he feared for his life. He went on to suggest that the thought of being fucked by Sir Butch was starting to arouse him.

"Sir Butch gracefully accepted Prince Orsino's invitation. They searched until they found a dry spot under a tree, where Sir lovingly removed the Prince's clothing and admired his big, beautiful belly, which was indeed covered with fur. They fell into each other's arms and kissed with an intensity that neither had ever known.

"After some time Orsino removed Sir's studded codpiece and felt a great happiness at the sight, which he expressed by drawing Sir's dick completely into his mouth and swallowing it, to the evident delight of the Knight. The Prince continued his own enjoyment until he noticed that Sir was perilously close to climax.

"Orsino looked into Butch's eyes and the Knight understood that the time had come to fuck the Prince. Being a very tender lover, Sir Butch laid him back onto the ground, wet his fingers, and inserted first one, then two fingers into Orsino's willing but tight asshole. For more than an hour he loosened the Prince, whose moans grew louder and whose cock grew harder with each thrust.

"When he judged that the time was right, Sir Butch withdrew his fingers and inserted his dick into the Prince's receptive asshole. To the tune of Orsino's ever-louder cries of delight and encouragement, Sir's initially measured thrusts gave way to their mounting passion. Time stopped until Sir noticed that he was again approaching his climax. Sir moved his face down to kiss the Prince and, just as he came in great waves inside the Prince, Orsino himself experienced an orgasm unlike any he had ever experienced.

"As they lay heaving for breath with bodies entwined, Prince Orsino felt an unknown lightness in his soul and contentment in his heart, and he smiled with overwhelming joy to realize his destiny as a Bottom with Sir Butch his Top. Noticing that the rain suddenly stopped, he looked up and saw the sun break through the clouds.

"Prince Orsino took Sir Butch's hand and they walked back to the castle, slowed in their progress by frequent stops for kissing. As the sun was beginning to set, they emerged from the enchanted forest and were greeted by the people of the village, dancing and cheering and throwing paperwork into the air.

"Acknowledging his faithful people, Prince Orsino waved and smiled his beautiful smile, then introduced Sir Butch, his new mate. As the cheering resumed, the Prince led his Knight to the castle where they lived together and came happily ever after."

"Wait a minute! What was the answer to the riddle? And are you saying that the Prince was really a Bottom all the time?"

"Roll over, my Prince, and let's start finding out."

Knowing Johnny
Bob Vickery

The single bulb that lights up the hallway is busted, and I have to negotiate my way to Rico's apartment by trailing my fingers against the wall, counting the doors. In the dark, the smells of the place seem a lot stronger: boiled cabbage, mildew, old piss. Heavy-metal music blasts out from one of the doors I pass, and I get a sickly sweet whiff of crack. Fucking junkies. I can hear loud voices arguing in the apartment across the hallway, then the sound of furniture breaking. Rico's apartment is the next one down. I grope my way to it and knock on the door.

I stand there for a minute, waiting. "Who's there?" a voice finally asks from inside.

"Open up, Rico," I say. "It's me, Al."

I hear the sounds of bolts being drawn back. The door opens an inch, still chained, and Rico's eye peers at me through the crack. He closes the door, undoes the chain, and opens it wide this time. "Get in," he growls. I slip in, and Rico bolts the door behind me. The room is small: an unmade bed, a beat-up dresser, a table by the window. The kid Rico told me about on the phone is sitting at the table, looking scared and trying not to show it. It's quieter in here than in the hall, even with the sounds of traffic coming in from the window. I can faintly hear above our heads the clicking of writergod's keyboard.

I keep my eyes trained on the kid. He's sitting in a shaft of light pouring in from the street, and I take in the shaggy blond hair, the strong jaw, the firm, lean body. "Where'd you find him?" I ask Rico, without turning my head.

"Out on the street, hustling," Rico says. "I convinced him he could do better with a little management." Rico walks into my line of sight. "He tells me he's eighteen." Of course, writergod has Rico say that to keep the censors happy.

"What's your name," I ask the kid.

"Johnny," he says. There's a slight quaver in his voice.

"Did Rico rough you up?" Rico stirs, but I silence him with a gesture. "Did he force you up here?" And again, writergod is having me ask this for the sake of the fucking censors. If there's coercion, the story won't sell.

Johnny shakes his head. "No," he says. "I wanted to go with him. Rico told me about you. I thought maybe you could help me." His voice is steadier now, firmer. But the wideness of his dark eyes still gives away his fear.

I look at him for a long moment, gauging him. "How good are you at taking orders?"

Johnny licks his lips and swallows. "Real good," he says.

This is the first sex scene of the story. Writergod usually limits it to oral only, saving butt fucking for the end-of-story finale. "Stand up," I say. Johnny climbs to his feet. "I always sample my merchandise first, Johnny," I say. "I want you to come over here and suck my dick. Suck it until I shoot my load."

Johnny's eyes flicker toward Rico, and then back at me again. He shifts his weight to his other foot, but doesn't move. He seems to be weighing his options. "Okay," he finally says.

He walks over to me and drops to his knees. His hands are all businesslike as they unbuckle my belt, pull my zipper down, and tug my jeans and boxers down below my knees. I keep my face stony, but my dick gives away my excitement. It springs up and swings heavily in front of Johnny's face. Johnny drinks it in with his eyes. "You got a beautiful dick," he says.

"Just skip the commentary," I reply.

Johnny leans forward and nuzzles his face into my balls. I feel his tongue licking them, rolling them around in his mouth, sucking on them. He slides his tongue up the shaft of my dick, as if it's some kind of Popsicle, and then circles the cockhead with it. I stand with my hands on my hips, looking down at the top of his head. Rico stands behind the boy, watching. His dick juts out of his open fly, and he's stroking it slowly.

Johnny's lips nibble their way down my meaty shaft (all our shafts are "meaty"; writergod won't let us in the story without a crank at least eight inches long, and thick—always thick—topped with "flared heads," or "fleshy knobs," or "heads the size and color of small plums"). When Johnny's mouth finally makes it to the base of my stiff cock, he starts bobbing his head, sucking me off with a measured, easy tempo. The boy knows how to suck cock—I give him that. He wraps one hand around my balls and tugs them gently as his other hand squeezes my left nipple. I close my eyes and let the sensations he's drawing from my body ripple over me.

Rico comes up next to me and yanks his jeans down. He strokes his dick with one hand while his other hand slides under my shirt and tugs at the flesh of my torso. I reach over and cup his balls, feeling their heft, how they spill out onto my palm so nicely. I lean over and we kiss, Rico slipping his tongue deep into my mouth. Rico lets go of his dick and Johnny wraps his hand around it, skinning the foreskin back, revealing the fleshy little fist of Rico's cockhead (another favorite phrase of writergod). He takes my dick out of his mouth, sucks on Rico's for a while, and then comes back to me. I spit in my hand and wrap it around Rico's thick, hard cock, sliding it up and down the shaft. Rico lets out a long sigh, a hairbreadth shy of a groan. He starts pumping his hips, fucking my fist in quick, staccato thrusts. Johnny pries apart my asscheeks and worms a finger up my bunghole, knuckle by knuckle, never breaking his cocksucking stride. I lose my cool, giving off a long, trailing groan. Johnny pushes against my prostate, and my groan increases in volume. I whip my dick out of his mouth just as the first stream of spunk squirts out, arcing into the air, slamming against Johnny's face. My body spasms as my load continues to pump out, splattering against his cheeks, his closed eyes, his mouth. Rico groans, and I feel his dick pulse in my hand. Johnny turns his face to receive this second spermy shower, and soon Rico's jizz is mingling with mine in sluggish drops that hang from Johnny's chin. Rico bends down and licks Johnny's face clean, dragging his tongue along the contours of the boy's face. The clicking sound of writergod's keyboard rises in volume and then suddenly stops.

We all look up. "Do you think he's done?" Rico finally asks.

I shrug. "With the scene, maybe," I say. "He still has to finish the story."

Johnny climbs to his feet and looks around the room. "Christ, what a dump. I hope we don't have to stay here long."

Rico laughs. "Hell, this is fuckin' swank compared to where I was before." He starts pulling on his clothes. "Writergod had me lying on some teahouse floor with a bunch of guys shooting their loads on me. Then he just left me there, stuck in that stinking piss-hole." He looks around. "I just wish there was a TV here."

I offer a handkerchief to Johnny. "Here," I say. "Rico

missed a few drops." Johnny takes it and wipes the last of my load off his face. I pull out a deck of cards from my jacket pocket and sit down at the table. "Poker, anyone?"

There are only two chairs, so Rico has to sit on the edge of the bed. We start with five-card stud. "It's no fun unless you play for money," Johnny grouses.

I shrug. "I don't have any money. Do you?"

Rico grins. "We could always play for sex." We all laugh. As if we don't already get nothing *but* that from each other. Johnny finds matchsticks in the drawer of the dresser, and we divvy them out.

I deal the first hand. "So what have you been up to, Johnny?" I ask, glancing at him. "Any interesting locales?" Johnny and I have worked together more times than I can remember. I've fucked him in locker rooms, in the backseats of cars, in alleys, on secluded beaches, once even on the torch of the Statue of Liberty. Johnny is always "the kid" in writer-god's stories, sometimes going by the name of Billy, sometimes Eddy or Andy—always a name that ends in *y*. I look at him across the table, feeling the old frustration. For all the hot sex we've had together, I hardly know the guy. No conversation, no snuggling together under the sheets—just fade to black and then the cycle starts all over again.

"Oh, I was in a great place last story," Johnny said, laughing. "I was a street hustler in Cozumel who hooks up with an American tourist. You know him; it was Cutter."

"Shit," Rico mutters. I glance at him but he keeps his eyes focused on his cards. Cutter's a stock character that writergod uses for his more upscale stories, usually about some married man straying to the other side, or a well-heeled gay yuppie partying in the Keys or P-town. I've only worked with him a couple of times, the last time being when I was rough trade that he picked up in a leather bar on a slumming expedition. Rico and I both think he's got his head up his ass.

"Did you have a good time?" I ask.

"Oh, yeah, it was great fun," Johnny says. I look for sarcasm, but his smile seems sincere. "After writergod wrapped up the fuck scene on the beach, we just hung out there, sunbathing, snorkeling, shell-collecting—the whole tourist thing." Johnny nods at the room around us. "Until I wound up here."

"I'm sorry you're disappointed," I say. I'm aware of how pissy my tone sounds.

Johnny grins. "Who said anything about being disappointed?" He looks across the table at me and winks. My throat tightens.

"Hey, are you guys going to flap your jaws or play cards?" Rico asks. He throws three cards down on the table, and I deal him three more. But the wheels are turning in my head. Writergod usually writes several stories at the same time. I glance at Rico sorting through his cards. Rico's all right, but I wouldn't mind it if writergod suddenly pulled him for another story and left Johnny and me alone.

Johnny drops two cards on the table, and I deal him two more. I keep what I have. Rico starts the betting off with five matchsticks. Johnny throws in his five matchsticks and raises five more. Outside the window, a police siren wails and then trails off into silence. "Which one of your past scenes would you most like to go back to," I ask Johnny, "if you had a choice?"

Johnny grins and shakes his head. "You'll just laugh."

"No, I won't, I promise." I throw in the ten matchsticks and raise another ten.

"It was a college story," Johnny says. "Writergod had me gang-fucked in the UC Berkeley library by the college football team. After he wrapped up the story, he didn't use me for weeks. I got to hang out there all that time, doing nothing but reading." He glances at me. "Have you ever read *Leaves of*

Grass, Al? Or any of Robert Frost's poems?"

I don't laugh, like I promised, but I do smile. "When would I read poetry?" I say. "Between blow jobs in a back alley?"

Johnny gives a rueful smile and shrugs. "That's my point. I hardly ever get to spend time in places where I can improve my fuckin' mind."

Rico sees my ten matchsticks and calls. We show our hands. Johnny's got a pair of eights, Rico two pairs, aces and fives. I win with a straight, jack high. I gather up my winnings and deal us all new hands. Rico leans back on the bed and stretches. "I wouldn't mind going back to the story where I was a ranger in Yosemite," he says, picking up his cards and sorting them. "I ended up fucking these backpackers on top of Half Dome." He shakes his head and gives a wistful smile. "It was my one time out in nature. I loved it—all that bitching scenery!" He nods toward Johnny, "I know what you mean, kid. That was an exception. Writergod usually sticks us in some pretty crummy places."

I open my mouth to comment, when I feel my feet begin to tingle. The tingling moves up my legs, my torso. I know only too well what that means. "So long, guys," I barely have time to say. "I'm off to another story."

There's a knock on the door, and then Old Bert sticks his head in. "I got the lad here for you, Captain," he says. "Just like you told me to." He knows better than to give me a wink. The last time he tried such impudence, I had him flogged, but his mouth still curves up into a randy leer. I can hear the rest of the crew off in the distance fighting over the *Magdalena*'s spoils.

"Bring him in," I say gruffly. I'm lying on the bed that belonged to the *Magdalena*'s former captain. Since we've tossed him overboard with a slit throat, I don't think he'll be needing it anymore.

Old Bert opens the door wider, pushes the *Magdalena*'s cabin boy in, and closes the door behind him. The lad stumbles forward and then straightens up to face me. His dark eyes glare at me for an instant, but I can see the fear in them as well. He quickly lowers them. *So Johnny's in this story too,* I think. *Poor Rico, stuck in that room by himself.* The boy stands in the middle of the cabin, his hands at his side, head lowered, waiting.

"*¿Hablas ingles?*" I ask him.

He nods, his eyes still trained on the floor.

"Look at me, lad," I say. He raises his eyes again, eyes that are as black and liquid as the sea on a moonless night. My gaze sweeps down his wiry, muscular body and then back to his face again. "What's your name?" I ask.

"Juan Francisco Tomas Santiago, sir," he says. His voice is barely audible.

I laugh. "That's quite a mouthful for such a young lad," I say. "I shall call you 'Johnny.'"

There's a moment of silence. I can faintly hear the clicking of writergod's keyboard. I've never been in a period story before; writergod usually confines me to slums and back alleys.

The heat of the tropical sun pours in, as thick as Jamaican molasses, and I feel my head grow light from it. I lie back indolently in the captain's bed, my eyes traveling up Johnny's body: There's a coltish quality to his muscular young frame that makes my dick swell and lengthen. Johnny watches silently, his eyes now never leaving my face.

"Get naked," I say.

The blood rushes to Johnny's face, and he shifts his weight to his other foot. *Writergod should watch that little bit of business he always has Johnny do,* I think—*it's getting repetitious.* Slowly, hesitantly, he unbuttons his shirt and lets it fall to the floor. His torso is as smooth and dark as polished driftwood, the muscles beautifully chiseled. Johnny slips off his shoes, pulls his breeches down, and steps out of them, kicking them aside. He stands naked at the foot of the bed, his hands at his sides, his cock lying heavily against his thigh. His face is as pure as any angel's, but he's got a devil's dick: red, fleshy, roped with blue veins. In the stifling heat his balls lie as low and heavy as tree-ripened fruit. My throat tightens with excitement. "Turn around," I say.

Johnny slowly turns around. His ass is a very pretty thing, high and firm, the cheeks pale cream against the darkness of his tanned back. My dick stirs in my breeches, swelling to full hardness. Johnny completes his rotation and faces me again, his mouth set in a grim line.

"Well, come over here, lad," I say, giving an exaggerated sigh as I slip off my breeches. "And give me a reason why I shouldn't just slit your throat and toss you overboard."

Johnny stands where he is, head bowed but with his hands curled into fists. The silence in the room is as oppressive as the heat. "Aye, Johnny," I say softly. "Is it coaxing you want instead of threats?" I sit up in the bed. "Please do an old sea dog a favor, lad," I say in exaggerated politeness, "and come join me in my bed."

Johnny looks me in the eye, still saying nothing. His mouth curls up into the faintest smile. He crosses the small room and climbs into bed with me. I wrap my arms around him and kiss him, and he kisses back, lightly at first, then with greater force, slipping his tongue into my mouth. I pull him tightly against me, feeling his hard, young cock thrust up against my belly. I wrap my hand around both our dicks and start stroking them slowly within the circle of my fingers. Johnny reaches down and cups my balls in his hand, squeezing them gently, rolling them around in his palm. I nuzzle my face against the curve of his neck. "Tell me, lad," I whisper in his ear. "Have you ever been buggered before?"

"Yes, sir," Johnny whispers back. "Many times." I don't doubt it. A young lad as handsome as Johnny would be fair game on any ship.

There's a jar of pomade on the table next to the bed. I reach over and scoop out a heavy dollop from it. "Well, maybe I can still teach you a few new tricks," I say, as I work my hand into his ass crack and begin greasing up his bunghole. I slip a finger in, and the muscles of Johnny's ass clamp around it tightly, like a baby sucking on his mother's tit. I push deeper in, and Johnny's body stirs under me. "Do you want more of the same, lad?" I growl.

Johnny nods his head. "If you please, sir," he says.

"Well, since you asked so politely..." I laugh. I grease up my dick with the pomade and hoist Johnny's legs over my shoulders. Johnny takes my dick in his hand and guides it to the pucker of his asshole. I push with my hips, and my dick slides inside him, Johnny thrusting his hips up to meet me. As I start pumping his ass, Johnny meets me stroke for stroke, moving his body in rhythm with mine, squeezing his ass muscles tight with every thrust of my cock.

I laugh from surprise and pleasure. "Aye, Johnny," I say. "Ye're a lusty young buck, I can see that clearly enough. And ye've learned your buggery lessons well." *This is the first story in which I've fucked without condoms,* I think. *Sweet Jesus, it feels good!*

I continue plowing Johnny's ass with long, slow strokes. A groan escapes his lips and I grin fiercely. "That's right, Johnny," I say. "Sing for me. I want to play you like a mandolin." *Where is writergod coming up with this fucking dialogue?* I wonder. I thrust savagely until my dick is full inside him and then churn my hips. Johnny groans, louder. I bend down and kiss him, and he returns my kiss passionately, thrusting his tongue into my mouth. As I skewer Johnny, he reaches up and runs his hands across my body, twisting my nipples hard.

He wraps his legs around me and rolls over on top. We're drenched with sweat, and our bodies thrust together and separate with wet, slapping noises. I wrap Johnny in my arms and we roll again, falling off the bed onto the deck below.

I pin Johnny's arms down and plunge my cock deep inside him. Johnny cries out. "Do you want me to stop, lad?" I ask.

"No, sir," Johnny groans.

I thrust again, and again Johnny cries out. I can hear the pirates brawling outside. They're probably drunk by now on the *Magdalena*'s cargo of spirits. "Louder, Johnny," I snarl.

"Don't stop, sir!" he cries out.

"That's better," I grunt. I wrap my arms around him and press him tight. My sweaty torso slides and squirms against him, as I pump my dick in and out of his ass. A groan escapes from Johnny's lips. I thrust again, and he groans again, louder. Johnny reaches down and squeezes my balls with his hand. They're pulled up tight, ready to shoot. He presses down hard between them, and my body shudders violently as the first of the orgasm is released. I throw back my head and bellow as my dick gushes my jism deep into his ass. Load after load of it pulses out, and I thrash against Johnny like a man whose throat has just been cut. After what seems like a small eternity, the last of the spasms end, and I collapse on top of him.

I push myself up again. "Climb up on my chest, Johnny," I say. "And splatter my face with your load."

Johnny seems only too happy to oblige. He swings his leg over and straddles me. I look up at him, at the tight muscular body, at Johnny's handsome face, at the hand sliding up and down the thick shaft of his dick. "Aye, there you go, lad," I mutter. "Make your dick squirt for me." I reach up and twist Johnny's left nipple.

I feel Johnny's body shudder, and he raises his face to the ceiling and cries out. A load of jism gushes out from his dick and splatters against my face. Another load follows, and then another. By the time Johnny's done, my face is festooned with the ropy strands of his wad. He bends down and licks it off tenderly, and I kiss him, pulling my body tight against his.

Writergod's keyboard suddenly falls silent. We wait expectantly for it to start up again, finish the story, but nothing happens. I look up at Johnny and we both burst out laughing. "Do you believe that fucking dialogue?" I say. I twist my face into comic fierceness. "Aye, Johnny," I growl. "You're a lusty young buck. How 'bout letting me bugger your ass?"

Johnny laughs again. He climbs off me and helps me to my feet. We hunt for our clothes strewn all around, and pull them back on. I feel as if I'm dressing for a costume ball. I look at Johnny appraisingly as he tucks his shirt into his breeches. "You look really good as a Spanish cabin boy," I say. "It suits you."

Johnny raises his eyebrows. "You're not putting the make on me, are you, Al?"

I have to laugh at that. "Right. Like I don't get enough sex from you as it is." Still, I'm feeling light and playful now that I'm alone with Johnny, between stories. I look around. The cabin is cramped, and a glance out the porthole shows nothing but sea and sky. The deck beneath our feet rolls gently with the movement of the waves. The tropical heat makes the small room feel like a sauna. I jump onto the bed and pat the empty side next to me. "Hop back in," I say to Johnny. "Let's just relax for a while. Maybe talk."

Johnny joins me on the bed, stretching his legs out and placing his hands behind his head. My heart is beating hard, and when I notice this I almost laugh. I've forgotten how many times I've fucked Johnny in how many countless stories, and yet I'm actually feeling nervous. I cautiously wrap my arm around Johnny's shoulders, and he snuggles against me. "This is nice," he says.

"I've been wanting to do this for a long time," I say. "All we do is fuck. We never talk."

Johnny looks up at my face, his eyes amused. "What do you want to talk about, Al?"

I think for a long time. The only subjects I can come up with are back alleys, docks, and quarter booths in the back of porno bookstores. I'm struck by a sudden thought. "Tell me about the poems you read in the UC Berkeley library," I say.

"Do you want to hear one?" Johnny asks, grinning.

"Sure." I nestle back against the pillows, my eyes trained on him.

Johnny pulls himself up to a sitting position and turns to face me. He clears his throat.

> *In Xanadu did Kubla Khan*
> *A stately pleasure-dome decree:*
> *Where Alph, the sacred river, ran*
> *Through caverns measureless to man*
> *Down to a sunless sea.*

Johnny squeezes his eyes in concentration for a second and then looks at me apologetically. "I don't remember much more. Just the last few lines."

> *His flashing eyes, his floating hair!*
> *Weave a circle round him thrice,*
> *And close your eyes in holy dread,*
> *For he on honey-dew hath fed,*
> *And drunk the milk of Paradise.*

He looks down at me. "Sorry, that's all I know."

I shake my head. "I don't get it." Johnny shrugs but doesn't say anything. "I mean, who would name a river 'Alph'? And who ever heard of hair floating?"

"I don't know," Johnny says, laughing. "I didn't write the damn poem." He lies back down in the bed, burrowing into my arms. "Just let the words create the pictures."

We lie in the bed together, Johnny's body pressed against mine. My arm lightly strokes his shoulder. I can smell the fresh sweat of his body, feel the heat of his skin flow into me. The rocking of the ship lulls me into half-sleep. "This is so nice," I say, half to Johnny, half to myself. Johnny says nothing, just lays his hand on my thigh and squeezes it. I close my eyes.

My feet start to tingle. "Fuck!" I cry out. I look up at the ceiling. "Writergod, you bastard! Can't you give me just a few fucking minutes of peace!" The tingling spreads up my body, and the ship's cabin fades out, along with Johnny.

I got Nash taking point twenty meters in front of the squad, and Myers and Benchly behind us working the radio, keeping the com line open with the base. The others are in different positions, waiting for orders. That leaves me alone, with the kid, Jamison. Earlier reconnaissance reports indicated enemy movement about five clicks north of the base, working its way toward us, but fuck, that was hours ago, and Charley could be anywhere. I look around. We're on elevated ground, with good cover, and I don't anticipate any action for hours; our best bet is to lie low and hope Charley walks straight into our ambush.

I crawl over toward Jamison. "How you doin', son?" I whisper.

Jamison looks back at me, his eyes wide, his mouth set in a tight line. He's a green recruit, just assigned to the squad last week, and this is his first combat action. He still wears the look of someone trying to wake up from a bad dream. "All right, I guess, Sarge," he says.

I put my gun down and squat beside him. "It's a hell of a business, ain't it?"

Jamison grins, and I feel my throat tighten. I've been sporting a hard-on for the kid since he was first assigned to the squad. "What's your name?" I ask. "I mean, what do you go by?"

Jamison looks at me, and a little crackle of energy shoots between us. "Johnny," he says.

I put my hand on his thigh and squeeze. I'm risking court-martial, but I'm sick and tired of this fucking war, and after all I may be dogmeat tomorrow. I bend down and plant my mouth on Johnny's. He doesn't hesitate for a moment; it's as if he'd been waiting for me to get the ball rolling. He kisses me back, pushing his tongue down my throat.

Oh, Johnny, I think.... *One of these days, between stories, we'll get that chance just to hang out, to talk, to get to know each other a little. I've got to believe it'll happen.* I look into Johnny's eyes, and for a moment I think he can read my thoughts. He gives a tiny smile and nods, a gesture out of character for the story.

As writergod's keyboard clicks away, I reach down, unzip his fly, and pull out his thick, hard cock.

Pink Triangle-Shaped Pubes

Alexander Rowlson

It's forty minutes into geography class and you've glanced at my chest five times. As soon as you realize that I'm looking at you, you avert your gaze. You try to make me think that you weren't looking at me, but I know the truth. I can see it in your eyes. Every time you look at me, you turn into a deer caught in the headlights. A blank expression falls across your face as you think about all the dirty things that you want to do to me, like taste my cum or tongue my hole. Whatever it is that you fags do to each other.

You make me sick and I think that you know that. I think that's part of the reason that you like me. It turns you on, doesn't it? Oh! Caught you looking again, naughty little boy. This time you're a bit bolder: I spy your little eye looking straight at my crotch. I'm half hard, so I decide to flex my dick so it bulges in my pants. Didn't see that one coming, did you?

You look at me, hopeful and nervous and timid. I look you straight in the eye and mouth the word *fag* and watch the pain and embarrassment wash over your face. You quickly turn your head toward your paper and try as hard as you can to ignore me. I just stare at you from across the room.

Your hair is bright pink and the dye is coming off on the collar of your shirt. I imagine you in the shower for the first time after dying your hair. Half the dye washes out, staining all the hairs on your body. You even have pink triangle-shaped pubes. Thinking about this makes me laugh out loud. The girl in front of me turns around and smiles. She looks like a slut. I could fuck her. That makes me laugh too. I try to picture my cock pushing through her cherry-painted lips. I imagine grabbing hold of her ears and ramming my pole into the back of her throat, causing her to gag. She hasn't sucked as much cock as you have, so she doesn't know how to take it all in like a good bitch.

And then you start looking at me again. I know because I've been watching your eyes as they turned away from your paper and slowly made their way toward my leg. I try to catch the eye of my man Stan, and Stan's thinking the same. We look at each other and I point at you and mouth, *Watch*. I let out a whistle like a beer-bellied construction worker, causing you to look up. When you catch my eye I smooch my lips together and make kissing noises. Stan the man laughs, as do most of the kids around him. Half of them don't even know why they're laughing, but do so out of boredom.

The ruckus causes the teacher to stop writing out some tired passage on the blackboard and turn to the class in a half-assed attempt to make us be quiet.

You are mortified, and your public humiliation gives me a full hard-on. Your face turns bright crimson (just like your candy-ass hair) and your bottom lip starts to quiver. I know you won't cry, though. You haven't cried yet, and I've seen you get a lot closer than this. Like that time in gym, when me and Stan pantsed you in front of the whole class and you weren't wearing any underwear ('cause gay boys are such skanks) so the whole class saw your flaccid friend. But the best part was when the coach gave you trouble for being a perv and you had to run laps. I thought I'd see you cry then, but you didn't. And you're not going to now.

Your face is pretty when you look like this. You're pretty like a girl. I can't stop staring at you, and you can sense it. It embarrasses you even more and you squirm in your seat. I think about you sucking on my cock. You'd do it well. You've had a lot of practice. And, you've got those cocksucker lips. I can see your lips around my dick when I close my eyes. I start to flex my PC muscle, causing my cock to push against my pants and send shivers up my spine.

I remember the first time I saw your lips around a cock. It was at Queen's Park. Talk about the right place at the right time. I like going down there to watch; you never know what you're going to see, or who. I was leaning against a tree and watching some queers suck each other off in the shadows. I tried to match their rhythm with my hand as I jacked off. Some old geezer tried to swoop in for the kill, coming toward me and grabbing at my cock. I pushed his hand away, but he was relentless. Soon he had whipped himself out of his pants. I looked up at him and said, "You dirty fucking faggot!" and I spit in his face as I pushed him away. It was a good one too, lots of mucus. As he scrambled away, I made my way to another tree and watched the scene more closely.

I didn't know it was you at first because you had a hat on. The other guy had just come and you were standing up to get your turn. The hat hid your face, but as soon as your pants were around your ankles, I knew. Pink triangle-shaped pubes in the glow of the streetlight. I watched as you were getting your cock sucked, and kept on jacking off.

I shot into my hand, wiped it on the tree, and started walking up to the subway. I haven't been able to stop thinking about it since. Suddenly the bell rings. I gather my things and make my way out of class. As I pass you, I cuff you on the back of the head. You look up at me as I walk out the door and I wink at you.

Cocky
Mel Smith

I was feeling cocky again. I got that way every once in a while. I don't know why, because the punishments got worse and worse. Maybe it was because I knew I was his all-time favorite.

He was magnificent, an indestructible, fucking god who had owned dozens of asses way hotter than mine. But I was his favorite. Pretty heady stuff for a nineteen-year-old piece of street shit.

It was Friday afternoon, late. He'd let me come to work with him, the first time he had ever taken one of his boys. I spent the day under his desk, eating that sculpture of his he calls a cock. It's a fucking work of art, and my throat and my ass fit over it like custom-made gloves.

I hid under his desk, with people walking in and out, while his meat filled my gullet, swelling and pulsing and teasing me. I wanted to eat him so bad I whimpered, but he held back all day, giving me nothing but a precum appetizer.

Of course, I wasn't allowed to come, either. My balls and my cock were harnessed to a chain around my neck. If

I misbehaved—if he thought I was too close to coming or if I touched without permission—he pulled the chain and tightened the harness.

When he didn't want me on his cock, I curled up on his feet, cleaning his boots with my tongue or losing myself in the scent of leather, cured with oil, piss, and cum. God, I loved that smell. It never tasted as good as it smelled, but the gritty feel of his boots against my tongue made the taste tolerable. They were *his* boots, and our cum and piss were mixed together on that leather, along with the fluids of those who had come before me. The ones who no longer mattered to him.

At the end of the day, he pulled me from under the desk without locking the door and kissed me until my lip bled. My tongue was swollen and raw. With the door still unlocked, he took off my harness and one of his boots. He gave me the boot and laid me across his desk, and I fucked that beloved boot while he fucked my ass.

He pounded me so hard my nipples were rubbed raw and my hip bones bruised. I drenched that boot with two loads of cum before he shoved me back under the desk, sat back in his chair, and pumped his juices into my face while his secretary asked him questions about the next day's schedule.

Jesus Christ! Why the hell wouldn't I feel cocky after a day like that?

Before we left, he put my harness back on and pushed in a butt plug. Then we started walking the four blocks to his car.

He wanted me behind him on his right, with my left hand in his back pocket. I was still too excited, though, and I got squirrelly and full of myself. I bounced around, pulled my hand out now and then, and talked to people as they passed. Everyone stared at him, as usual, wanting him and envying me. I just smiled and said, "He's mine."

I knew he was getting pissed but thought he couldn't do anything. We weren't in the real world. We were in that fantasy land where people believe they are their own masters. No doubt he would whip me when we got home, but I felt too good to care.

We were a block from the car when I drifted to his left side. He stopped and gave me a look that should have ended it right there, but I didn't even lower my eyes. I just smiled.

He turned and started to walk again, but, like lightning, spun and slapped me so hard I was knocked to the ground. He kneeled and punched me in the face. He pulled his switchblade out and it snapped open.

I was too shocked to be scared, as blood ran into my mouth and down my shirt.

He sliced his own arm with the knife, then laid it on the ground. He hissed at me under his breath as a crowd formed. "Now you're going to find out what real punishment is." He looked up. "Someone call the police. This little asshole just tried to mug me."

My shock was gone and I felt fear. Plenty of it.

I pleaded with my eyes, but he just stared at me.

Someone had a cell phone and called 911.

I tried to touch him, but he slapped my hand away. He reached under my shirt collar and pulled my chain, stretching my balls to the limit.

I wanted to vomit.

How far would he let this go? What if he actually let them take me in? I didn't want to think about the cops' reactions to my harness and butt plug. Worse, though, was the thought of being separated from him. In our two years together, I was never away from him, except while he was at work. Then I was safe in our home, wearing his clothes to keep his scent close to me.

Out in this world, before he'd taken me in, I was terrified all the time. Out here, I didn't know what was expected of me.

Two police cars arrived.

I whispered, "Please," but he didn't flinch. I didn't want to shame him even more, but I couldn't keep from crying.

The police took his statement. He said I'd come up from behind him with the switchblade and demanded money. We struggled over the knife, he got cut, he punched me and seized the knife. He refused their offer of an ambulance.

They asked for my version, but he knew I wouldn't talk.

He said he wanted to press charges. "Maybe it'll teach the little shithead a lesson."

They cuffed my hands behind my back and led me to a police car. One officer patted me down before putting me in. He felt the harness.

"What the fuck…?" He pushed my face onto the trunk of the car and pinned my head. "I think he's got a shoulder harness on. Hold him while I do a better search."

The other cop held my head and twisted my wrist.

"I don't know what the fuck this thing is. It feels like he's got something up his ass, too. Follow me in. I'm going to have to strip search him."

I choked back a sob.

"What the hell are you carrying, boy? Are those weapons?"

I shook my head, no.

They shoved me into the car. I looked for him, but he was gone.

At the station, they stripped me as much as they could with my hands cuffed.

"Oh, Jesus Christ! What kind of a freak are you?"

One officer pulled hard on the chain around my neck and I almost passed out.

"And look at that tattoo. God, there are some fucking sick people in this world."

Luckily, my *Property of…* tattoo displayed only his club

name. He'd get in trouble if the cops found out about our relationship.

Other cops came and looked at me.

"Get him in front of the camera so dispatch can see, too."

They paraded me in front of a security camera. They laughed.

"I really, really don't want to know what's up his ass."

They took me to the cell and bent me over.

"Oh, fucking A."

"What a fucking freak."

"Get Landers's trainee in here. We'll make her pull it out."

There were four cops by now and they were enjoying themselves, but all I could think of was "her." They were going to have some female cop take out the plug.

I cried. As much as I didn't want to, I couldn't help it. I had never been so humiliated and, without him near, I was more frightened than I ever had been on the street.

I wanted only to be home with him. How long would he punish me?

While waiting for the female officer, my head was kept down and my ass up and spread. They laughed at and ridiculed me nonstop.

Then I heard a woman's voice. "Oh, Jesus, Cal. Don't make me do this."

The male cops laughed harder.

"You're the trainee, Simms. I have to be able to evaluate your performance in a wide range of situations."

"Fuck you."

"Besides, if one of us tries to get it out, he'll probably get so excited it'll take the Jaws of Life to unplug him."

"Fuck you. Give me all your gloves, at least. I ain't touching that thing without several layers of latex."

She put on six pairs of gloves, then removed the plug.

"Holy shit. Look at the size of that thing."

"There should be a place where we can deposit garbage like him so the rest of society doesn't have to deal with them."

The female officer finished her cavity search, and I was uncuffed and allowed to dress.

The arresting officer asked a lot of questions. Where did I live? Who should be contacted in case of emergency? I told him I was homeless and had no one. Without him, that was true. He found me on the street and he could send me back there.

I was processed and interrogated, then transported to the county jail. Several other prisoners from other places were brought in at the same time.

When my name was called, my arresting officer gave the jail deputy my property.

"What the hell is this shit?"

"My boy's into bondage."

"He didn't actually have this thing up his ass, did he?"

"Wedged in tighter than a drum."

Even the other prisoners laughed.

"Fucking pervert. I know exactly which cell to put him in. A parolee came in earlier who couldn't even make it a full week on the outside. He'll be more than happy to replace this one's butt plug for him."

I dribbled in my pants.

I was processed and taken to my cell. The deputy pushed me in and said, "Dixon. Got a present for you." He tossed something in behind me. A handful of condoms landed on the cell floor.

I knew which one was Dixon. He was huge, and both of his arms and his neck were completely tatted out. The other prisoners gave him plenty of space.

He stared at me and licked his lips. "I got me some real pussy while I was out, but this looks almost as good."

He bent over and grabbed some rubbers.

I wanted to fall at his feet and give myself to him, hoping

he would show some mercy. At the very least, he might protect me from the other prisoners.

It was my dishonor, though, that had brought me here. I would not make it worse by being unfaithful.

The other prisoners moved to the front of the cell, preventing anyone from seeing in.

Dixon pushed me down onto a bench and raped me. The other prisoners took turns until the rubbers were gone. One guy didn't get a turn, so he beat me up instead.

I huddled on the floor in a corner of the cell, too scared to sleep, and thought about him.

I was seventeen when I first saw him. My dad had just been arrested. My mom had gotten mad at my dad, so she turned him in for the things he'd been doing to me all of my life.

After the police took my dad away, my mom didn't want anything to do with me. I ended up on the streets.

I was on my own for about two weeks when I saw him coming out of the club. He was beautiful and powerful. I had never seen anyone like him before. Men hovered around him, just to be in his presence. A young man followed close behind, led like a willing, devoted dog.

He glanced at me when he came out the door, and I knew instantly that he would save me—that he was where I belonged.

I pushed through the crowd and stood in front of him. He looked down at me and he knew it, too.

I went to the faithful young dog and I punched him in the face. I took off his collar, put it around my neck, and stepped into my rightful place.

He took me home and he trained me. He gave me boundaries and showed me what was expected of me. When I earned it, I was rewarded with his affection. When I overstepped my boundaries, the punishment was severe but controlled. It was never the random violence I'd known from my father.

I had never known that kind of love before, and I would have done anything for him.

After our first week together, he took me to the club and handed me over to his friends. He was the only man, besides my father, I had ever been with. I hated being touched by them, but I submitted to everything, wanting to make him proud.

When they had finished with me, I crawled to him. I curled around his feet, my face pressed to his boots, and I cried like a baby.

No one else was allowed to touch me after that. No boy before me had received that honor. He even broke a guy's arm once after the man had grabbed my ass and made a degrading comment about me.

Now I sat in a jail cell and thought about what he was going through. He had known there was a good chance I'd be used by others. I saw his face when the police searched and handled me. If he never took me back, I had no one to blame but myself. I had taken his love for granted, and I didn't deserve another chance.

In the morning, though, I was released. All the charges, except the weapons charge, had been dropped. The deputy gave me a court date and sent me out the door. My property was not returned.

I had no money, so I hitchhiked home. I didn't have a key to the house—I'd never needed one—so I knocked on the door.

He answered.

I fell to the ground, crying. I laid my head on his boots and begged for his forgiveness.

He yelled. "Ryan! Come here."

I looked up in horror.

Ryan Black appeared and stood beside him. He was wearing my collar. Ryan was the young man I had punched out two years before.

"Ryan, piss on this piece of shit for me, then show him the right way to suck my cock."

I lay on the ground and looked at my beloved boots while Ryan's stream soaked my hair. Then he pushed me aside, with a boot to my face, as he made room for Ryan.

Ryan knelt in my spot and swallowed what was rightfully mine.

The door slammed in my face.

I felt empty and amputated.

I heard his orders from the other side of the door. "Don't just suck it, asshole. I want you to fucking inhale it. I want this meat of mine to end up in your fucking lungs. If you're still conscious when this is over, cunt-boy, you ain't doing it right."

He was talking to Ryan, but the message was mine. If I wanted to come home, I had to earn the right.

I got off the ground, slammed open the door, and kicked Ryan as hard as I could. He fell to the floor.

I went to my knees, wrapped my arms around my god's body, and slid his sculpture into my throat. It was still a perfect fit. They would have to kill me to get it away from me.

Ryan got up and kicked me several times, but I wouldn't budge. They both slugged me in the face and head, over and over, but I refused to let go.

His cock grew and filled me even more. Dazed and bleeding, I felt complete again.

I was close to passing out when I heard him say, "You can go now, Ryan. I won't be needing you any more."

The door slammed as my collar landed next to my knee.

He whipped me until I was raw. He took me to the shower, cleaned me, and treated my wounds. He put my collar back on, then he took me to bed.

He sat on the edge and I sat on the floor, nestled between his legs. I laid my face against his cock. It beat like a heart and wept precum onto me.

He petted my head, then took a handful of my hair and made me look at him. "Don't make me do that again. I swear to God, I won't drop the charges next time."

I began to cry. I took his cock into my mouth and pacified us both.

He pulled me off by my hair and I got on my hands and knees on the bed. He stood at the end, entered me with a single thrust, and reclaimed ownership of me.

He pounded me until I fell off the bed, then he pounded me into the floor. He came inside of me, after I came for the second time.

He pulled out, took off his full rubber, tied it closed, and gave it to me.

I curled up on the floor next to his bed. His hand hung down and rested on my head. I held his sac full of semen to my face and fell into a deep, peaceful sleep.

Six months later, I got cocky again. He kept his promise, and I went to prison.

Once inside, I refused to serve any other master. There was only one way to keep from being someone else's bitch: I fought like hell.

Before long, nobody messed with me. Eventually, I ruled my section of the population. First choice of all fresh white meat that came through the door was mine. If I craved something darker, I worked a trade.

I was a fucking god in there, training my bitches to do exactly what I wanted. When I snapped my fingers, they squatted and pissed. When I whistled, they pulled out their dicks and came. They could suck my cock with every trick known to man, or they could open wide and give me a tunnel to ream. They could sit on my dick and do all the work, or they could hang on tight to the toilet while I ripped their fucking asses in two. Whatever I wanted, they gave on command. And if anyone touched one of my bitches without my permission, they didn't live long enough to enjoy it.

I worked hard, battled nonstop. Someone always wanted to take control of my slice of the population, or some new bitch couldn't get it right. Decisions had to be made—who's too much of a threat to live, who's worth retraining, who should be tossed into the yard? I couldn't relax for a second.

I modeled myself after him. I thought about him every minute. I realized how much work and worry he'd put into me, and how much crap he'd put up with. I now appreciated just how much he had loved me.

I got out four years later. The scared nineteen-year-old was gone. I was buffed to perfection, and my muscle and my passion had ruled my kingdom almost the entire time. He hadn't visited me in those four years. I knew he wouldn't recognize me.

I went straight to the club. He was there, with people still hovering around him and a faithful young pup following behind.

Our eyes locked and there was a type of recognition in his, but I don't think he knew for sure.

I pulled my switchblade and snapped it open. The crowd moved away from him. The puppy dog moved closer for protection.

I stabbed the dog in his thigh and he dropped to the floor, screaming. I took off his collar and held it in my fist. I wiped the bloody knife on my shirt and turned to look at the man who had been my master those four long years ago. My reign in prison had been playacting. I now stood before the real god.

I was hard.

Doubt was still in his eyes, so I offered him the knife and he took it.

He sliced open my shirt. Below the tattoo he had given me was a new one: *I Will Serve No Other Master.*

I dropped to his feet and found his boots. I closed my eyes and breathed in. A few unfamiliar scents clung to them, but I would eliminate those soon.

I licked every inch of those boots, getting harder with each taste.

He pulled me to my feet by my hair, laid the knife against my throat, and put his face in mine. "This is the last time I'll take you back."

He kissed me hard, the blade drawing blood, and I felt invincible.

He turned me around and I bent over. He opened the ass of my jeans with the knife, then put my collar back on me.

The crowd moved in closer while he slid his armor onto his cock.

With our world watching, he gripped my collar and reclaimed ownership of me.

He pounded me onto my knees, then into the floor. I bled from the nose and mouth. I felt safe and whole.

I covered myself with cum more than once, and the crowd added theirs to the floor around me. No one dared get a drop on me.

He came inside my ass, then pulled out and removed the full rubber. He tied it closed and dropped it onto me. I hung it from my collar.

I stood to follow him, but stopped and pissed on the bleeding bitch on the floor. As I turned to follow my master home, I said, "You can go now, cunt. He won't be needing you anymore."

Warm-up
Matt Bernstein Sycamore

It's finally spring, so of course I walk all the way across town to Stuyvesant Park. I swear I've got a hundred pounds of shit in my backpack, not to mention a shopping bag full of file folders and computer disks, but listen, it's warm outside and there's no way I'm gonna miss the park. I get two blocks away and it starts to drizzle but who cares, I get to the entrance and suddenly I'm wired.

I walk right over to this couple in the middle, this guy in a blue warm-up suit or what do they call those stupid things. Jogging suits? Running suits? Whatever—he's with someone else but he's working me hardcore. I walk around but there's no one else I'm in the mood for, so I sit down next to a guy by the entrance who's not bad; I'd suck his dick. I say hi and he looks away, smokes a cigarette. After a few minutes he gets up and leaves. Bitch. I stay seated and the guy in blue walks over and I stare right at him and say hey. He says aren't you cold, because I've only got a T-shirt on, but I'm warm. He walks past me and then back, then looks around and goes across the street to the other side of the park. Does he want me to follow?

I do one more go-around, but there's no one I'm hot for. I pass this older guy who's standing in the shadows, say hello, and he's surprised—probably because no one's said a word to him. People are so damn serious in these places. I cross the street and there's the guy in blue right in the middle of the park getting blown by first one guy and then another. My heart's literally racing, or maybe it's not my heart, but whatever it is means I've got to get over there immediately or I might die.

I sit down right next to the guy in blue, he's got this huge, beautiful dick, and one guy's on his knees sucking it. The third guy is grabbing the other guy's dick. The guy sucking takes a break so I lean over and take that beautiful dick in my mouth, then I get on my knees so that I can get a better angle. The guy who was sucking grabs my dick, but I'm not hard yet, then the guy I'm sucking pushes my head down and his dick thrusts into my throat. It's too big and the force gets me hard and I'm gagging but wanting more and more, he's pushing my head all the way down and it's amazing I'm hard and the other guy's sucking me.

Then I choke and some food comes up, I press up to breathe, and the guy just pushes my head down, oh that amazing feeling of him pressing down, finally I can't take it anymore, I push up hard and he releases. I swallow my vomit then go back down on the guy, put his hand on the back of my neck, but then the other guy wants some, I sit up and the fourth guy (what's he been doing?) starts sucking my dick. Then the guy in blue says I'm gonna come and I put my hand on his chest, he comes in the guy's mouth and damn I want that cum so bad.

The other guy gets up and starts spitting out the cum, I wouldn't mind him spitting it into my mouth. Then the guy in blue gets up and I take his place, now my dick's looking large too, he looks back and I look him right in the eyes with heat. The fourth guy's still sucking my dick and the other guy's sitting next to me, I bend over and take his dick in my mouth, he pushes my head all the way down. His dick starts out medium but pretty soon he's huge too and I'm rock hard in the other guy's mouth though he's sort of hurting me.

I ask the guy whose dick I'm sucking to stand up and put his dick in my mouth. He hesitates, but then he's fucking my face, I pull his hand down to my neck and oh I'm so hard in the other guy's mouth, but I pull his head away so that I don't come. I want the other guy to come in my mouth and I say so, but he already came—probably better that way for me anyway. I pull his head down and we start making out.

The guy who used to be the fourth guy—but now he's the third guy, I guess—he's jerking my dick and I could come but I hold his hand to stop. I pull up my shirt and the third guy rubs my chest—yes—and I'm sucking the other guy's dick. Then he takes out his dick and starts smacking my face, he's grabbing my chest and holding my neck and the other guy's got a finger pumping at the edge of my asshole and his other hand jerking my dick. And I don't even know where I am anymore or what I'm doing and then I feel myself coming but I can't even tell if I've come yet, no there I'm coming no I've already come but my orgasm just goes on.

When I open my eyes, there's just me and the guy standing up and he grabs my head to make out but I'm coughing, a dryness in my throat like all this stuff is stuck there. I start laughing, it's spring yes it's spring and then I'm kissing the guy again and pulling up my pants, what's your name, his name's—now I can't remember—and I get up and there are guys wandering all over and good, my bags are still there. I start walking and I'm coughing and laughing, I'm so high from coming, I'm walking down the street with my eyes sometimes rolling back and sometimes I'm just laughing, thinking how amazing sex can be, the insane high, how I need some throat lozenges.

Going Down, Going Down Down
Simon Sheppard

The things I find on AOL. Jesus. Twenty-one. He was twenty-one, which even for *me* is young. He'd warned me he'd want to smoke crack before he played with me. Or was that a promise? Anyway, let's face it, the only real problem with drug addiction is that it totally fucks up people's lives, sometimes beyond redemption, so who was I to say no? Right?

After all, lots of things fuck up lives. Lots. And he *was* twenty-one.

When he showed up at my door—and he actually did show up at my door—he was as cute as his online pictures. The pictures didn't show the dark circles under his eyes, but I'm used to that, that look of perfect young boys who don't get enough sleep. Not enough sleep. He was considerably more fragile-looking than his power over me would have suggested.

He tugged at his baseball cap and made himself at home, nervously. Tweakers talk too much, then apologize for talking too much. I assure them it's okay. I stroke their drug-blank faces, pull down their pants. I'm such a nice guy.

God, he was so beautiful. And he seemed intelligent and sweet, but then, that's how I wanted him to be. Sweet and twisted and horny. So that's how he was, then.

Twisted. Fucked-up. Why would a young, beautiful boy want to have sex with someone damn near old enough to be his grandfather? (Funny how the opposite question almost never gets asked. At least not by me.) Well, let's look at it another way: why would someone want to be put into diapers and treated as though he were an infant, all the while on a drug-fueled rush?

Because he was, in a word, fucked-up. But it was best not to dwell too much on that, at least not while he was draped across my sofa, the already-open fly of his baggy pants thrust forward. He took off his baseball cap.

My partner? My partner was at work. I wasn't cheating on him; it's a really, really open relationship. My boyfriend, whom I love with all my heart and soul, doesn't want me to remain sexually monogamous with him, no more than I mind when he fucks around with other guys. He wants me to be happy. And he wants me to be safe. I feel the same about him.

wrong, Bucko

He even knew this particular boy was due to come over. I hadn't shown him the pictures, though, the way I've sometimes shamelessly done. Okay, clearly, doing a diaper scene with a young boy on crack doesn't qualify as "safe," at least not in the minds of normal people. Maybe it even squicks *you*, I don't know. I do know that as the beautiful young man reached into his shoulder bag and pulled out his paraphernalia, assembled the crack bong, heated the bowl, sucked in and puffed out big clouds of demonstrably toxic smoke, I felt like I was just one horrible step from the predatory old fags in Dennis Cooper's stories. And I could live with that.

"Oops, my shoe's up against your pillow. You mind?"

I reached down and untied his battered sneaker.

"I'm really sweaty. My feet probably stink. You mind that?"

214

Quite the opposite. "That's fine," I said, "I'm pretty kinky." I was saying that to a boy who liked to put on a diaper and piss in it.

His socks were moist. I bent over and took a sniff. I felt like the luckiest chickenhawk in town. Who knows? At that moment maybe I was. Lucky.

His cell phone beeped. He took it. A woman's voice. Though I discreetly left the room so he could talk, I could tell from his tone of voice that he was making excuses.

"Sorry about that," he said when I got back. "My mom."

Quicksand. "That's okay. No problem."

He reached for the crack pipe again. I was starting to get the feeling this was one adventure I wasn't going to discuss with my partner.

I stood up between the diaperboy's spread legs, my knees pressing out against his thighs. After he'd taken the hit, he asked me, semi-blissfully, what was wrong. Nothing, I assured him. And almost nothing was.

"Want some?"

It had been years, many years, since cocaine had entered my system, and I hadn't missed it at all. But I didn't want to be standoffish. Nope, I didn't want to be left out, not where a cute young guy was concerned. Nope. I sat down beside him, thigh to thigh on my sofa. While he heated the bowl with a Bic, I inhaled a smallish hit of the dope.

There was a rush, yes, but it didn't feel particularly good. After the first few seconds, I just felt edgy. I was glad, in a way, that I didn't enjoy the coke. Guess I'm getting old.

I wanted to see his dick. I reached down to his unzipped crotch. Nice handful. It was easy to undo the drawstring and pull his pants down. He had on black jockstrap-style underwear. I felt the hefty, semi-curled shaft through the thin cloth, knowing that this next second was the moment I would first see his cock, a moment that, whatever came later, was never going to be repeated. Undies down. His dick was half-hard and bigger than it had any right to be. And his crotch was shaved; not a surprise, not a turn-on. Just shaved.

He yawned. "I don't know, I'm sleepy, you'd think with all this crack I wouldn't be, huh?" He laughed, then yawned again. I was playing with his cock. It was getting harder. Damn, I almost never get a chance to suck such pretty young dick. I took it between my lips, filled my mouth with it. A treat. Like full-fat ice cream—delicious, but bad for me at my age. He got kind of harder, kind of.

"Stop," he said, jumpily. "I'm not really into that. The diaper scene, that's what I came here for. We talked about that online, right? You agreed?"

I took my mouth away. "Sorry," I said.

"Why'd you do that, suck my dick?" he said, suddenly urgent, as though it were a genuine puzzle, one that pissed him off.

"Jesus. Sorry, okay?"

I tugged his shirt up. He didn't stop me. His lean chest was entirely hairless, his nipples pink and symmetrical and as yet untouched by time.

"You have any stuff?" By "stuff" he meant: diapers, training pants, baby wipes, talcum powder, baby oil. Well, no.

"I left my stuff over at a friend's house. It's not far from here, I'll go get it."

Speedfreaks always seem to be between apartments. Their stuff is always at someone else's house. Crackheads. Speedfreaks. The things I find on AOL…

"We can go buy diapers at Walgreens."

"No problem, I won't be long."

I knew damn well what that meant. To boys who use illicit central nervous system stimulants, time is flexible. As flexible as morality.

I knew damn well. He wasn't the first twenty-something

speedfreak I'd met. I thought back to Corey, how I'd gone over to his house for the first time way after midnight, a couple of years back, how I had played with his pale, skinny body and limp little dick for hours. He snorted, I sucked. But then he'd gone out to score more crystal, a process he figured would take a half-hour, since he'd just arranged by cell phone to meet his dealer a few blocks away. It was four in the morning. Of course. I let him borrow my black leather jacket. Otherwise I would have left his place earlier, way before seven, but there I lay for hours, there in his unsprung bed, wondering what the fuck had happened to him. And to my leathers. When he finally got back, around eight, the world outside his window was wide awake, facing the new day. He returned with stories of not finding the dealer, getting propositioned by some old guy, being stopped and questioned by the cops. He was still wearing my jacket. He looked beautiful.

That was Corey. That had been last year, the year before. Now I wanted to see this new cracked-out boy, naked except for a diaper, lying in my bed. I wanted to watch his face as he let his piss flow, as he wallowed in a feeling that went way the hell back to when he was a newborn. I wanted to reach down and feel the warm stiffness of his crotch through the plastic diaper, to undo the diaper, open it to the whiff of pee, change him, sprinkle his pretty young butt with sweet-smelling baby powder.

These were things I could never do with my boyfriend, things I could do with, well, nearly no one (and certainly not, dear reader, with you). I looked down at him lying there, his big dick lolling against a pale, skinny thigh, his scrawny chest rising and falling with each drugged breath. I wondered what he was like when he was sober. I wondered how long it had been since he was. Sober. I wondered what the hell had gone wrong in his life, in my life. I wondered if I could fuck his ass.

"Where are my shoes?"

I handed them to him, though I wanted to steal them, throw him out on the street in his sweaty white socks.

"I'll be back soon, less than an hour," he said, pulling himself together. "Just have to get my stuff. I really want to do this."

"So do I," I said, and most of me meant it. My boyfriend would be out till early evening. Even allowing for delays, the kid might be back with his diapers and training pants in time for a scene. If he got back at all.

I could have stopped him from leaving, said, "No really, let's just walk out to buy some diapers." But, like lending Corey my leather jacket, letting diaperboy go was a test of sorts. Corey had passed that test, but then, all he'd had to do was get back to his own messy house, something he'd have been sure to do sooner or later regardless. Later, during our subsequent hookups, Corey had passed other tests, but he'd failed a lot, too, and he was so thoroughly fucked-up that when he moved away to get the hell away from his speedfreak friends, I was happy to see him go. My partner was glad to see him go, too; he always has my best interests at heart. But my joy was not unalloyed. I figured I'd maybe never touch the flesh of such a beautiful young man again.

Diaperboy was disassembling his crack pipe, looking for his cell phone, pulling his baseball cap down over his shock of unruly hair. I looked at him, hard, and I could suddenly imagine him in some future, an adult, much older. I hoped he would get through all this in one piece. I'm just too sentimental to be in a Dennis Cooper story, I guess.

He made for the door, telling me once again that he'd be back soon, that he was "really into this." It might have been true, might not. A loose grasp on truth is yet another of your typical crackhead's dubious charms. My hard-on was fading.

When he left, I pressed a button on the CD changer, went

from Radiohead to Led Zeppelin. Something about the levee breaking. Just right. Still edgy from the crack, I read the Sunday paper for a while, then did the dishes. I phoned up Corey's ex-roommate, left a message asking if he'd heard lately how Corey was doing.

Three-plus hours later, I'd finished the newspaper, the dishes, and writing the first part of this story. The boy still hadn't returned. I didn't know exactly *how* I felt about that. And you know what? I still don't.

Natoma Street
JT LeRoy

It's like I'm pushed from behind, pulled down the slope of Natoma Street like a ramp down into another world. All the buildings are low and tight huddled around me. Heavy-gated sweatshops, sunken-down tenements, windows filled with dusty laughing Santas and graying fake snow and ancient slaughterhouses with rusted metal beams jutting suddenly out above me. I watch my shadow slip underneath them, sharpen under the piss-colored street lamp, and slide unsliced over the green and white pebbles of glass almost worn smooth from streams of urine. And behind me somewhere is the rainlike sound of a car window being smashed, and in front of me the crunch-crunch under my boots, pulling me forward. I tilt my head to listen to the blood in my own ear, and all I hear, and all I feel, is my cold ache. The sheet metal door glistens in front of me like an ax on a fire blade, and the sound of my pounding fist on the door echoes through me and down Natoma Street. Each split second of contact with the frozen metal is like a jolt trying to wake or stop me but all that's racing in my blood is too old and too known and too mechanical to be turned back.

I stand and wait and watch delicate white puffs of air float out from me. And it's amazing anything can come out of me. Soon nothing will. I bang the door as hard as I can, bruising my knuckles, and wait a few seconds.

"C'mon...."

My teeth are clamped. I kick at the door with my boot. They're gonna find me collapsed here as drained and as empty as if a vampire had fed on me. I kick the door again and again, and it shudders. I feel the panic and desperation in my stomach spread as my blood roars away, feeding on itself.

"You're supposed to...."

I kick and hit the metal door.

"Be fuckin' here!" I yell. From behind me a window slams open.

"People sleeping, people sleeping!"

I turn and look up to see a bald Chinese guy, his face so chubby and squished he looks like a smiling Buddha. Christmas lights flash like a strobe around him.

"You go 'way, go 'way!"

From behind me I hear heavy latches and bolts moving, and I twist around, and it's like an opening in the world, with cars, lights, and people passing the mouth of Natoma, and they have no idea I'm here, and waiting to be.

"Goddamn, you're eager...." The door pulls open like a bank vault, and blue light reflects onto the sidewalk.

"It's just eleven-thirty now, I don't start early," he says in a deep radio announcer tone. My ears pound and I look back up to the Buddha man, but he's gone, just the empty flashing space of his gaping window.

"Let's go," he orders, and I turn to face him, but he's gone too. I climb into the blue lights and the door that's framed in steel, and it slams behind me.

"Bolt it," I hear from ahead of me. I stare at a puzzle of red-and-black-painted locks and bolts. "The bottom," he says. It's a lock that will need a key to unlock. I feel it clink in my stomach as I watch my hand seal me in.

I walk down an unpainted narrow Sheetrock hall with bare blue bulbs poking out like lights in an arcade. The ground is concrete and cracked.

"C'mon!" he says impatiently. "Off to the right."

The hall opens into a huge warehouse with two giant Harleys parked in the middle and a maze of other halls, lofts, ladders, and doors surrounding it. I follow the blue lights into a smaller room that smells of rubbing alcohol and something else I recognize but can't recall.

"Over here."

He's sitting in a director's chair in the middle of the room, holding two Fosters. He holds an open one out to me. I watch my shadow like a black fog moving toward him. My shadow head hits his feet, black in engineer boots, and I trace up faded Levi's, to a leather vest half revealing shining silver hoops through his nipples. His arms are like air-drawn traces of a woman's figure. I avoid his face. I reach out for the beer.

"Uhh, thanks."

"How old are you?"

He crosses his legs.

"Eighteen," I say automatically, and sip some foam. He laughs.

"Try again."

His boot wags.

"Fifteen," I mumble.

"Fifteen?" he repeats. I follow the floor to a brick wall to my right. There are things hanging, attached, from the wall. A warm wave rushes over me; I swallow loudly.

"Fifteen, I like that."

I nod my head.

"But I have ID in case."

"In case of what...? Huh?!!"

I look up at him. His cheekbones are cut too sharply, his lips are small, tight, and curled up like old newspaper. His hair is black and slicked straight back. His eyes are the reddish brown of dried blood.

"This is between you and me, got it?"

"Mmm-huh." I feel awkward and stupid. "I got your money!" I say too loudly, and start to reach back to my pocket with my beer hand but spill some. He laughs, shakes his head.

"Sorry...shit!"

It takes me a few seconds too long to figure out how to maneuver my money out with only one free hand.

"Blonds," he sneers. "Fuckin' geniuses!"

He takes a big gulp of beer. I hand him $100.

"So, how's it feel being on the other side?" He smiles, crooked little teeth.

"Huh?"

He holds the money up and shakes it, eyebrows raised.

"I had to borrow it." I look away.

"Jesus, you're quick," he snorts. "And stop rocking."

I didn't know I was. I feel like my eyes are telescopes I'm peering through, somewhere far away.

"Uhh, sorry."

"You will be." He smiles sarcastically.

"Huh? Oh." I nod. "Yeah." I feel my face getting hotter and hotter.

He nods, grins, and says, as if I don't speak English, "You are paying me...how does that make you feel?" He starts fanning the money.

"I dunno...." I sigh. His foot taps.

"Umm...weird."

"How?" He leans in.

"Uh...." I rub my face, it feels red.

"Embarrassed, I guess," I mumble.

"Would you be, humiliated, if your friends knew…? Hey, hey!!" He snaps his fingers. I look up.

"Stop rocking!" He puts his arm out and waves his hand like he's trying to move something aside to see me.

"I dunno…yeah…I guess."

I can't explain it. Paying for it does humiliate me, and I want that, I need that part, it calms me in some way. You can't trust people you don't pay.

He sighs loudly.

"Just…just sit down." He leans back. I look around me.

"Right there."

"Yeah…sorry." My left eyelid starts twitching. I sit on the cold concrete and chew on the inside of my cheek.

"I've heard about you," he says with a little laugh, and stuffs the money away.

"Uh-huh," I nod. My blood swirls around faster and faster.

"No limits for you, right?" His beer clanks on the wooden chair arm. My eyes shift from side to side, back and forth.

"No safe word right?"

"Mmm."

"You can take it all, huh?"

My head twitches in a nod.

"Coz you"—he points at me and laughs—"don't give a fucking shit, right?"

"Well…." My voice sounds too high. "I'd like, umm, I'd like it if, uh…. I'd like…." I twist my mouth from side to side.

"Sssay it," he says, singsong.

"Ummm…I'd like it if you would…." My head jerks.

"Would what?" He leans forward again.

"Um…give a shit, I mean, ya know…." I swallow hard. "Sorta like, care, um, ya know." My bottom lip starts to quiver.

"Yeah." He sighs. "You know I care…shall we get going?"

He gets up. "I don't got all night."

I take a few huge gulps of the beer and rise up like I'm pulling myself out of a pool and follow him to the exposed brick wall.

"So what do you need?" He waves his arm like a model on a game show at the collection of belts, paddles, whips, and crops displayed on the wall. He smiles proudly.

"I dunno," I mumble.

There's a jungle gym-looking metal thing, with wrist restraints hanging down, in the middle of the wall.

"Whatta ya think of this?" He reaches for a short whip and starts fondling it. I'm starting to feel nervous-sick.

"It's cool, but uhh...."

"Not into whips, right?" He replaces it gently. I shake my head. My eyelids twitch nonstop. "No cats?"

I shake my head, no, again and notice that under the metal bars there's a drain.

"Look, I know talking is a drag," he says, like I won't eat broccoli or drink my milk or something. "But you'll be happy for it later." He pats my shoulder. "I'm not a mind reader, you know. I haven't heard everything about you."

I want to ask him what he's heard but I'm afraid it'll hurt too much.

"C'mon." His voice is soft. He moves over to me and places his hand on the back of my neck and massages it lightly.

"Let me help you," he whispers into my ear, and I feel it all start to melt. "Let me help."

"That one," I say softly, and motion with my head.

"That?" He points to it. I nod and stare at the drain.

"Good boy!" he says enthusiastically, and I should be embarrassed, but I feel sort of proud. He goes over to it, I hear him take it down, and it's all starting.

"Take your clothes off, you can put 'em on that chair." A chill jerks my head, and I close my eyes. "Yes, sir," I whisper, and start to undress quickly.

"That's right, you call me sir," he responds. I hear him moving things, setting things up. "Any other special words?"

"I dunno." I lean down to unlace my boots. He comes over to me and I feel his hands sliding along my naked back, down my open jeans and underwear.

"You do take a lot, huh?" he says.

"Fuckin' knot!" I pull and slap at the tight knot at the top of my boot.

"Dad…? Stepfather, right?" He's running his hands across the little gullies and streams lining my back and ass.

"Can't get this fuckin' knot!" I yell, and punch my boot top, and stomp.

"Hey!" He grabs my face between his hands and leans over me from behind. I keep stomping. "Hey, hey, hey, not yet, stay calm…it's okay…." His voice is soothing. I hear a moan escape me. "It's okay, it's okay, it's okay." Like a lullaby.

Ouch!

"Please…" I half whisper, and reach one of my hands up to his holding on to my face.

"Tell me," he says into my ear. His breath smells like warm beer and saliva. I bring my other hand up around his other hand, cupping my face. I feel his hard cock leaning into me from behind and I release into containment.

"Tell me," he whispers. We breathe together, him leaning over me, in-out-in-out.

"Fix me," I murmur. "Fix me."

"What's it say?" He points to the words cut on my stomach, ass, thighs.

"Bad boy," I pant. "Evil…." I feel like I've hooked on to a train that's speeding away from me, or with me.

"You are a bad boy, aren't you," he says above me, squeezing my head.

I feel it loosening.

"Sinner, aren't you."

226

I close my eyes and my stomach cramps and a chill runs through me. He wraps his arms, crisscrossed, around me. I moan.

"Tell me, now," he says quietly.

"Punish me," I pant.

"How hard?" His chin digs into my shoulder.

"Till I learn...please? I need you to, please?" My body is shaking.

"Safe word?" he whispers.

"No, no, not till you're done, okay?" I pant, "Just, okay, please not my face, okay?"

"It's a very pretty face." He pats my cheek, and I try to lean my head into his touch.

"Yeah, yeah, tell me that," I gasp, and he rubs against me through his jeans. "Tell me I'm beautiful...please...."

I can't stop.

"You are, and that's why I need to help you," he whispers, like a kiss.

"Save me," I groan, and he squeezes his arms tightly around me, and I hope he'll never let go.

"I will, you beautiful, conceited, bad evil bitch."

"Yes...please...yeah...."

He reaches down between my legs and grabs my thing. "Call me sir!" His voice becomes throaty and harsh. He twists me hard and fast. It's all coming back, like being lost in waves of wheat, just rolling by, rushing me, soothing me, caressing me.

"Make me cry, I need to...cry...." He twists his hand, harder.

"Sir!" he shouts in my ear.

"Sir," I whisper, and I feel the tears swelling in my gut. "Sir...hold me after, please, I'll pay extra, please, after hold me." He says nothing. "I'll pay extra...." I sound pathetic but I can't shut up. "Please."

"Let's go," is all he says, and reaches behind to bring out a long switchblade. I suck in air.

"You like this?" He leans down, slices open my laces, then helps me kick off my boots and step out of my jeans. He presses the switchblade against my thing, and I'm spiraling away inside myself.

"It's a dirty, evil thing," I whisper. "And I hate it! I hate it!" The blade presses harder, I feel my skin ready to slit gracefully, like a paper cut. "I hate it, I hate, I hate it!" I'm hyperventilating.

"Well, we'll take care of it, don't you worry.... C'mere."

I feel suddenly embarrassed, exposed, stupid.

"Get over here now, now!" He stands by the rack contraption. I walk as if in a dream and face the bricks. I hand him my arms and watch him Velcro the restraint cuffs around my wrists so they hang above me spread apart on the bar. I look down at my chest heaving up and down, too quickly from my heart or my breath, I don't know. He stands beside me, the thick black leather belt unfurled, swinging back and forth like a pendulum. He steps close to me and raises the belt to my face. I panic.

"Please, not my face!" I plead. "Please!"

"Shut up." He brings the belt closer. "Kiss it."

I look at him. He grabs a handful of my hair. "Kiss it!" He shoves the belt up to my mouth. It smells faintly of bleach.

I begin to kiss it. I feel relief and excitement surge through me.

He knows. He understands.

"You're a nasty cunt, aren't you?" He pulls my head back by my hair. The belt disappears.

"Yes, sir." My eyes roll up. He drops my head with a shove, and I hear him pacing an arc behind me. My body hangs limp like a swing wanting to be pushed.

"You're a very nasty, evil, bad, sinful boy, aren't you?!"

"Yes…yes, sir." I correct myself and moan, my butt muscles flexing in anticipation.

"Say it!" he orders loudly from behind me.

"I'm a bad, disgusting, evil boy." I hear him pace.

"Again!"

"I'm an evil faggot, sir!" I can hardly swallow. "Please punish me…severely…sir." The heat spreads down my legs, into my toes. No sound, not even his breath. "Oh, God… please!" I yell.

"You need it, don't you?" His voice is heightened and tight.

"Yes, please." I'm starving, ravenous.

"You're a pig." The word someone once carved on my stomach. I freeze and taste sour spit-up. I nod my head. "Say it!" he screams in my ear.

"I'm a greedy pig, sir!" I shout breathlessly. He laughs.

"So beautiful," he whispers, and caresses my face. "Beautiful."

I gasp, and it's perfect. He moves back behind me, and I watch the shadows. The strap is hurled back, like he's throwing a football, whole arm into it, and I hear the familiar sound of air being thrashed through, and the cymbal-like crash across my ass. My body rocks.

"Thank you, sir." My mouth hardly moves.

"I have to punish you, don't I?" I nod. It crashes down again. My body sways in disagreement and my butt skin puckers. How can you crave something your whole body rejects, and even increase the cravings the greater the protest from the body?

"I bet you're a fucking cocktease, aren't you?" The strap slices into my ass.

"Yeah." My head rocks back.

"Sir!" he corrects. The strap lands on my upper thighs.

I lift my head.

"Punish me, sir…teach me."

"Beg." He walks behind me.

"Please, sir…." He laughs, I hear the belt drop.

"You're not worth my fuckin' time." I hear him walking away.

"No! Please! God, please! Don't leave me, I can't take that, please, God!" I hear him open drawers. "Sir, punish me!"

I howl, and shake my arms, rattling the jungle gym thing.

"You don't order me, spoiled cocktease brat!" He's next to me.

"Yes, yes, yes."

"What?!"

"Sir!"

He's jingling something in his hand. My stomach hardens.

"Close your eyes, cunt." I stare down at his closed hand. "Now, you bitch!" His open hand slaps hard at my thing. Air spits out of me, and I can't fold over. My eyes clamp shut. He laughs. "You're not too fuckin' bright, are you?" I sort of swing, letting my arms hold me. I feel something cold against my left nipple. I hold my breath.

"You want me to fix you? Discipline you?" I hear it snap down around my right nipple, and it feels like a needle being driven in. "You have to learn obedience."

"Yes." The heat rushes through me. "Please, sir, I want to be yours…." My left nipple erects next to the open clamp. "Please. I'll do anything!" He snaps it shut on my tit. I grunt.

"I know you will, you fucking nasty, spoiled brat, cock-tease, bad, bad boy." Cold heavy chains hang from the clamps, and he gives them sharp swift tugs as if in a bell tower. I feel his hand caressing my cheek and I push my face into it like a dog searching for scraps. I kiss his palm, lick it.

"Say it, beautiful." I feel the cold metal by my thing. My mind swirls away, and I feel his hand slap hard across my cheek. My eyes jerk open at him, surprised. He's inches in front of me.

"I won't scar your pretty face..." he says flatly. "If you're lucky." My face stings. He caresses the other cheek. "Close your eyes," he whispers. I hear the metal chink-chink and his other hand snaps a clamp on my thing. I jump and whimper.

"Tell me what you are." He snaps another one on, but continues to caress my cheek.

"Uhh...a dirty whore...." I want to bury my face in his palm as his other hand begins to twist the clamps and snap more on. How can I explain pain that burns like torture but soothes and excites more than a caress or kiss? His finger traces my lips and dips in and out of my mouth. The rest of his fingers tap on the outside. I suck his finger as it slides in and out of my mouth.

"You fucking cocktease!" His hand pulls away and slaps my other cheek loudly, and it feels like a punch. I blink away the tears rimming my eyes. He pulls at the chains. "Tell me! You faggot whore!"

"I'm a fucking dirty whore cocksucker...." My chest tries to curl up against the pain like warped plywood. He walks behind me.

"It's time for you to learn."

"Yes." I ball my fists in the air and open my eyes wide to the brick wall in front of me. "I need to repent." My blood throbs.

"Yes, you do, 'cause you've been a very naughty boy, haven't you?"

"Make me pay, sir," I whisper. I hear him pick up the belt.

"It's time for you to cry."

"Oh, he'll cry!" My mother squeezes and twists my wrist.

"Never done seen a thief, young or old, so bold-face remorseless," the white-haired security guard says, and wags his finger at me. The steak and beer six-pack from my knapsack sit on the table in front of me. "See all the trouble you put your poor mother to?"

The young frizzy blonde checker that busted me shakes her head at me.

"Steals it for his no-good gang friends."

"Oh, we don't let gang members in this store, ma'am." The manager quickly shines his shoes on the back of his pants legs.

I feel my mother smiling at him. She fans herself with her hand. "Well, that's a good thing, sir…." She crosses her legs.

"We have special services for them at our church, the Virgin of Perpetual Love and Mercy, but all in vain, I reckon."

She sniffles, and I can't help but laugh. Her hand reaches out fast and slaps my cheek. I keep my grin despite myself; I know I'll pay later.

"Yes, ma'am, the police won't do a thing to help you, ma'am, 'cause his age…he is amazin'." The manager leans down over my face. He smells of tuna and pickles. "Have you no shame, boy?"

My mother clears her throat. "He's been a bad boy since his father passed, few years back, that big blaze? Was a firefighter, over Tallahassee." Murmurs of sympathy. "Thank you, Lord rest his soul. Boy hasn't had the father he badly needs to give guidance and discipline."

I spurt out a laugh at the thought of her being married to a firefighter. Her hand smashes across my face again.

The manager clears his throat. "Well, I think this is the best way to handle this, ma'am."

"Mary." My mother nods.

"Mary, Howard." He reaches out, and shakes my mother's hand a little too long.

"Howard, sorry we meet in such a way, but I'm sure it will help save my boy more than police or I can."

I roll my eyes and groan. My mother's nails dig into my wrist. "You're an evil boy, you thank Mr. Marsh."

"Thanks," I say flatly, and grind my teeth.

The checker girl flashes her braces and flips her hair. "We should whoop all the shoplifters like him."

"Way it used to be, and hardly anybody thieved," the guard grumbles. I look up and see two bag boys, a little older than me, peering in wide-eyed through a broken, small, one-way mirror. "Well, no time like the present."

My mom stands and pulls me over to the table. My heart pounds louder. "Please," I whisper.

"Oh, now we see the remorse," Howard gloats. He opens his belt. "Soon you'll see the tears."

My mother jerks me forward. "Take down your pants."

I look up at her, and her eyes flash a private message of rage. She didn't tell me to get caught.

"Excuse me," Howard says to my mother as he pulls the belt from the loops.

I stare at the checkout girl biting her lip. "Oh, I'll leave...." She starts to get up.

"Oh no, darling!" My mother waves her back. "He stole in front of you, so he'll pay in front of you."

I look over to the boys in the mirror and point. My mother shakes her head and smiles slightly at me. I feel everyone's stares and it's like heat, my body shivers, and like Batman sliding down his tunnel, I am suddenly transformed to endure the impossible. I am able to lean over the table and pull my pants below my underwear. But I pull as much as possible of my jeans in front of me, and I pray and pray. At some point I feel Howard's belt beating me, as he will almost every other day as my new loving father, till we move out of his trailer three and a half months later, stealing all his cash, gold cuff links, and school ring.

I pray during my punishment. I pray so hard, I drown out the horrible whipping sound. I pray that God, or Satan, or whoever, won't let them see how sinful and repulsive and bad I truly am. I pray something won't let them see what my mother knows and has tried to punish me for but which only worsens. And the tears that eventually come burn through me and only heighten it all.

For hidden in my bunched-up jeans is my erection, like a gleaming badge of guilt, waiting to be discovered and ripped from me.

The belt is slamming into me all over, my back, ass, and thighs, and the tears are streaming, and confessions of every sin and every evil thought or action I ever did or almost did pour out from my mouth. But I cry harder and harder as the truth washes over me. Even as he takes the belt to between my legs and the pain is unbearable, I'm like the opportunistic mosquito, sucking blood down from the punishing hand of God, reaching down from heaven. I am still excited even though my thing has long been cured of its ability to have erections. I beg for it harder and harder so perhaps I can outrun it, but like my shadow, it is always next to me. It follows me.

As I hang from the gray bars, swaying, wet, and throbbing, I recognize the scent from earlier as blood. His switchblade at my crotch slices like I begged him, to try and help save me. One hand caressing, one hand cutting.

I remember when I saw *Peter Pan* when I was little. After all the other kids wanted to reenact the battles of the lost boys, pirates, and Indians, all I could think about was the part where Peter Pan sits still while Wendy takes a sharp needle and, with concern and maybe love, sews his shadow onto his feet. And I wonder if the pain excited him as much as it excited me to watch.

I hang here, the voices still bleeding in my ears. I watch my shadow, solid like a murdered body's outline, and I pray. Maybe one more slice, just one more, will sever it forever.

About the Authors

Since **DIMITRI APESSOS**'s story was originally published, he has moved even closer to the world's greatest gay diner, but he hardly eats there anymore. Having finished his first novel, he has come to realize that when people say "write what you know" it does not automatically mean that they will believe or approve of what it is that you know. While he's still making half-assed attempts at getting it published, he is enjoying cowriting screenplays, DJ-ing on the radio, and pouring drinks for people who don't wear beads.

OTTO COCA is a writer living in New York City. His journalism and book reviews have appeared in *HX*, *New York Blade*, and *LGNY*, among other publications. More of his fiction can be found on his website, www.ottococa.com.

JAIME CORTEZ is a writer and visual artist in the San Francisco Bay Area. Jaime's writing has appeared in numerous anthologies, and he was the editor of the groundbreaking queer Latino anthology *Virgins, Guerrillas & Locas*. Jaime's transgender graphic novel, *Sexile*, was nominated for the National Library Association award for queer writing. He is currently pursuing his MFA in Art Practice at UC Berkeley.

JAMESON CURRIER is the author of a novel, *Where the Rainbow Ends*, and two collections of short fiction, *Dancing on the Moon* and, most recently, *Desire, Lust, Passion, Sex*. "Snow" first appeared online in the first issue of *Velvet Mafia* and was included in *Best Gay Erotica 2003* and *Best American Erotica 2004*.

TREBOR HEALEY is the author of *Through It Came Bright Colors*, which received the 2004 Ferro-Grumley Award. His erotic fiction has most recently been anthologized in *Law of Desire, Fratsex, M2M, Quickies 3, Best Gay Erotica 2003* and *2004*, and *Pills, Thrills, Chills and Heartache*, as well as online at *Ashe* and *Velvet Mafia*. Trebor lives in Los Angeles. Find out more on www.treborhealey.com.

JT LEROY is the author of the international best-sellers, *Sarah* (being made into a film by Steven Shainberg) and *The Heart Is Deceitful Above All Things* (being made into a film by Asia Argento). *Harold's End*, an illustrated novella showcasing the work of Cherry Hood, was published in 2004 by Last Gasp Books, and a third novel is coming later this year from Viking. LeRoy was associate producer on Gus Van Sant's film *Elephant*, the Palme d'Or winner at Cannes in 2003; he is also part of the rock band Thistle (www.thistlehq.com), recording their debut with producer Jerry Harrison. He is a contributing editor for *Index, Flaunt, 7x7,* and *i-D*, and writes for *Spin, GQ, Sunday London Times*, and other publications. www.jtleroy.com.

JEFF MANN's work has appeared in many publications, including *Rebel Yell, Rebel Yell 2, The Gay and Lesbian Review*, and *Best Gay Erotica 2003* and *2004*. He has published a full-length collection of poetry, *Bones Washed with Wine*; a collection of essays, *Edge*; and a novella, *Devoured*, in the anthology *Masters of Midnight*. He lives in Charleston, West Virginia, and Blacksburg, Virginia, where he teaches creative writing at Virginia Tech.

DOUGLAS A. MARTIN's first novel, *Outline of My Lover*, was named an International Book of the Year in the *Times Literary Supplement* and adapted in part by the Ballet Frankfurt for their multimedia production *Kammer/Kammer*. He is also the author of two collections of poetry and a coauthor of *the haiku year*. Forthcoming is a collection of stories, *They Change the Subject*, and a second novel, *The Brontë Boy*.

DAVID MAY first made his mark writing for *Drummer* and other gay skin magazines in the 1980s. He is the author of *Madrugada: A Cycle of Erotic Fictions*. His work has appeared in numerous magazines and more than a dozen anthologies, including *Mentsch, Afterwords: Real Sex from Gay Men's Diaries, Kosher Meat*, and *Flesh and the Word 3*. He lives with his husband in Seattle where he is trying to finish that damn novel.

ALISTAIR MCCARTNEY was born in Australia in 1971. His writing has appeared in such fine places as *Fence, The James White Review, Mirage #4/Periodical, Wonderlands: Good Gay Travel Writing, Aroused*, and *4th Street*. His book of flash fiction, *The End of the World Book*, is forthcoming from the University of Wisconsin Press. Currently teaching literature and creative writing in the BA program at Antioch University, Los Angeles, Alistair has lived in Venice since 1995 with his partner Tim Miller.

SEAN MERIWETHER's fiction has been defined as dark realism, his subjects rooted in the peculiar nature of everyday life. In addition to *Best Gay Erotica*, his work has been published in *Lodestar Quarterly*, *Out of Control: Erotic Wild Rides*, and *Quickies 3*. He is the editor of *Outsider Ink* (www.outsiderink.com) and *Velvet Mafia: Dangerous Queer Fiction* (www.velvetmafia.com). Sean lives in New York with his partner, photographer Jack Slomovits. For pictures by Jack Slomovits of the men in "For Hire," visit http://seanmeriwether.com/forhire/index.php.

MARSHALL MOORE is the author of the novel *The Concrete Sky* and the short story collection *Black Shapes in a Darkened Room*. For more information about him, please visit his website: www.marshallmoore.com.

When it comes to men, JAY NEAL's favorite adjective is *husky*, and those best described as Big Lugs are lovingly treated in his fiction. Basically a geeky, vanilla kind of guy, he enhances his sex life by making things up. His dirty stories have appeared in *American Bear, American Grizzly,* and *100% BEEF* magazines, and in the anthologies *Best Gay Erotica 2002, 2003, 2004,* and *2005; Bearotica; Kink; Friction 7; Bear Lust;* and others. He and his partner are celebrating twelve years of suburban contentment together in Washington, D.C.

MIKE NEWMAN's first novel, *Secret Buddies*, is back in a new edition from GLB Publishers, with the entire first chapter available for sampling at www.GLBpubs.com. His short story, "Wolfie," about a werewolf on San Francisco's Folsom Street, can be downloaded from GLBpubs for a modest fee. "Wake the King Up Right" is excerpted from his second novel, *Detour*, which he hopes to finish in 2005. He has lived in and around San Francisco since 1970.

JOHN ORCUTT grew up in Maine and Wyoming and graduated from Tufts University. He lived in San Francisco from 1989 to 1996 where most folks remember him holding court behind the counter at A Different Light Bookstore. He was the manager of A Different Light in New York from 1996 to 1998. He has published numerous works of nonfiction under a different name. He lives and works in Manhattan, summers in Fire Island Pines, and is currently attending law school.

ANDY QUAN, Canadian-born, lives in Sydney, Australia and is the author of *Calendar Boy* and *Slant*. His first full-length collection of erotica is *Six Positions*. Other writing and smut has appeared in anthologies such as *Law of Desire: Tales of Gay Male Lust and Obsession*, *Best American Erotica*, and *SEMINAL: The Anthology of Canadian Gay Male Poetry*. He is proud to make his eighth appearance in the *Best Gay Erotica* series and he welcomes the curious and intrigued at: www.andyquan.com.

ALEXANDER ROWLSON knows how many licks it takes to get to the center of a Tootsie Roll pop. Born and raised in the frigid city of Toronto, he has been writing professionally since the age of eighteen as *fab magazine*'s youth columnist, covering such pressing twink issues as sugar daddy etiquette and the pros and cons of body hair. When he's not quilting throw pillows and baking brownies, he enjoys drinking in his local breeder bar. He would choose Brian Krakow over Jordan Catalano any day of the week.

SANDIP ROY has lived in San Francisco for more than a decade, where he works as an editor and host of *UpFront*, a show on ethnic communities. He has been published in various reputable and sleazy anthologies like *Men on Men 6*, *Quickies*, *Q & A: Queer in Asian America*, *Contours of the*

Heart, Desilicious, Best Gay Asian Erotica, and *Chick for a Day.* He writes regularly for the *San Francisco Chronicle, San Jose Mercury News, India Abroad, India Currents* and *Trikone Magazine.* Born in India, trained to be a software engineer, he is still trying to undo his "good boy" image.

DOMINIC SANTI is a former technical editor turned rogue whose latest erotic work is the German language collection *Kerle Im Lustrausch.* Santi's fiction is available in English in *Best Gay Erotica 2000* and *2004, Best American Erotica 2004, Best Bisexual Erotica,* various volumes of *Friction, Tough Guys, His Underwear,* www.nightcharm.com, and dozens of other smutty anthologies and magazines and websites. www.nicksantistories.com.

SIMON SHEPPARD, whose work was also selected for the first volume of *Best of the Best Gay Erotica,* is the author of *In Deep: Erotic Stories,* the nonfiction work *Kinkorama: Dispatches from the Front Lines of Perversion,* and *Sex Parties 101.* His work appears in more than one hundred anthologies, including five editions of *Best American Erotica* and nine editions of *Best Gay Erotica.* His first short story collection, *Hotter Than Hell,* won an Erotic Authors Association Award, and he coedited *Rough Stuff* and *Roughed Up.* He also writes the syndicated column "Sex Talk" and the column "Perv" for gay.com. He lives in San Francisco with his honey and loiters at www.simonsheppard.com.

MEL SMITH's stories have appeared in numerous print anthologies, online at *Suspect Thoughts* and *Velvet Mafia,* and in magazines such as *In Touch* and *Indulge.* She is the author of a collection of erotic stories, *Nasty.*

Mattilda, a.k.a. **MATT BERNSTEIN SYCAMORE,** is a prancer, a romancer, and a fugitive. She is the author of *Pulling Taffy*, from which "Warm-up" is excerpted. Mattilda is the editor of *That's Revolting! Queer Strategies for Resisting Assimilation, Dangerous Families: Queer Writing on Surviving*, and *Tricks and Treats: Sex Workers Write About Their Clients*. Visit www.mattbernsteinsycamore.com.

BOB VICKERY (www.bobvickery.com) is a regular contributor to various websites and magazines, particularly *Men, Freshmen*, and *Inches*. He has five collections of stories published: *Skin Deep, Cock Tales, Cocksure, Play Buddies*, and most recently, *Man Jack*, an audiobook of some of his hottest stories. Bob lives in San Francisco, and can most often be found in his neighborhood Haight Ashbury cafe, pounding out the smut on his laptop.

JAMES WILLIAMS is the author of *...But I Know What You Want*. His stories have appeared widely in print and online publications and anthologies, including several editions of *Best American Erotica, Best Gay Erotica*, and *Best SM Erotica*. He was the subject of profile interviews in *Different Loving* and *Sex: An Oral History*. He can be found in the ether at www.jaswilliams.com.

RON WINTERSTEIN is a California native who has been accused of being a lazy writer. He is unqualified to list glowing credits, unlike his prolific, diligent colleagues in this book. Perhaps he'll tame the fiddlin' grasshopper before too many more liver spots appear. In the meantime, he's perfectly content listening to a story or two over coffee, a beer, or fluffed-up pillows.

About the Editor

RICHARD LABONTÉ has edited the *Best Gay Erotica* series since 1997. After working with A Different Light Bookstores in Los Angeles, San Francisco, and New York from 1979 to 2001, he moved home to Ontario, Canada, where he divides his time between a communal farm near Calabogie and the rural town of Perth. He shares both with his partner of twelve years (and his husband of two years), Asa Dean Liles, who can't take the winters, and their loving pooch, Percy, who has never met a squirrel he didn't hate. He reads many books, writing about some of them in the syndicated review column "Book Marks," for Q Syndicate (www.qsyndicate.com), and in the Gay Men's Edition of the *Books to Watch Out For* newsletter (www.btwof.com). Reach him at tattyhill@sympatico.ca.